Sherlock Holmes – A Study in Illustrations

Volume 3

(In Glorious Colour)

A Collection of Early Illustrations from various publications

And this time not a Single Sidney Paget illustration in sight –

Promise

Michael J. Foy

Paperback ISBN 978-1-80424-064-9

Published by MX Publishing
335 Princess Park Manor, Royal Drive,
London, N11 3GX
www.mxpublishing.com

Cover design by Brian Belanger

Revision 1

I am indebted to Alexis Barquin, curator of *The Arthur Conan Doyle Encyclopaedia* (**arthur-conan-doyle.com**), for source material and help in the writing of this book, many of his illustrations do not appear anywhere else on the internet.

Foreword

A picture is worth a thousand words (Apparently), a cliché of course attributed to Frederick R. Barnard, rather than Telly Savalas (Shudder!), so with this book we get to my 1000th collected picture and beyond, that's equivalent to one million words all about Sherlock Holmes -wow! I never knew I could write so much and it's here at last, the volume I have been looking forward to from the very start and it's finally here, the long awaited (I hope, you have awaited for a long time) colour or is that color Volume! Whichever way it is spelt, it's in wonderful

Now, this is going to be a slightly smaller volume in order to keep the book cost to a manageable level, Colour printing costs so much more and we don't want you selling volume 1 & 2 in order to purchase number 3 (There's a story here about hair and combs, but I digress). It's small but packed with Sherlock Holmes goodness and on the bright side, that does mean that Volume 5 will probably also be in colour so that I can include the Postal stamps, I was going to put into this book. (Sorry Alderney, no stamp pages this time[1]) as well as other colour Sherlock Holmes images that I have had to be leave out this time.

But let's live in the present and talk about this volume and its contents, It's going to be a mixed hodgepodge of Images, graphics gleaned from the four corners of the Earth, and there was me, thinking that the world was a globe, anyway since many illustrations are from unattributed one-off book covers or dust-jackets, unrelated to further images within, I will be presented them without any context apart from where they can be found, no biography of the artist, nothing, but it is better to include them because they exist and I am trying to be inclusive.

In colour books, such as this one, every page whether it be in colour or black and white is priced as a colour page, so if an artist produces one colour image and ninety-nine monochrome ones, the book cost would be the same as if there were one hundred colour pages, so with that explained Let us make a start.

---

[1] Please have a look at the Alderney Sherlock Holmes stamp collection, it is so impressive, every Sherlock Holmes fan should have these 6 stamps in the booklet.

We start this book, and quite rightly with the cover of, perhaps, the most famous and also the most expensive Magazine. It's position in the Sherlock Holmes lore is beyond measure. It is the Beeton's Christmas annual of 1887, I have to admit it is probably not an image which shows any Sherlock Holmes character, but this is such an important item in the world of Holmes, that it would be churlish not to include it here and given its historic importance, it is the first image in this book.

We next have a nice French Cover by André Galland, sadly a one hit wonder as far as Holmes illustrations are concerned, but it is a nice image and he, by all accounts, seems to have lived an interesting life, see his short biography.

Our cover section continues with three from Gaston Simoes da Fonesca and because of the high ratio of monochrome to colour images (128:3), you will have to wait for Volume 4, when the rest of his images will be published, I know I am splitting an artist over two volumes, but since only 3 of his images were in Colour and the rest were in black and white, this seems a smart thing to do and I hope this volume will be a nice little taster for the rest of his work. Monsieur Gaston is one of my favourite illustrators and needs to have much more exposure, I discovered his work will preparing images for my Sherlock Holmes Character books, and his drawing of little Edward Rucastle (next volume) always makes me smile (smack, smack, smack!), Gaston certainly marched to his own drum when it came to the subject matter of his illustrations, drawing some of the most obscure characters named in the Canon. Do you know who Francis Prosper[2] is? unlikely, (but then again, perhaps not, since you must be a Sherlock Holmes Super fan, owning Volume 3 of this multi-volume collection, so I take this back!), Now Mr. Prosper was never seen nor heard and who's existence was only deduced by Sherlock Holmes' observation of a footprint, yet Gaston chooses to do an image of him.

The next collection of images has me breaking with tradition, and showing photographs rather than drawings, but these are of the Great William Gillette with photographs and posters for his Play and film. This is in way of an introduction to our featured artist, who will be following directly after, I have to admit that I have slipped in a couple of other actors, who appeared around the same time and took over Gillette's Sherlock Holmes' role, it was either put them in here or have them lost on their own in Volume 5. This section includes Gillette's Play programme with a few drawings by Pamela Colman Smith, a

---

[2] He was the one-legged greengrocer who visited the maid on the evening of the disappearance of the Beryl Coronet.

very interesting young lady, I don't think her images do Holmes justice, but beauty is in the eye of the beholder.

So why put in all these photographs of William Gillette, I hear you ask, well, it is an excellent introduction to Frederic Dorr Steele, Steele's drawings of Holmes WERE William Gillette. The First Avatar? Maybe. Look at Steele's drawings and tell me this isn't William Gillette, anyway this leads us on to the next set of illustrations, Our featured artist.

About time too, I hear you cry, the great Frederic Dorr Steele and boy, do we have a Bonanza of 210 of his illustrations, now sadly only 30 of them are in colour, however these colour illustrations are crackers and graced the cover of the famous Collier's Magazine. They are truly some of the best and iconic (and I don't use that term lightly) Sherlock Holmes images. I have also included some of Steele's initial sketches too, which show Steele's thought processes before he handed over his finished work for publishing and these are a nice bonus. So savour these wonderful images.

We finish up with some Sherlock Holmes collecting cards and a beer mat.

- Set of 40 cards from a Spanish Chocolate company brought out in 1920
- Set of 25 cigarette cards from Alexander Boguslavsky (1923)
- one card from a Set of 25 cigarette cards from the tobacco company Players (1933) Thank you John Player & Sons for permission to print this.
- And finally, a beer mat for the Sherlock Holmes Pub in London.

The Spanish Cards are a strange set, 10 cards for the Musgrave Ritual, 10 cards for the speckled band and just 20 (yes 20) for the Sign of Four. Of course, the backs were in Spanish, but I have attempted a loose translation, very loose, I have to admit (no hablo español), which is sometimes a problem living in Florida.

The Boguslavsky card illustrations are interesting, I must say that these are not my idea of what the Conan Doyle Characters would have looked like, but who am I to say that they are wrong, clearly the Artist thought that the hound of the Baskerville was a Black Labrador (here boy, fetch the stick, or better still push that convict off the Tor). I know many of the cards are unrelated to Holmes, but in my defence, they are Conan Doyle characters, so I have included all 24 cards here, but don't moan, you would have firmer ground for complaint if I had included the other 24 cards from the Players Cigarette collections, as page after

page in this book would have been filled with cards of Captain Kettle, Adam Bede, Colonel Newcome and Little Lord Fauntleroy (and other really well know characters – Not!)
Just a couple of more items, a beer mat from The Sherlock Holmes Pub in London and right at the end we have some images from Wladyslaw Teodor "W.T." Benda.

Oh and a controversial John French Sloan, did he copy Pamela Colman Smith image and then did Frederic Dorr Steele copy one of his images from them, you must decide, and there is a puzzle here for you to solve too.

I have as promised, not included a single Sidney Paget image here, I was tempted to include a few of the more recent colorized illustrations, but not for long, because being a purest I thought this was just not right, I am also against the colorization of old films.

You will find a special 1000th picture page.

If I may quote from Emerson, Lake, and Palmer at this point;

"Step inside!
Hello!
We've a most amazing show
You'll enjoy it all we know
Step inside! Step inside!
Let the show begin"

Mike Foy, Florida.
        please contacted me at SherlockHolmesImages@gmail.com

Index

Some Covers

Before we move onto the main event (FDS), we present a collection of Magazine and book covers and of course start with the first ever and probably the most famous Sherlock Holmes Cover, from Beeton's Christmas Annual of 1887.

The only clue to the artist is their initials in the bottom left-hand corner of the drawing, which look a bit like S H. S., but who can tell with signatures.
Clearly this image is not the work of D.H. Friston, who did the 4 Sherlock Holmes illustrations inside. (Volume 1, page 21)

Perhaps one day the name of this artist will be revealed, until then, we are left with a mystery to just enjoy.

Beeton's Christmas Annual 1887

We have to start this book with the first image associated with Sherlock Holmes, the cover of the much sought-after Beeton's Christmas annual of 1887

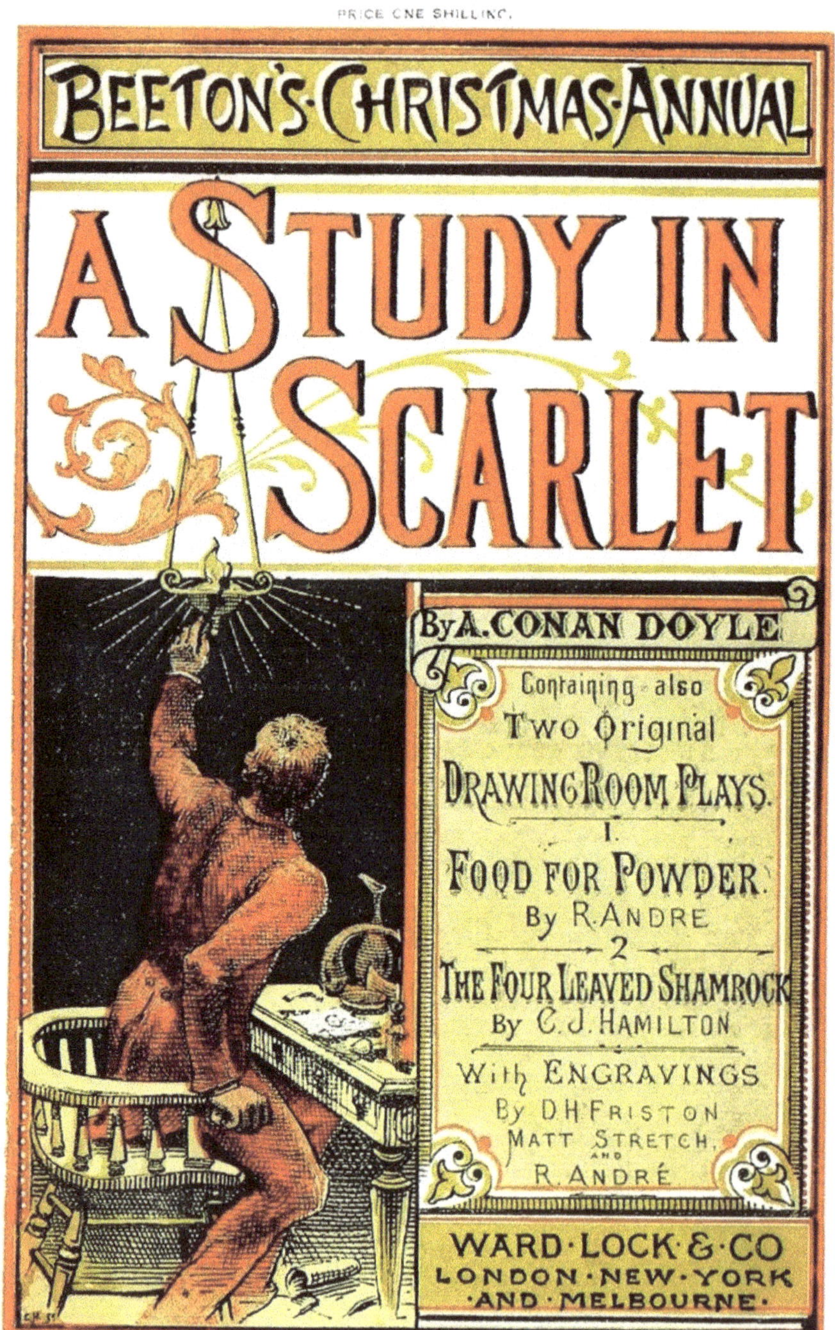

There were 4 illustrations in the publication by D.H. Friston (See Volume 1, Page 21)
Ref. SH-BCA1

Andre Charles Galland

11

Born 29th July 1886 in Sedan
Died 12th September 1965 in Paris

French artist and illustrator of children's books. During World War II, he made posters for the Vichy government and illustrated for L'Espoir français, after the War he covered the Nuremberg trial and later founded the Union des Artistes et Dessinateurs Français (U.A.D.F.) He produced just one Sherlock Holmes image, which was for the Grande Collection National series, and it was a cover of the Les Debuts de Sherlock Holmes issue, published 31st December 1913.

The Story 'A Study in Scarlet' was translated by Albert Savine.

André Galland's Cover for Les Debuts de Sherlock Holmes from 31st December 1913

Ref. SH-ACG1

Gaston Simoes da Fonseca

Gastão Simões da Fonseca (or Gaston Simoes da Fonseca)

Born 16th October 1874 in Brazil.

Died 18th June 1943 in France.

A Brazilian-born French artist.

Between 1909 and 1913, he did 151 illustrations for Arthur Conan Doyle stories.

See Volume 4 for the next 128 images

He illustrated three Sherlock Holmes covers for Félix Juven in 1909.

- Les Premières Exploits de Sherlock Holmes (1909, Félix Juven)
- Premières Aventures de Sherlock Holmes (1909, Félix Juven)
- Nouvelles Aventures de Sherlock Holmes (1909, Félix Juven)

CONAN DOYLE
LES
PREMIERS EXPLOITS
DE
SHERLOCK HOLMES
PARIS
Librairie F. JUVEN

SH-GSF1

BIBLIOTHÈQUE ILLUSTRÉE
PRIX 0 fr 95 NET
A. CONAN DOYLE
PREMIÈRES AVENTURES DE
SHERLOCK HOLMES
G. S. Fonseca
PARIS
Société d'Édition et de Publications
LIBRAIRIE FELIX JUVEN
PARIS

SH-GSF2

Gaston Simoes Da Fonseca – Nouvelles Aventures de Sherlock Holmes (1909, Félix Juven)

SH-GSF3

Pamela Colman Smith

Born 16th February 1878 in Pimlico, London
Died 18th September 1951 in Bude, Cornwall

Cousin of William Gillette, many of her works are
on display in Gillette's home (Castle)
she illustrated his Sherlock Holmes Play programme
in 1900.

Nicknamed Pixie, she was a British artist, illustrator,
writer, publisher, and occultist.

She is probably best remembered for her 78
illustrations that formed the Waite-Smith Tarot
deck, which even to this day are the world's most
popular Tarot cards.

I suggest you read up the rest of her interesting life
and who she collaborated with in her art, try
Wikipedia.

Albert George Morrow

Born 26th April 1864 in Comber, Country Down, Ireland.
Died 26th October 1927 in West Hoathly, England.
Just a brief biography for Mr. Morrow here rather than just before his artwork, which would otherwise disturb the narrative of the Gillette collection.

Very talented Irish illustrator who had seven brothers, four of which were also illustrator and all but one were artists. He illustrated for a number of publications and had nine works at the Royal Academy of Arts between 1890 and 1904. He illustrated books, but is best known for the hundreds of Posters he designed for theatres like the one for the Gillette play on page 51.

William Hooker Gillette as Sherlock Holmes

Born 24th July 1853 in Hartford, Connecticut
Died 29th April 1937 in Hartford, Connecticut

What can we say about William Gillette, for a generation, he was the living, breathing embodiment of Sherlock Holmes, so much so that Frederic Dorr Steele's drawings of Holmes were images of Gillette.
He is credited for linking Sherlock Holmes with his Calabash pipe. Producing a highly successful play not to mention a movie. So, we will break with convention here and instead of showing illustrations drawn by an Artists, we will instead have a collection of images related to a real person playing Sherlock Holmes.

So here he is William Gillette.

He played Sherlock Holmes on stage more that 1300 times, which strangely only ranks him 3rd in appearances. (H. Hamilton Steward {1[st] with 2000} and Harry Arthur Saintsbury {with 1400}

The Following are some posters from William Gillette's play 'Sherlock Holmes'. This play was premiered at the Star Theatre, Buffalo, New York on 23rd October 1899 with 3 previews before moving to the Garrick Theatre in New York and then touring the United States. The London Lyceum posters date from September 1901, with H.A. Saintsbury taking over Gillette's role in 1903. Gillette revived the play in 1905, 1906, 1910, 1915 and 1929.

William Gillette also appeared in a 1916 Silent movie of Sherlock Holmes, which has recently been rediscovered.

While on the subject of the Sherlock Holmes Play, over 130 people have played the role of Sherlock Holmes, but we are really interested only in those actors who appeared in early posters and flyers.

Strangely William Gillette was not the first person to play Sherlock Holmes in his own play, that honour goes to Herbert Waring, who took the part in a special copyright performance in front of an audience of three people: Charles Frohman (producer, whose name keeps appearing on the posters), William Gillette (playwright) and Annie Russell at the Duke of York Theatre, London 12th June 1899. William Gillette then travelled back to America and appeared in his play as mentioned above.

Other Notable performances.

From 1903-1910 in London
Harry Arthur Saintsbury (H. A. Saintsbury)
Born 18th December 1867 in Chelsea, London
Died 19th June 1939 in Westminster, London

From 1905-1906 UK tour company
H. Lawrence Leyton (real name Henry Jacob Allmann)
Born 20th November 1873 in Mile End, London
Died 1952 in Kensington, London
He appeared as Dr. Watson to H. A. Saintsbury's Sherlock Holmes, before taking on the role of Sherlock Holmes

Harrison. Hamilton Stewart 1906-1918 England
Born 9th December 1857
Died 15th May 1924 in Oxford, England

Royce, Julian (born William Leonard Gardener)
Born 26th March 1866 in Chorlton-upon-Medlock
Died 10th May 1946 in Hailsham
Appeared in a number of films as well as appearing as Sherlock Holmes several times over a number of years.

Sherlock Holmes (With William Gillette 1899)

Charles Frohman promoted many of these plays worldwide.
SH-WHG1

This is supposed to be a 1900 play poster, but the actress looks like Marjorie Kay, who played Alice Faulkner in 1916. Inspired by image *SH-WHG27*
SH-WHG2

William Gillette Broadway Production of play 1899

The name of the page-boy, was unknown until he was named Billy in
William Gillette's play. Arthur Conan Doyle later used the name in his
Mazarin Stone story.
SH-WHG3

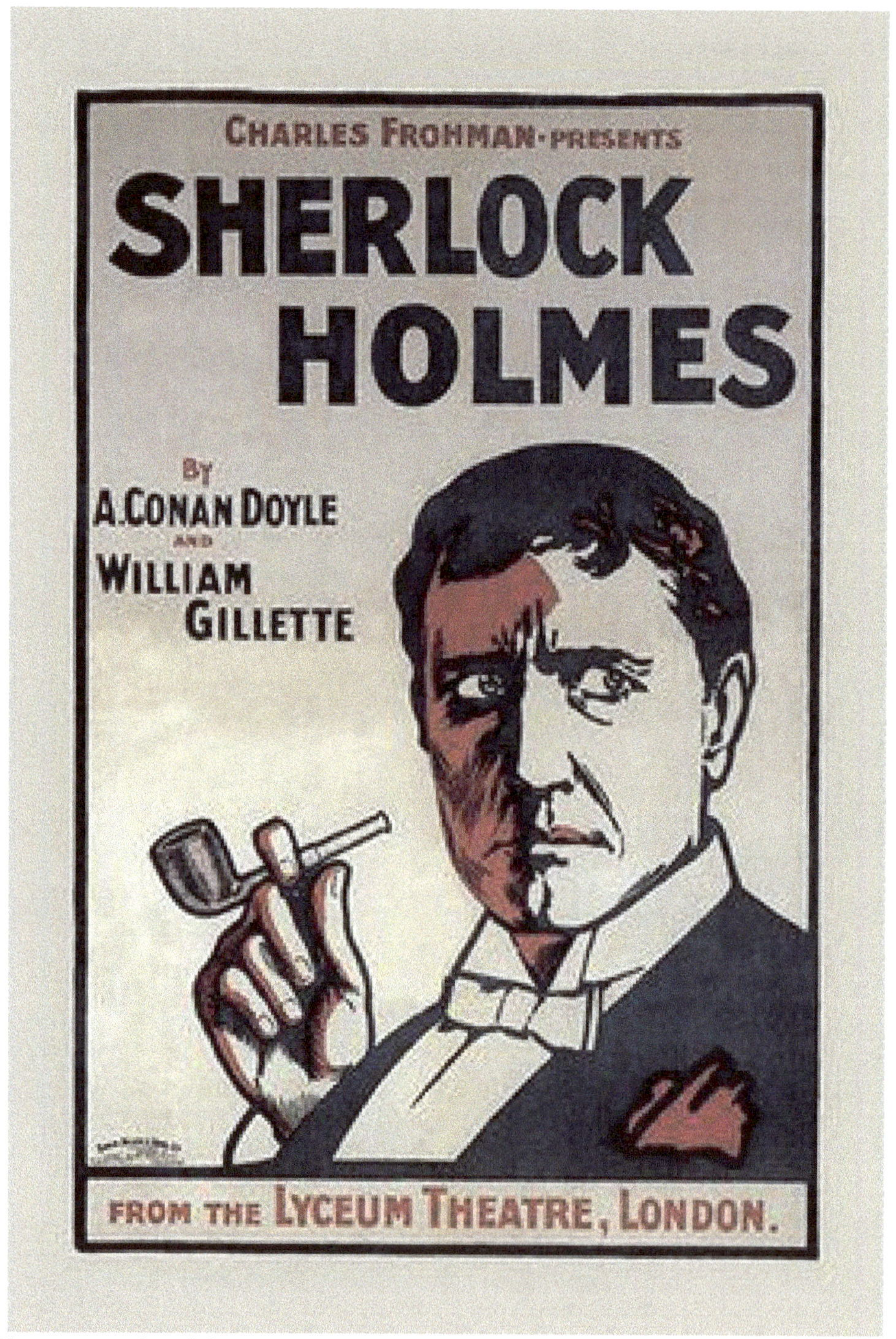

Play poster dated from 1901, when the play moved over to London.
SH-WHG4

Another play poster dated from around 1901,
SH-WHG5

William Gillette Broadway Production of play 1899

Play poster for the 1899 Broadway production
SH-WHG6

From August 1905 until February 1906 Harry Yorke's Company had H. Lawrence Leyton as Sherlock Holmes in the UK
SH-HLL1

In 1929 William Gillette returned for a 45-performance run, This Poster is from 1930 and drawn by Frederic Dorr Steele.
SH-WHG7

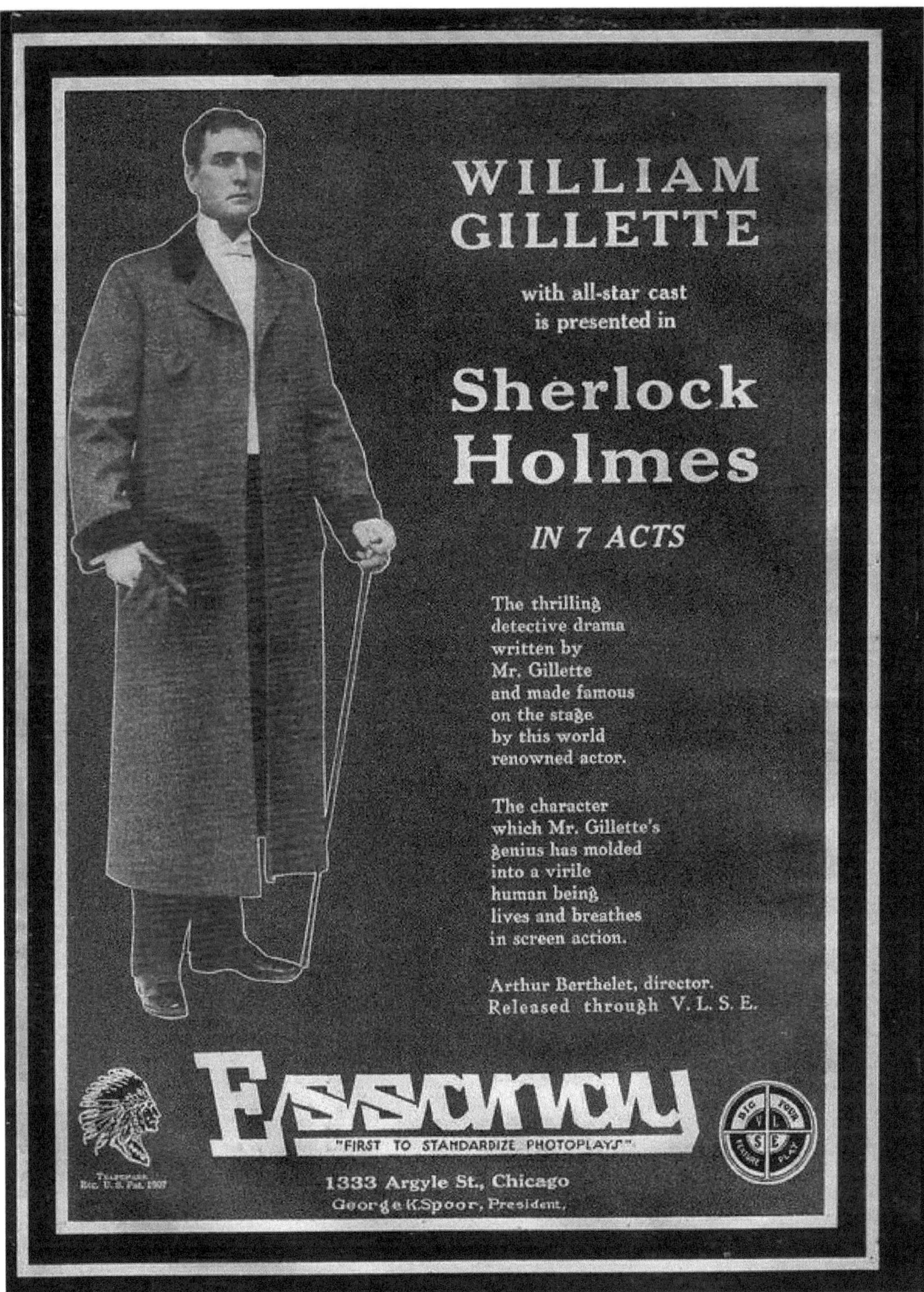

Poster for the 1916 movie, showing William Gillette as Sherlock Holmes
SH-WHG8

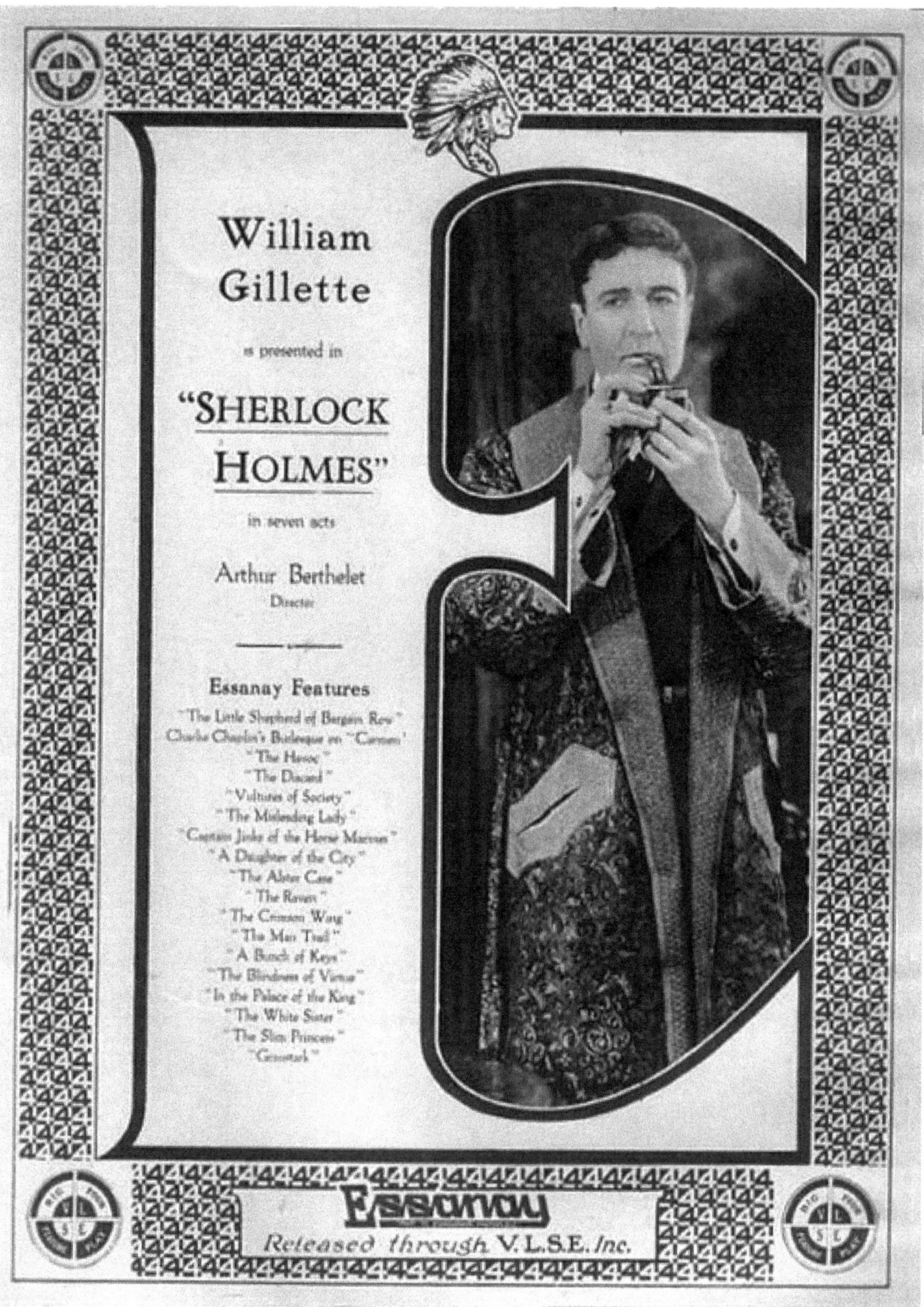

Another poster for the 1916 Silent Sherlock Holmes movie.
SH-WHG9

William Gillette Movie and Play posters

The Black and White Sherlock Holmes Movie were produced by Essanay Film Manufacturing Co.
SH-WHG10

William Gillette Movie and Play posters

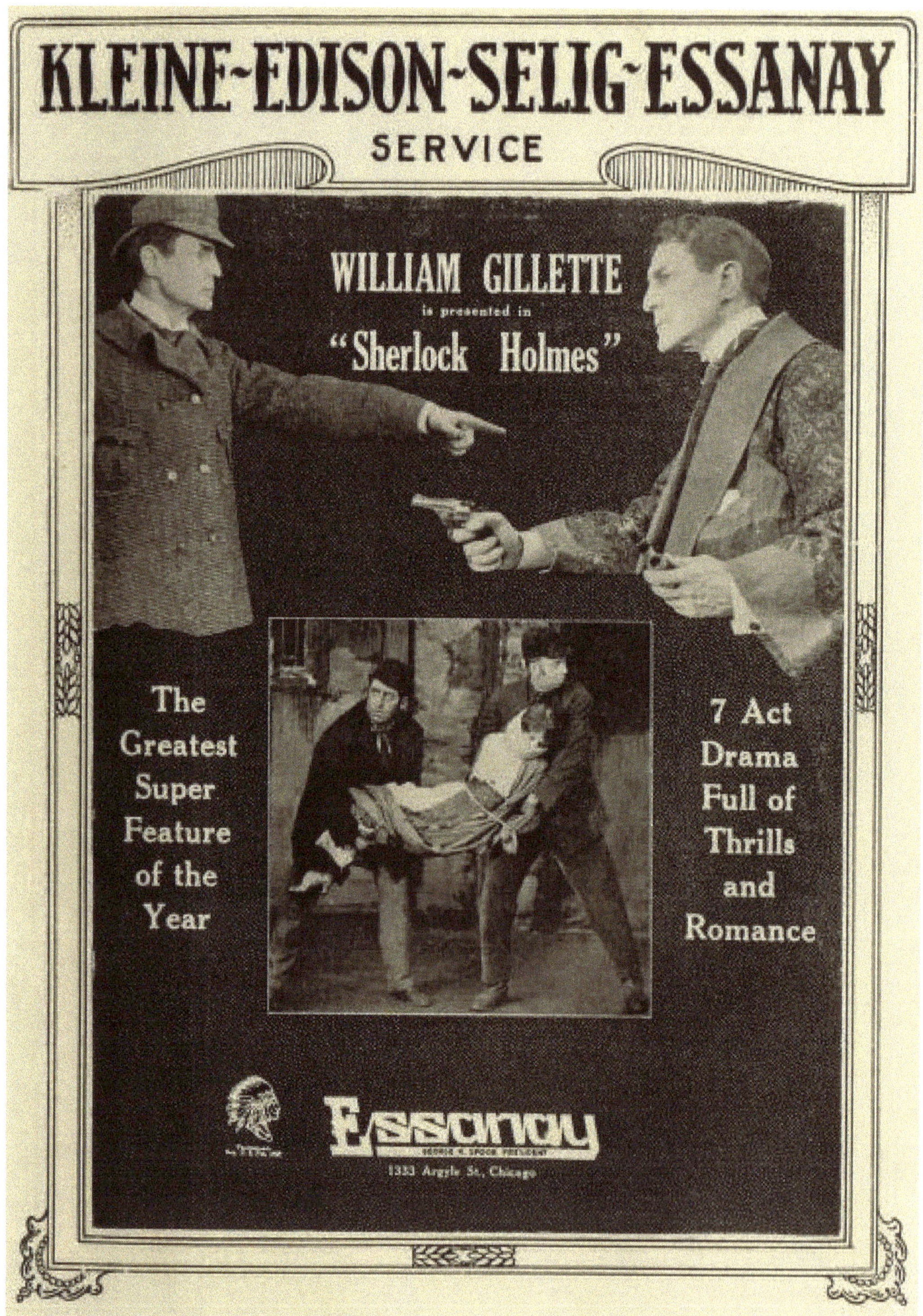

Last Movie Poster from 1916
SH-WHG11

William Gillette's Sherlock Holmes contemplates the characters that appear within the play.
SH-WHG12

William Gillette Play program 1900, printed in New York

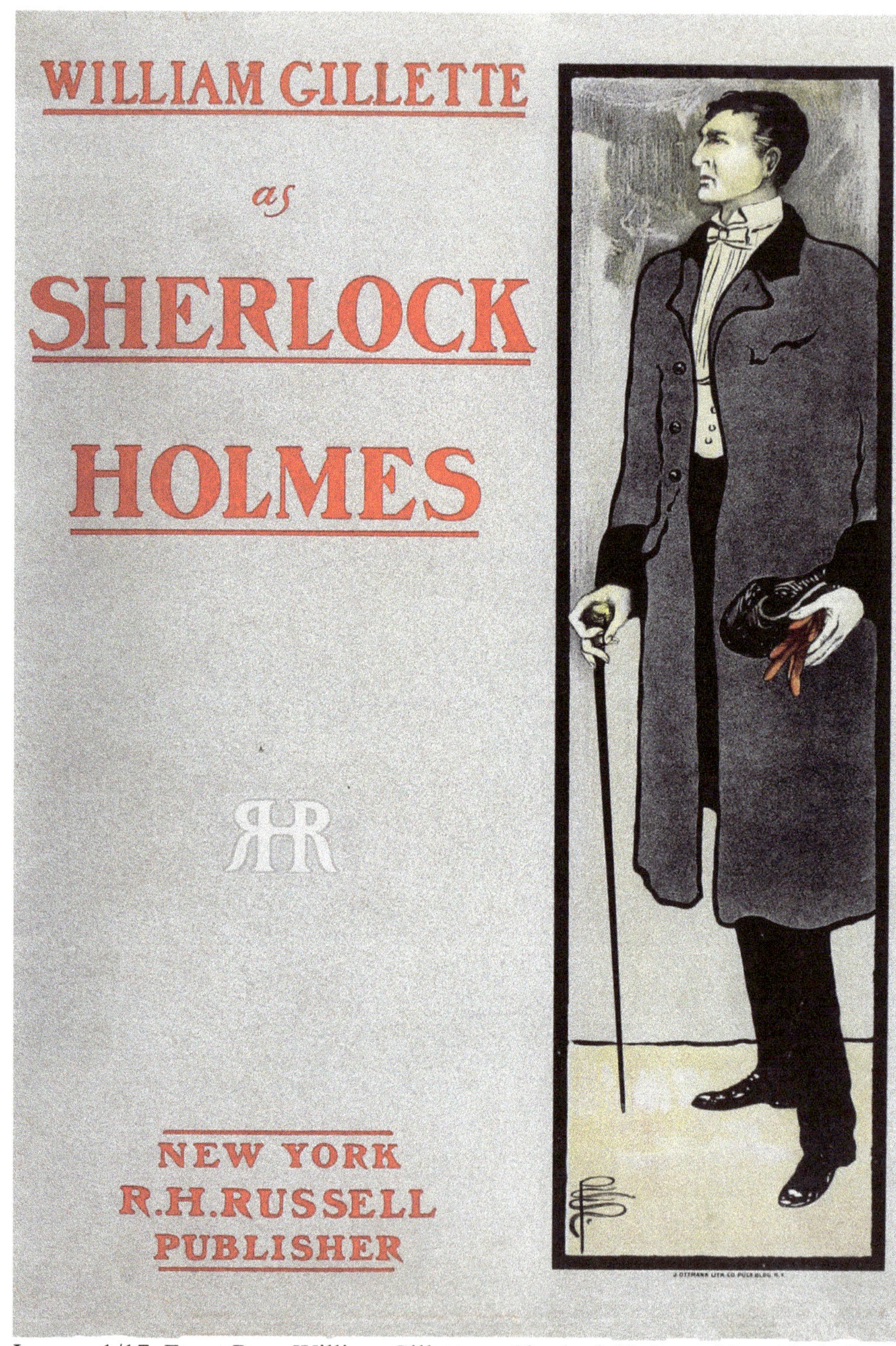

Images 1/17. Front Page William Gillette as Sherlock Holmes. New York, R. H. Russell Publisher. (Illustration by Pamela Colman Smith (1878-1951) *SH-WHG13*

William Gillette Play program 1900, printed in New York

Images 2/17. Page 1 William Gillette as Sherlock Holmes
SH-WHG14 & SH-PCS1

William Gillette Play program 1900, printed in New York

Images 3/17. Page 2 William Gillette.
SH-WHG15

William Gillette Play program 1900, printed in New York

WILLIAM GILLETTE

IN

SHERLOCK HOLMES

AS PRODUCED AT THE GARRICK THEATRE
NEW YORK

*Published with the Authorization
of Mr. Charles Frohman*

NEW YORK
R. H. RUSSELL, PUBLISHER
1900

Copyright, 1900, by ROBERT HOWARD RUSSELL

Images 4/17. Page 3 William Gillette as Sherlock Holmes as produced at the Garrick Theatre New York. Published with the authorization of Mr. Charles Frohman. New York, R. H. Russell, Publisher, 1900
SH-WHG16

Images 5/17. Page 4. Sherlock Holmes – Act l.
SH-WHG17

William Gillette Play program 1900, printed in New York

Images 6/17. Page 5. Sherlock Holmes – Act l.
SH-WHG18

William Gillette Play program 1900, printed in New York

Images 7/17. Page 6. Holmes returning the packet to Miss Faulkner – Act l
SH-WHG19

William Gillette Play program 1900, printed in New York

Images 8/17. Page 7. Sherlock Holmes – Act II.
SH-WHG20

William Gillette Play program 1900, printed in New York

Images 9/17. Page 8. Character sketch of Sherlock Holmes – Act II. (See John Sloan story at end of this book regarding this illustration by Pixie, clearly it's a copy of the previous photograph.
SH-PCS2

William Gillette Play program 1900, printed in New York

Images 10/17. Page 9. Holmes and his "Hypodermic" with Dr. Watson – Act II.
SH-WHG21

William Gillette Play program 1900, printed in New York

Images 11/17. Page 10. Sherlock Holmes and Jim Larrabee in the Gas Chamber –
Act lII.
SH-WHG22 & SH-PCS3

44

William Gillette Play program 1900, printed in New York

Images 12/17. Page 11. Sherlock Holmes– Act lII.
SH-WHG23

William Gillette Play program 1900, printed in New York

Images 13/17. Page 12. The arrest of Professor Moriarty– Act III.
SH-WHG24

46

William Gillette Play program 1900, printed in New York

Images 14/17. Page 13. Sherlock Holmes– Act IV.
SH-WHG25

William Gillette Play program 1900, printed in New York

Images 15/17. Page 14. The Counterfeit Packet– Act IV.
SH-WHG26

William Gillette Play program 1900, printed in New York

Images 16/17. Page 15. The End
SH-WHG27

William Gillette Play program 1900, printed in New York

Images 17/17. Back Page. William Gillette as Captain Thorne in "Secret Service"
SH-WHG28

William Gillette Play program 1900, printed in New York, Artist Albert George Morrow

London Sherlock Holmes Show poster, printed in Paris in 1902.
Artist was Albert George Morrow
SH-WHG29 / SH-AGM1

William Gillette as Sherlock Holmes as he appeared in Vanity Fair.

Vanity Fair dated 27th February 1907
SH-WHG30

William Gillette as Sherlock Holmes

Vanity Fair dated 27th February 1907
SH-WHG31

William Gillette as Sherlock Holmes from 21st August 1091 The Sketch

MR. WILLIAM GILLETTE AS SHERLOCK HOLMES
IN DR. CONAN DOYLE'S POPULAR DRAMA OF THAT NAME, DUE AT THE LYCEUM THEATRE ON SEPT. 9.
" Pull down the blinds, Doctor ; I don't care to be shot from the street this evening."

Mr. William Gillette as Sherlock Holmes.
In Dr. Conan Doyle's popular drama of that name, due at the lyceum theatre on September 9.
"Pull down the blinds, Doctor; I don't care to be shot from the street this evening."
SH-WHG32

William Gillette as Sherlock Holmes

Vanity Fair dated 27th February 1907
SH-WHG33

William Gillette as Sherlock Holmes

Vanity Fair dated 27th February 1907
SH-WHG34

Vanity Fair dated 27th February 1907
SH-WHG35

William Gillette as Sherlock Holmes

Vanity Fair dated 27th February 1907
SH-WHG36

William Gillette as Sherlock Holmes on a Cigar label

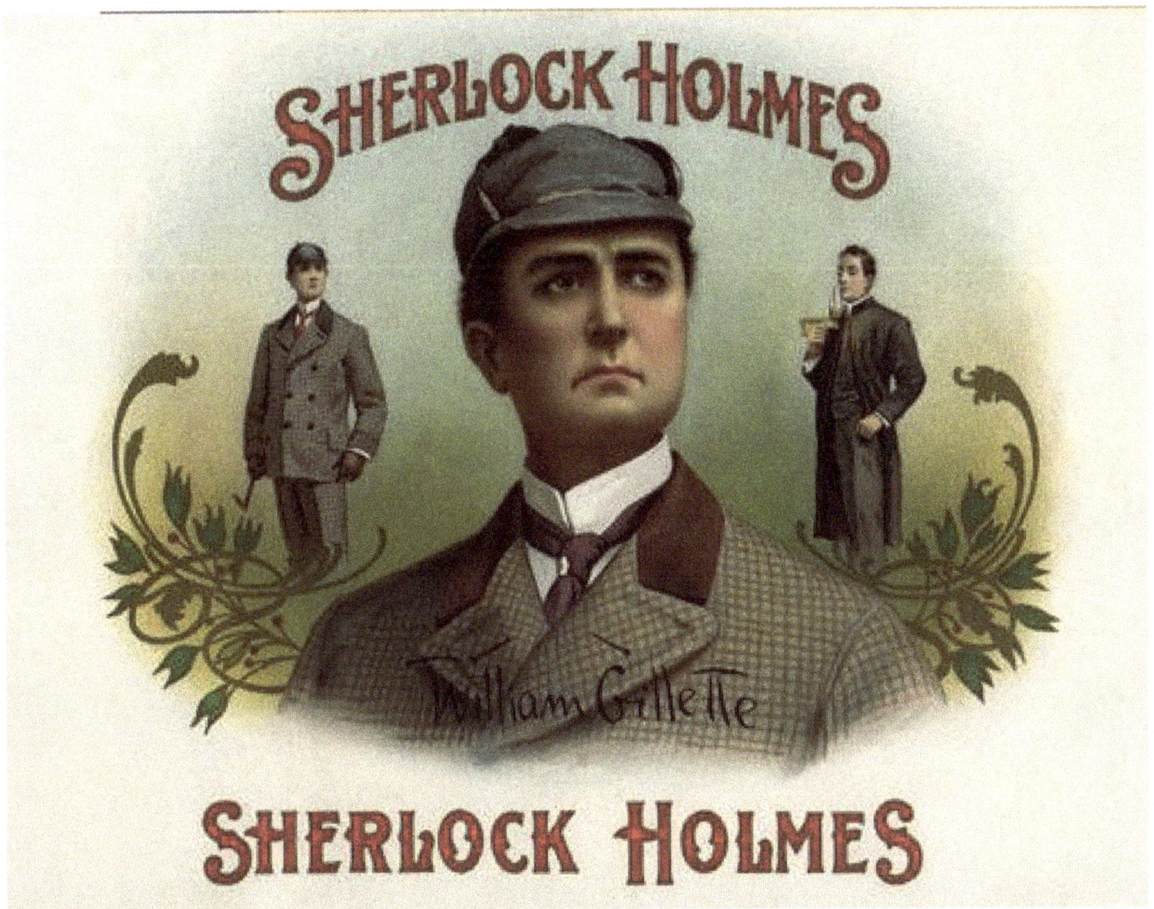

Variation on a Sherlock Holmes cigar box, Rum Soaked Crooks from 1920s
SH-WHG37

Julian Royce Play program from 1902, for Lyceum Theatre

Julian Royce took over the role of Sherlock Holmes in 1902 for one year. *SH-JR1*

Frederic Dorr Steele

Born :6th August 1873 in Eagle Mills, Michigan
Died 6th July 1944 in New York.

From the age of 16, Steele studied art at the Art Students'
League and the National Academy of Design and supported
himself by working as an architectural draftsman.
He worked for The Illustrated American from 1896 to 1897
before becoming a freelance illustration.

He was invited in 1903 to do the Sherlock Holmes
illustrations for Collier's Magazine's 'The Return of
Sherlock Holmes' He used the likeness of American actor
William Gillette for his drawings of Holmes, who was
appearing as Sherlock Holmes on stage at the time.

He was later quoted about this.

> "Everybody agreed that Mr. Gillette was the ideal Sherlock Holmes, and it was
> inevitable that I should copy him. So, I made my models look like him, and even in two
> or three instances used photographs of him in my drawings. But while the actor was
> seen by thousands, the magazines and books were seen by millions; so, after a score of
> years had gone by, few could remember which "did it first." Even so well informed a
> historian as Mr. Clayton Hamilton has tried to give me credit which belongs entirely to
> Mr. Gillette."

Steele was a fan of Sherlock Holmes and wrote four short Sherlock Holmes parodies.

1. "The Adventure of the Missing Hatrack" (1926)
2. "The Adventure of the Missing Artist" (1928)
3. "The Attempted Murder of Malcolm Duncan" (1932)
4. "The Adventure of the Murdered Art Editor" (1933)

In 1915 Steele produced 4 illustrations for Carolyn Wells' Sherlock Holmes Parody called
"The Adventures of the Clothes-line", these 4 images have been included at the end, (I know
I am really breaking the rules by having non-canon work, but hey it's Frederic Dorr Steele and
it is a Sherlock Holmes story)

There is one Thor Bridge illustration that appeared in 1944, which isn't included here because of possible copyright issues.

Mr. Steele illustrated most of the later Sherlock Holmes short stories, starting with The Empty House and continued until Shoscombe Old Place, there are a couple of stories he did not illustrate, namely the Devil's Foot and the Red Circle.

Extra sketch images have been included to show the development of the some of the illustrations.

In 1904 Conan Doyle's best books: in three volumes was published which featured A Study in Scarlet as well as A Scandal in Bohemia and A Case of Identity and other non-Sherlock Holmes stories, 5 of Steele's illustrations were used, but there was nothing original, just modified versions of other images, mainly Covers. I have briefly listed them in row 1 of the table on the next page.

Details of Frederic Dorr Steele's Sherlock Holmes Illustrations appear in the table on the next page.

My sources have been of course Alexis Barquin's excellent www.arthur-conam-doyle.com site but also

- Archive.org
- The University of Minnesota UMedia libraries umedia.lib.umn.edu (particularly for the development sketches)
- Hathi Trust Digital library babel.hathitrust.org
- Various search engines, Google is good, and they have scanned a number of printed books, but Google, can you please rescan some of your pages, we don't really need to see the people's fingers and it would be nice to have some images straighter and not blurred because the operator snatched the page away halfway through the scan. (what's that? Don't look a gift horse… quite right, thank you Google)

Although the majority of Steele's illustrations appeared in the Collier's Magazine, his Sherlock Holmes illustrations did appear in other publications.

C = Collier's magazine

A= The American Magazine

H= Hearst's International

J= The Courier-Journal

S= The Sun (Baltimore)

T= The Los Angeles Times

L= Liberty

	Code	Publishing Date	details	Magazine
1	HOUN	Unpublished 1901-2	3	-
2	SIGN	Unpublished	1	-
3	STUD	1904	5 (EMPT,NORWx3, PRIO)	Book
4	EMPT	26th September. 1903	Sketch, Cover & 6 others	C
5	NORW	31st October. 1903	Cover & 5 others	C
6	DANC	5th December 1903	6	C
7	SOLI	26th December 1903	Cover +4	C
8	PRIO	30th January 1904	Cover+5	C
9	BLAC	27th February 1904	Cover+5	C
10	CHAS	26th March 1904	Cover+5	C
11	SIXN	30th April 1904	6	C
12	3STU	24th September 1904	Cover+5	C
13	GOLD	29th October 1904	Cover+5	C
14	MISS	26th November 1894	Cover+4	C
15	ABBE	31st December 1894	Cover+5	C
16	SECO	28th January 1905	Cover+5	C
17	WIST	15th August 1908	Cover+6	C
18	BRUC	12th December 1908	5	C
19	LADY	December 1911	Cover+4	A
20	DYIN	22nd November 1913	Cover+3	C
21	LAST	22nd September 1917	Cover+4	C
22	MAZA	October 1921	4	H
23	CREE	March 1923	7	H
		15th March 1925	1	J
24	SUSS	8th March 1925	1	J
25	3GAR	22nd March 1925	4	S
26	ILLU	29th March 1925	6	J
27	3GAB	18th September 1926	6	L
		13th February 1927	1	T
28	BLAN	16th October 1926	6	L
		30th January 1927	1	T
29	LION	27th November 1926	7	L
		6th February 1927	1	T
30	RETI	18th December 1926	4	L
		22nd May 1927	1	T
31	VEIL	22nd January 1927	5	L
		15th May 1927	1	T
32	SHOS	5th March 1927	7	L
		29th May 1927	1	T

Images 1/3. The magazine's Cover page. Hound with floppy ears.
Ref. SH-FDS1

Images 2/3. Hound. Looking left with pointed ears
Ref. SH-FDS2

Images 3/3. Another Hound image. This time looking right
Ref. SH-FDS3

Images 1/1. The text along the side reads
Sign of the Four

At the Lyceum Theatre the Candidate

"We had hardly reached the third pillar, which was our rendezvous, before a small, dark, brisk man in the dress of a coachman accosted us.
Facing page 142
Ref. SH-FDS4

Images 1/8. Initial sketch for the cover of the Collier's Magazine.(see next image for published version.)
Ref. SH-FDS5

Images 2/8. The magazine's Cover page. (isn't this just a wonderful image?)
Ref. SH-FDS6

Images 3/8. Page 12. The title of the story
Ref. SH-FDS7

Frederic Dorr Steele – The Empty House
Collier's Magazine 26th September 1903

Images 4/8. Page 12. The 'I' in this image is the first letter of the story 'It was in the spring of the year 1894 that all London was interested….'
Ref. SH-FDS8

Images 5/8. Page 12. "With a snarl he turned upon his heel"
(This image was also used as an illustration for 'A Study in Scarlet' in the 1904 book
'Conan Doyle's Best Books' (in three volumes on Page 19 with the captions 'Sherlock
Holmes in disguise')
Ref. SH-FDS9

Images 6/8. Page 13. Sherlock Holmes stood smiling at me over my study table.
Ref. SH-FDS10

Images 7/8. Page 14. "My collection of M's is a fine one"
Ref. SH-FDS11

Images 8/8. Page 16. Colonel Moran sprang forward with a snarl of rage.
Ref. SH-FDS12

Images 1/11. Cover.(of course it should only have been a thumb print, but you have to admit is is a great picture)
Ref. SH-FDS13

Images 2/11. Page 16. Title of story.
Ref. SH-FDS14

Images 3/11. Page 16. The 'F' in this image is the first letter of the story ''From the point of view of the criminal expert,' said Mr Sherlock Holmes, 'London has become a singularly uninteresting city since the death of the late lamented Professor Moriarty:' "
Ref. SH-FDS15

Images 4/11. Early sketch of the next published illustration on page 16.
Ref. SH-FDS16

Images 5/11. Another sketch of that illustration
(This image was also used as an illustration for 'A Study in Scarlet' in the 1904 book
'Conan Doyle's Best Books' (in three volumes on Page 43 with the captions 'A visit from
Lestrade')
Ref. SH-FDS17

Images 6/11. Page 16. "I arrest you for the wilful murder of Jonas Oldacre".
Ref. SH-FDS18

Images 7/11. Early sketch for the next published illustration, notice John Hector McFarlane isn't actually in this first sketch.
Ref. SH-FDS19

Images 8/11. Page 17. "A mass of documents, which we went over together"
Ref. SH-FDS20

Images 9/11. Page 18. "It was more than a stain. It was the well marked print of a thumb"
Ref. SH-FDS21

Images 10/11. Continuation image at top of page 28.
Ref. SH-FDS22

Images 11/11. Page 29. "There was a sort of sulky defiance in her eyes"
Ref. SH-FDS23

Images 1/9. "Steele's initial thought for the title page, it seems that he removed the Sundial,
but kept the skeletons, as you can see in the next image."
Ref. SH-FDS24

Images 2/9. Page 11. Dancing Skeleton's anybody?
Ref. SH-FDS25

Images 3/9. Page 11. The 'H' in this image is the first letter of the story 'Holmes had been seated for some hours in silence, with his long, thin back curved over a chemical vessel in which he was brewing a particularly malodorous product. "
Ref. SH-FDS26

Images 4/9. Page 11. "Well, Mr. Holmes, what do you make of these?"
Ref. SH-FDS27

Images 5/9. Sketch 1 for group illustration.
Text "Mr. Hilton Cubitt has been shot through the heart."
Ref. SH-FDS28

Images 6/9. Sketch 2 for group illustration.
Ref. SH-FDS29

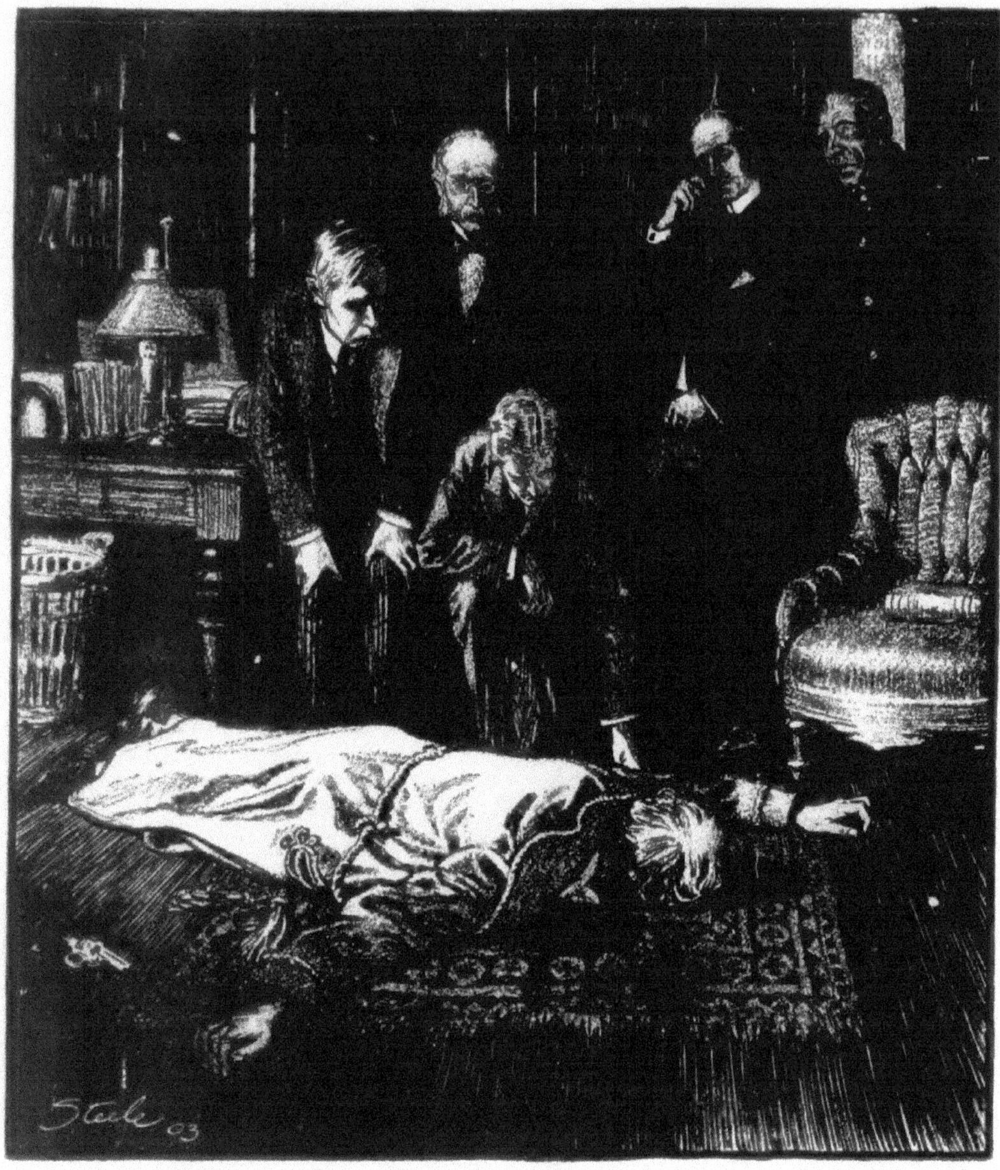

Images 7/9. Page 12. "Our first attention was given to the body of the unfortunate squire"
Ref. SH-FDS30

Images 8/9. Page 13. "He sank with a deep groan on the settee."
Ref. SH-FDS31

Images 9/9. Page 14. "Well, Gentlemen, you have the drop on me this time"
(These last two images are actually in the wrong order, Abe Slaney has this dialog before
he sits down on the settee, maybe the pictures fitted better this way around in the
Magazine.)
Ref. SH-FDS32

Images 1/6. Cover. (See Pamela Colman Smith & John French Sloan's images)
Ref. SH-FDS33

Images 2/6. "Steele's initial thought for the title page, showing Miss Violet Smith being followed."
Ref. SH-FDS34

Images 3/6. Page 16. Miss Violet Smith followed by a skeleton!
Ref. SH-FDS35

Images 4/6. Page 16. The 'F' in this image is the first letter of the story "From the years 1894 to 1901 inclusive, Mr Sherlock Holmes was a very busy man."
Ref. SH-FDS36

Images 5/6. Page 16. "Miss Violet Smith, Teacher of Music."
Ref. SH-FDS37

Images 6/6. Page 17. "It was a straight left against a slogging ruffian."
Ref. SH-FDS38

Images 1/8. Sketch of Cover.
Ref. SH-FDS39

Images 2/8. Cover.
Ref. SH-FDS40

THE ADVENTURE OF THE PRIORY SCHOOL

Images 3/8. Page 18. Miss Violet Smith followed by a skeleton!
Ref. SH-FDS41

Images 4/8. Page 18. The 'W' in this image is the first letter of the story "We have had some dramatic entrances and exits upon our small stage at Baker Street, but I cannot recollect anything more sudden and startling than the first appearance of Dr Thorneycroft Huxtable, M.A., Ph.D., etc."
Ref. SH-FDS42

Images 5/8. Page 18. "I can not imagine how I came to be so weak"
Ref. SH-FDS43

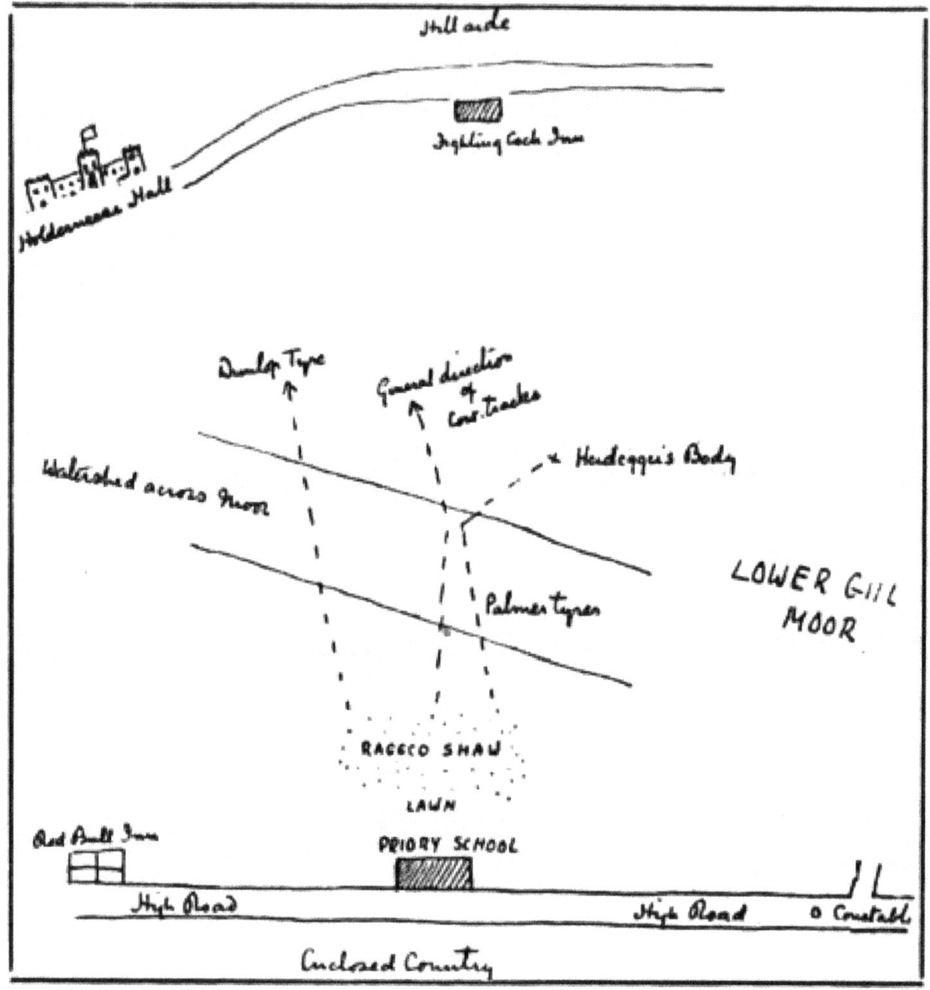

HOLMES' MAP OF THE NEIGHBORHOOD OF THE SCHOOL

Images 6/8. Page 18. "Holmes' map of the Neighbourhood of the school."
Ref. SH-FDS44

Images 7/8. Page 18. "The duke and his secretary."
Ref. SH-FDS45

Images 8/8. Page 20. "You infernal spies!" the man cried
Ref. SH-FDS46

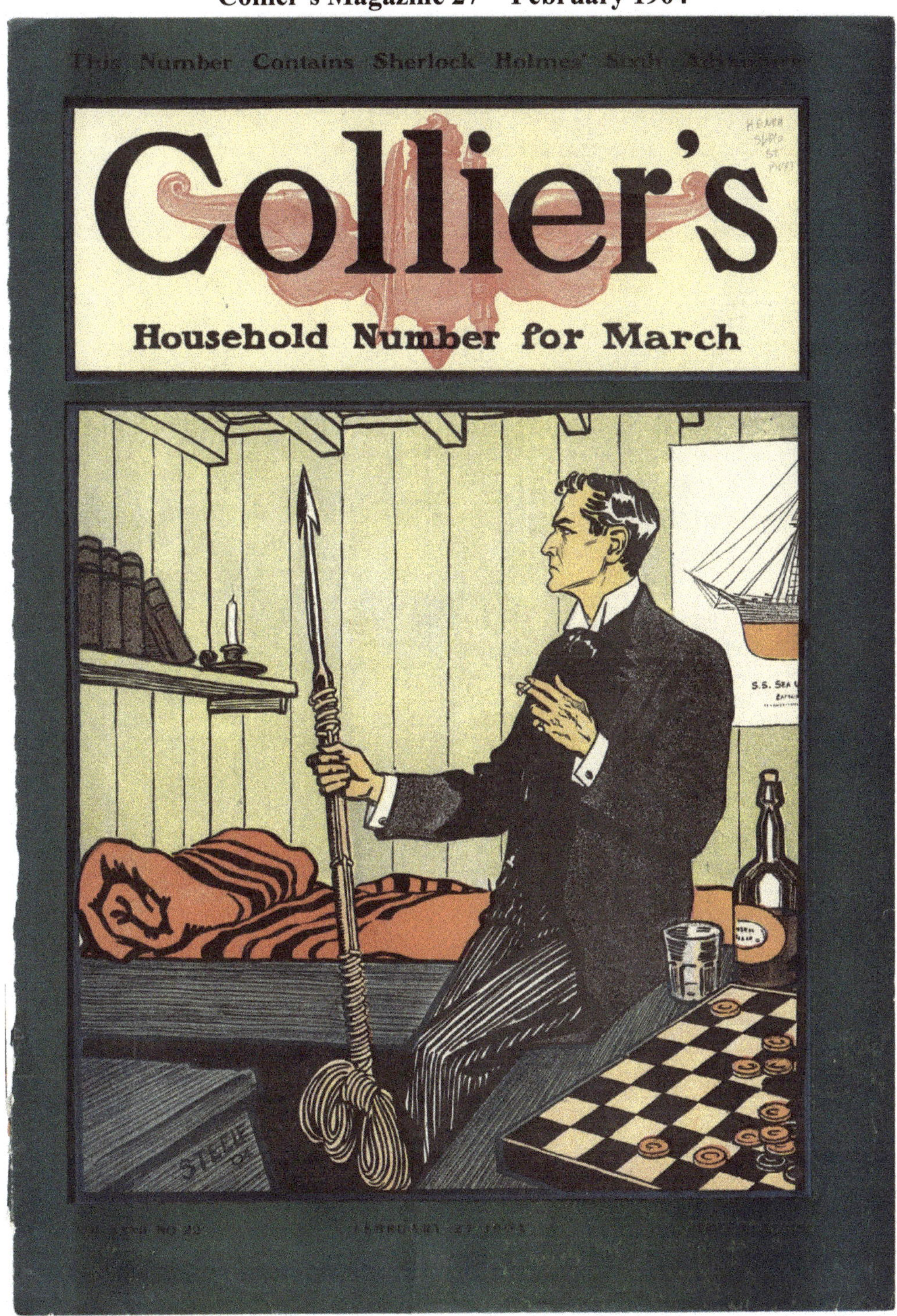

Images 1/7. Cover.
Ref. SH-FDS47

Images 2/7. Sketch of part of title.
Ref. SH-FDS48

THE ADVENTURE OF BLACK PETER

Images 3/7. Page 18. Miss Violet Smith followed by a skeleton!
Ref. SH-FDS49

Images 4/7. Page 18. The 'I' in this image is the first letter of the story "I have never known my friend to be in better form, both mental and physical, than in the year '95..."
Ref. SH-FDS50

Images 5/7. Page 18. "We watched him ... He returned with a large book"
Ref. SH-FDS51

Images 6/7. Page 19. "Then how do you account for that?"
Ref. SH-FDS52

Images 7/7. Page 19. The third applicant was a man of remarkable appearance
Ref. SH-FDS53

Images 1/9. Cover.
Ref. SH-FDS54

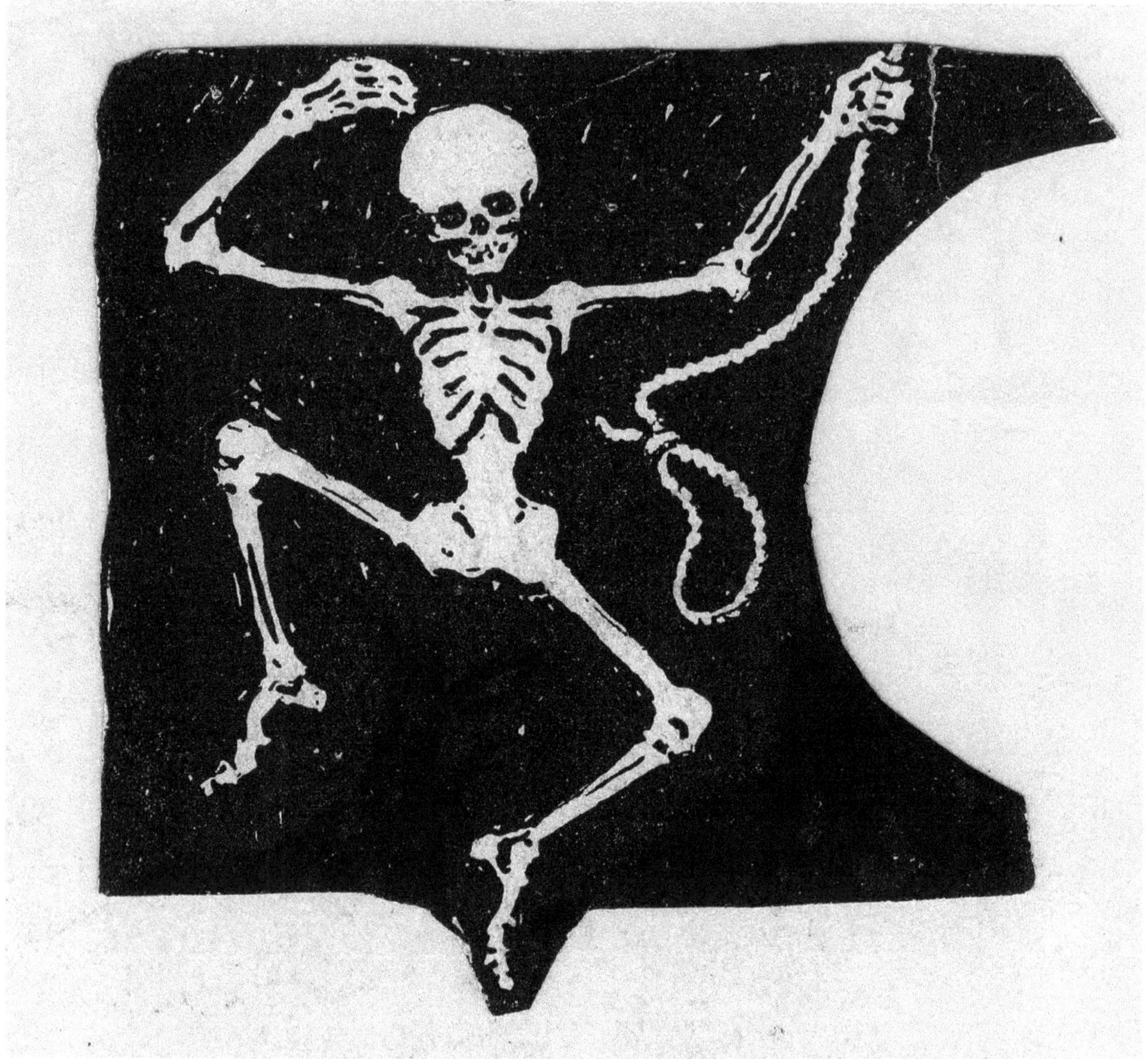

Images 2/9. Sketch that was actually used in the title of the Dancing men, there is a pencilled notation found on the original at the University of Minnesota Umedia Library, that does link it into the Milverton story, The note reads
"(Milverton - single in top hat) See Heritage Version Vol 2 P. 914 Milverton (alone) This drawing denigrated by Steele as a "duplicate drawing" as essentially similar to the Heritage Version "redrawn" therefore. But many minor differences (the best of them."
Ref. SH-FDS55

Images 3/9. Sketch of Charles Augustus Milverton that was never used in the Collier's magazine.
Ref. SH-FDS56

Images 4/9. Page 13. Steele drew a spider for this title as Milverton's victims were caught and squeezed and squeezed and drained dry.
Ref. SH-FDS57

Images 5/9. Page 13. The 'I' in this image is the first letter of the story "It is years since the incidents of which I speak took place, and yet it is with diffidence that I allude to them."
Ref. SH-FDS58

Images 6/9. Another sketch which unlike the previous one was adapted and appeared
Collier's Magazine as the next image.
Ref. SH-FDS59

Images 7/9. Page 13. There was something of Mr. Pickwick's benevolence in his looks
Ref. SH-FDS60

Images 8/9. Page 14. "You couldn't come any other time- Eh?"
Ref. SH-FDS61

Images 9/9. Page 27. Sherlock Holmes in disguise
Ref. SH-FDS62

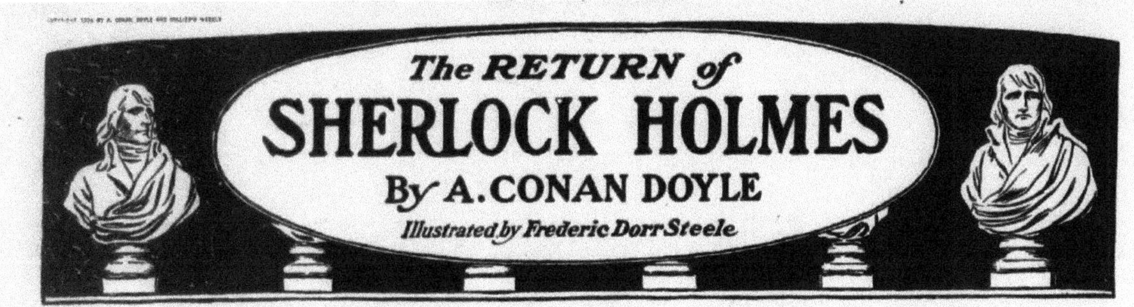

Images 1/6. Page 14 There was no Sherlock Holmes cover illustration for this story, but we have six full and partial Napoleons
Ref. SH-FDS63

Images 2/6. Page 14. The 'I' in this image is the first letter of the story "It was no very unusual thing for Mr Lestrade, of Scotland Yard, to look in upon us of an evening"
Ref. SH-FDS64

Images 3/6 Page 14. Holmes had just completed his examination when the door opened
Ref. SH-FDS65

Images 4/6. Page 15. He picked up his hunting-crop and struct Napoleon
Ref. SH-FDS66

Images 5/6. Page 28. Image at the top of page 28 where the story continues.
Ref. SH-FDS67

Images 6/6. Page 30. He carried a large old-fashioned carpetbag.
Ref. SH-FDS68

Images 1/10. Cover.
Ref. SH-FDS69

THE ADVENTURE OF THE THREE STUDENTS

Images 2/10. Page 14. A nice title for the story.
Ref. SH-FDS70

Images 3/10. Page 14. The 'I' in this image is the first letter of the story "It was in the year '95 that a combination of events, into which I need not enter, caused Mr. Sherlock Holmes and myself to spend some weeks in one of our great University towns,"
Ref. SH-FDS71

Images 4/10. Page 14. Daulat Ras
Ref. SH-FDS72

Images 5/10. Page 15. Miles McLaren
Ref. SH-FDS73

Images 6/10. Page 15. Gilchrist
Ref. SH-FDS74

Images 7/10. Early sketch by Steele for the next illustration.
Ref. SH-FDS75

Images 8/10. Page 15. "I trust, Mr. Holmes, that you can spare me a few hours."
Ref. SH-FDS76

Images 9/10. Page 27. Images at the top of Page 27 where the story continued. *Ref. SH-FDS77*

Images 10/10. Page 29. Bannister Explains
Ref. SH-FDS78

Images Advert 1. Page 22. Not strictly speaking an image from a story, but this advert appeared to have a Frederic Dorr Steele illustration.
Ref. SH-advt1

A SLEEPLESS WATCHMAN

FOR 1 CENT A DAY

Sherlock Holmes Says:

"The Prevention of Theft is Infinitely Better and Cheaper Than Its Detection and Punishment."

A prominent resident of Dayton, Ohio, speaking before the Retail Grocers' Association of Ohio, related the following incident:

"The first night after I introduced cash registers into a coal store in Dayton, our cash was short $2.00. My partner and I thought a mistake had been made and paid no attention to it. We had two clerks. Next day we were short $2.00 more, and the next day $2.00 more. We came to the conclusion that the machine was wrong and sent it back to the factory, but they assured us it was all right. Again we were short $2.00. We found after TWO MONTHS' investigation by the police, that our janitor, who had left us two years before, had been coming into the store at midnight. The policeman on duty thought he was a night watchman and so did not question his entering. He probably had stolen $2.00 a night for two years. The entire sum lost amounted to probably $1,400.00 which was a pretty big draw upon our small capital."

Now, Mr. Merchant, you, like this gentleman, have doubtless availed yourself of

Unknown hands may rifle YOUR cash register or stock.

many devices for safeguarding your interests through the day,—for checking your goods,—for recording your sales and registering your cash, but who guards your property during the night and during these periods when you and your trusted employees are away?

His cash register didn't save him from loss and it took two years to locate the thief.

Cases daily come to light where discharged employees with duplicate keys, have organized and carried out systematic robbery, and it has taken years to catch them.

How do you know who unlocks your doors in your absence? Or what unknown leak may be making inroads into your profits?

Wouldn't a lock which combined within itself all the good features of a bank vault

Inside Face of Lock.

time lock—together with a keenness of action almost human in its skill—appeal to you?

Our booklet, "A Sleepless Watchman," which explains how to secure a Sleepless Watchman for a cent a day, sent upon request.

CUT ON THIS LINE AND SEND TO

COLUMBUS RECORDING LOCK, Columbus, Ohio

Please send me your booklet, "A Sleepless Watchman."

Name

Firm name

Address

Images Advert 2. Page 28. Another advert from the same Collier's Magazine. (Not a Steele illustration.)
Ref. SH-advt2

Images 1/7. Cover.
Ref. SH-FDS79

THE ADVENTURE OF THE GOLDEN PINCE-NEZ

Images 2/7. Page 15. Page The title image shows the wild, tempestuous night towards the close of November.
Ref. SH-FDS80

Images 3/7. Page 15. The 'W' in this image is the first letter of the story "When I look at the three massive manuscript volumes which contain our work for the year 1894 …..."
Ref. SH-FDS81

Images 4/7. Page 15. "Now, my dear Hopkins, draw up and warm your toes"
Ref. SH-FDS82

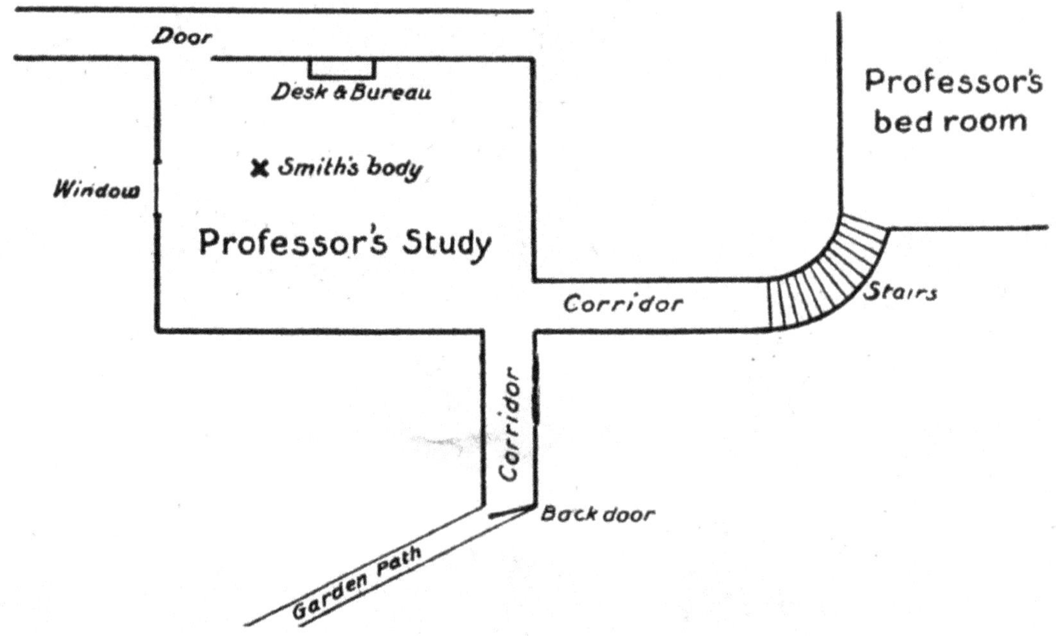

Images 5/7. Page 18. "Map of Yoxley Old Place"
Ref. SH-FDS83

Images 6/7. Page 18. "Yes, sir it is a crushing blow," said he old man
Ref. SH-FDS84

Images 7/7. Page 28. "The Professor was seated by the fire"
Ref. SH-FDS85

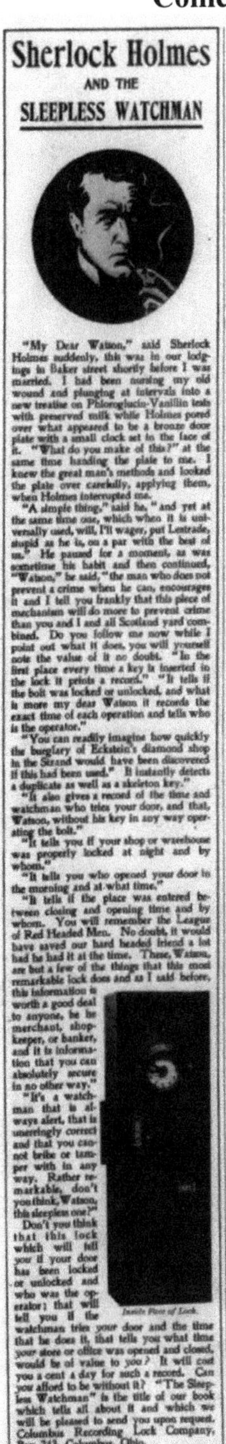

"My Dear Watson," said Sherlock Holmes suddenly, this was in our lodgings in Baker street shortly before I was married. I had been nursing my old wound and plunging at intervals into a new treatise on Phloroglucin-Vanillin tests with preserved milk while Holmes pored over what appeared to be a bronze door plate with a small clock set in the face of it. "What do you make of this?" at the same time handing the plate to me. I knew the great man's methods and looked the plate over carefully, applying them, when Holmes interrupted me.

"A simple thing," said he, " and yet at the same time one, which when it is universally used, will, I'll wager, put Lestrade, stupid as he is, on a par with the best of us." He paused for a moment, as was sometime his habit and then continued, "Watson," he said, "the man who does not prevent a crime when he can, encourages it and I tell you frankly that this piece of mechanism will do more to prevent crime than you and I and all Scotland yard combined. Do you follow me now while I point out what it does, you will yourself note the value of it no doubt. "In the first place every time a key is inserted in the lock it prints a record." "It tells if the bolt was locked or unlocked, and what is more my dear Watson it records the exact time of each operation and tells who is the operator."

"You can readily imagine how quickly the burglary of Eckstein's diamond shop in the Strand would have been discovered if this had been used." It instantly detects a duplicate as well as a skeleton key."

"It also gives a record of the time and watchman who tries your door, and that, Watson, without his key in any way operating the bolt."

"It tells you if your shop or warehouse was properly locked at night and by whom."

"It tells you who opened your door in the morning and at what time."

"It tells if the place was entered between closing and opening time and by whom. You will remember the League of Red Headed Men. No doubt, it would have saved our hard headed friend a lot had he had it at the time. These, Watson, are but a few of the things that this most remarkable lock does and as I said before, this information is worth a good deal to anyone, be he merchant, shopkeeper, or banker, and it is information that you can absolutely secure in no other way."

"It's a watchman that is always alert, that is unerringly correct and that you cannot bribe or tamper with in any way. Rather remarkable, don't you think, Watson, this sleepless one?"

Don't you think that this lock which will tell you if your door has been locked or unlocked and who was the operator; that will tell you if the watchman tries your door and the time that he does it, that tells you what time your store or office was opened and closed, would be of value to you? It will cost you a cent a day for such a record. Can you afford to be without it? "The Sleepless Watchman" is the title of our book which tells all about it and which we will be pleased to send you upon request. Columbus Recording Lock Company, Box 743, Columbus, Ohio.

Inside View of Lock.

Images Advert 3 Page 27.
Ref. SH-advt3

Images 1/8. Cover.
Ref. SH-FDS86

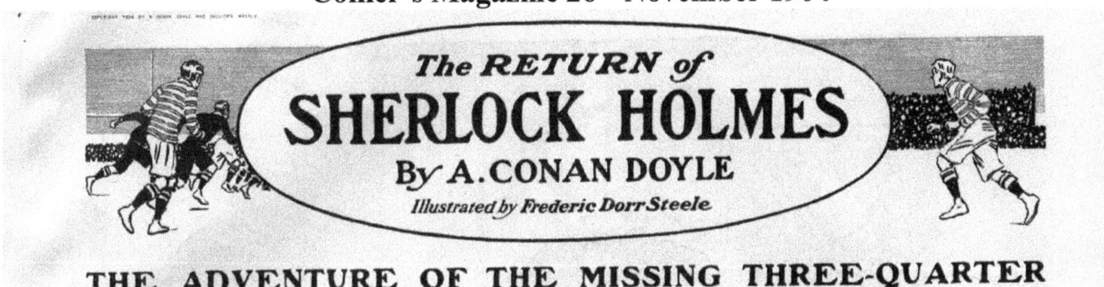

Images 2/8. Page 15. The title image shows the players who didn't go missing.
Ref. SH-FDS87

Images 3/8. Page 15. The 'W' in this image is the first letter of the story "We were fairly accustomed to receiving weird telegrams at Baker Street, but I have a particular recollection of one which reached us on a gloomy February morning some seven or eight years ago…."
Ref. SH-FDS88

Images 4/8. Page 15. We looked up to find a queer little old man, jerking and twitching in the doorway.
Ref. SH-FDS89

Images 5/8. Page 18. Part of the message, Holmes found on the Blotting Paper (it was of course reversed)
Ref. SH-FDS90

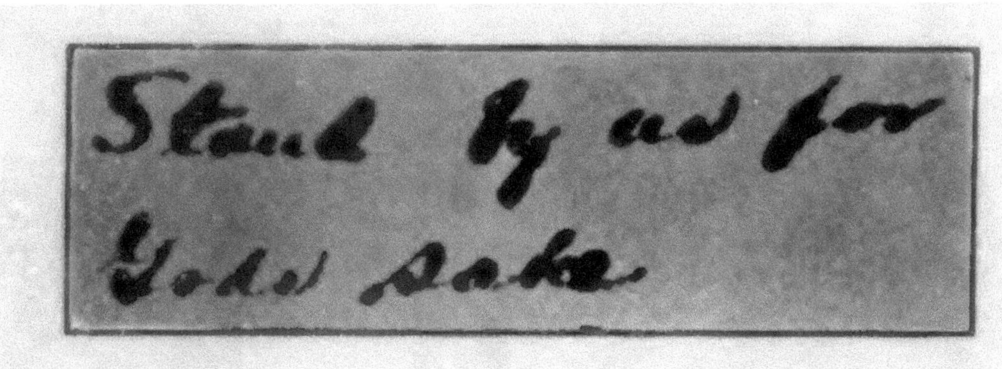

Images 6/8. Page 18. This is the message Holmes and Watson read.
Ref. SH-FDS91

Images 7/8. Page 18. Dr. Leslie Armstrong
Ref. SH-FDS92

Images 8/8. Page 27. Image at the top of the page where the story continued.
Ref. SH-FDS93

Images Advert 4. Page 6. Advert for a new game called "Sherlock Holmes"
Ref. SH-advt4

Images 1/6. Cover.
Ref. SH-FDS94

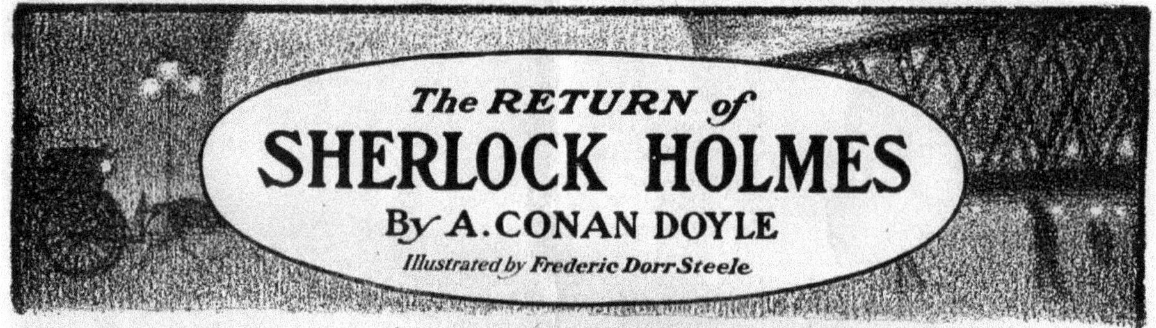

Images 2/6. Page 10. The title image shows the players who didn't go missing.
Ref. SH-FDS95

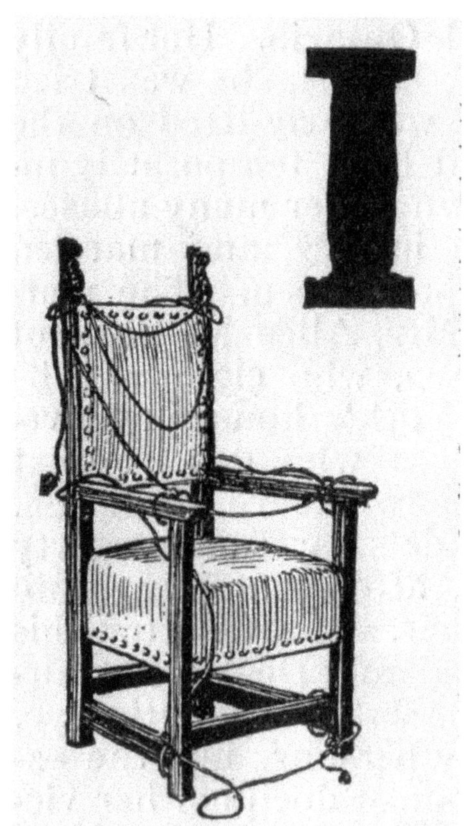

Images 3/6. Page 10. The 'I' in this image is the first letter of the story "It was on a bitterly cold and frosty morning during the winter of '97 that I was wakened by a tugging at my shoulder."
Ref. SH-FDS96

Frederic Dorr Steele – The Abbey Grange
Collier's Magazine 31st December 1904

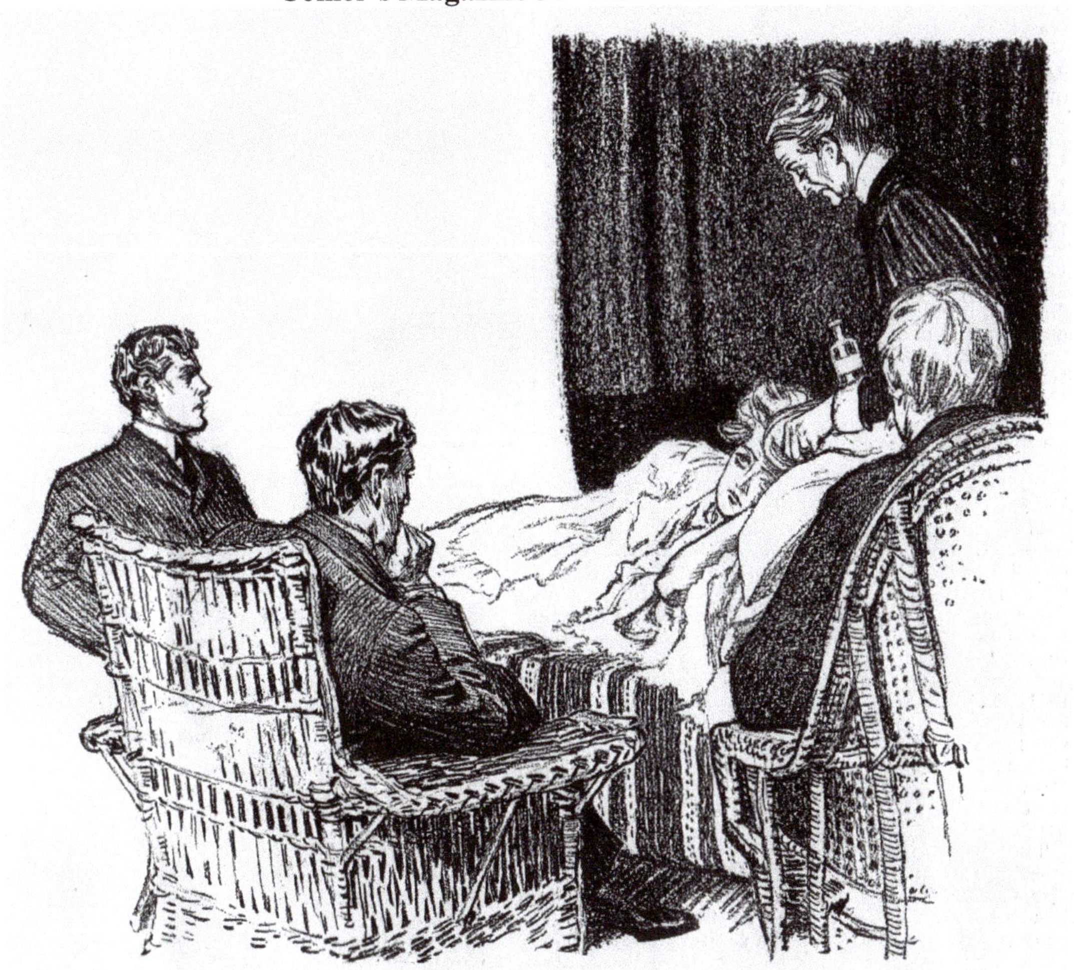

Images 4/6. Page 10. The lady lay back exhausted upon a couch enveloped in a loose dressing-gown of blue and silver.
Ref. SH-FDS97

1000th Image

Images 5/6. Page 11. Sherlock Holmes examines the glasses.
Ref. SH-FDS98

Images 6/6. Page 12. he stood with clinched hands and heaving breast.
Ref. SH-FDS99

Images 1/7. Initial sketch for front cover.
Ref. SH-FDS100

Images 2/7. Cover.
Ref. SH-FDS101

Images 3/7. Page 13. The second stain story was thought to be the final Sherlock Holmes, hence this title page. (In fact, Wisteria Lodge appeared in August 1908)
Ref. SH-FDS102

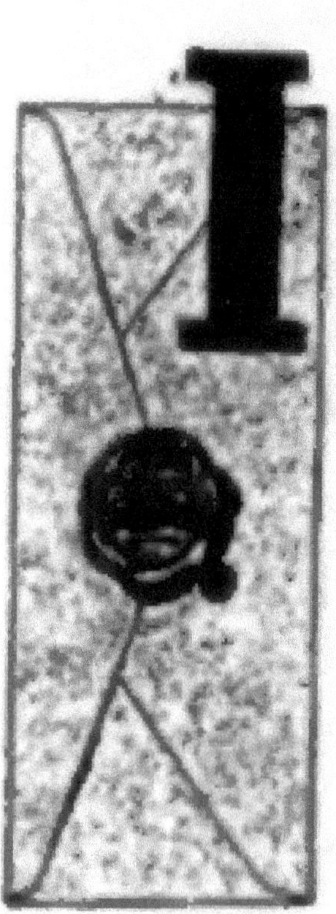

Images 4/7. Page 13. The 'I' in this image is the first letter of the story "I had intended 'The Adventure of the Abbey Grange' to be the last of those exploits of my friend, Mr Sherlock Holmes, which I should ever communicate to the public."
Ref. SH-FDS103

Images 5/7. She seated herself with her back to the window
Ref. SH-FDS104

Images 6/7. "There is a second stain!"
Ref. SH-FDS105

Images 7/7. "Madam, I have been commissioned to recover this immensely important paper"
Ref. SH-FDS106

Images Advert 5. Page 3. Advert for a new game called "Sherlock Holmes"
Ref. SH-advt5

Images 1/3. Page 67. A slightly modified version of the cover of November 1903 issue of Collier's Magazine. (*SH-FDS9)*
Ref. SH-FDS107

Images 2/3. Page 67. A slightly modified version of *SH-FDS17*
Ref. SH-FDS108

Images 3/3. Page 115. A slightly modified version of the cover of February 1904 issue of Collier's Magazine *Ref. SH-FDS34*
Ref. SH-FDS109

Images 1/8. Sketch of Cover.
Ref. SH-FDS110

Images 2/8. Final Cover.
Ref. SH-FDS111

Images 3/8. Page 16. "Sacrifices to propitiate his unclean gods"
Ref. SH-FDS112
(Historically, this story was first published in Collier's as 'The Singular Experience of Mr.
J. Scott Eccles and then printed in The Strand over the next two months with the second
part being called 'The Tiger of San Pedro'. It was later retitled 'The Adventure of Wisteria
Lodge'

Images 4/8. Page 17. Our client sat up with staring eyes
Ref. SH-FDS113

Images 5/8. Page 18. The queer thing in the kitchen
Ref. SH-FDS114

Images 6/8. Page 19. The light from the window streamed across the shrubbery
Ref. SH-FDS115

Images 7/8. Page 20. "They had gagged me, and Murillo twisted my arm around"
Ref. SH-FDS116

Images 8/8. Page 21.
(The death of Marquess of Montalva and Signor Rulli.)
Ref. SH-FDS117

"We were to go to the theater. . . .   Suddenly he darted away into the fog"

Images 1/5. Page 15. Title drawing. "We were to go to the theatre . . . Suddenly he darted away into the fog"
Ref. SH-FDS118

Images 2/5. Page 16. "This is where the young man's body lay"
Ref. SH-FDS119

Images 3/5. Page 17. "Yes," she said, "I had a feeling there was something on his mind""
Ref. SH-FDS120

**Frederic Dorr Steele – Bruce-Partington Plans
Collier's Magazine 15th August 1908**

Images 4/5. Page 18. I stowed them all discreetly away in my overcoat
Ref. SH-FDS121

Images 5/5. Page 18. Holmes swept his light along the window-sill
Ref. SH-FDS122

Images 1/7. Sketch of cover.
Ref. SH-FDS123

Images 2/7. Final cover.
Ref. SH-FDS124

Images 3/7. Page 133. "What has happened to the Lady Frances? Is she alive or dead? There is our problem"
Ref. SH-FDS125

Images 4/7. Page 135. "See!" she cried, "The miscreant follows still! There is the very man
of whom I speak"
Ref. SH-FDS126

Images 5/7. Page 138. The door had been opened to admit the men and their burden
Ref. SH-FDS127

Images 6/7. Missing illustration. "There is surely some mistake here, gentlemen," he said
Ref. SH-FDS128

Images 7/7. Page 141. "Quick, man, quick! It's life or death"
Ref. SH-FDS129

Images 1/5. Cover.
Ref. SH-FDS130

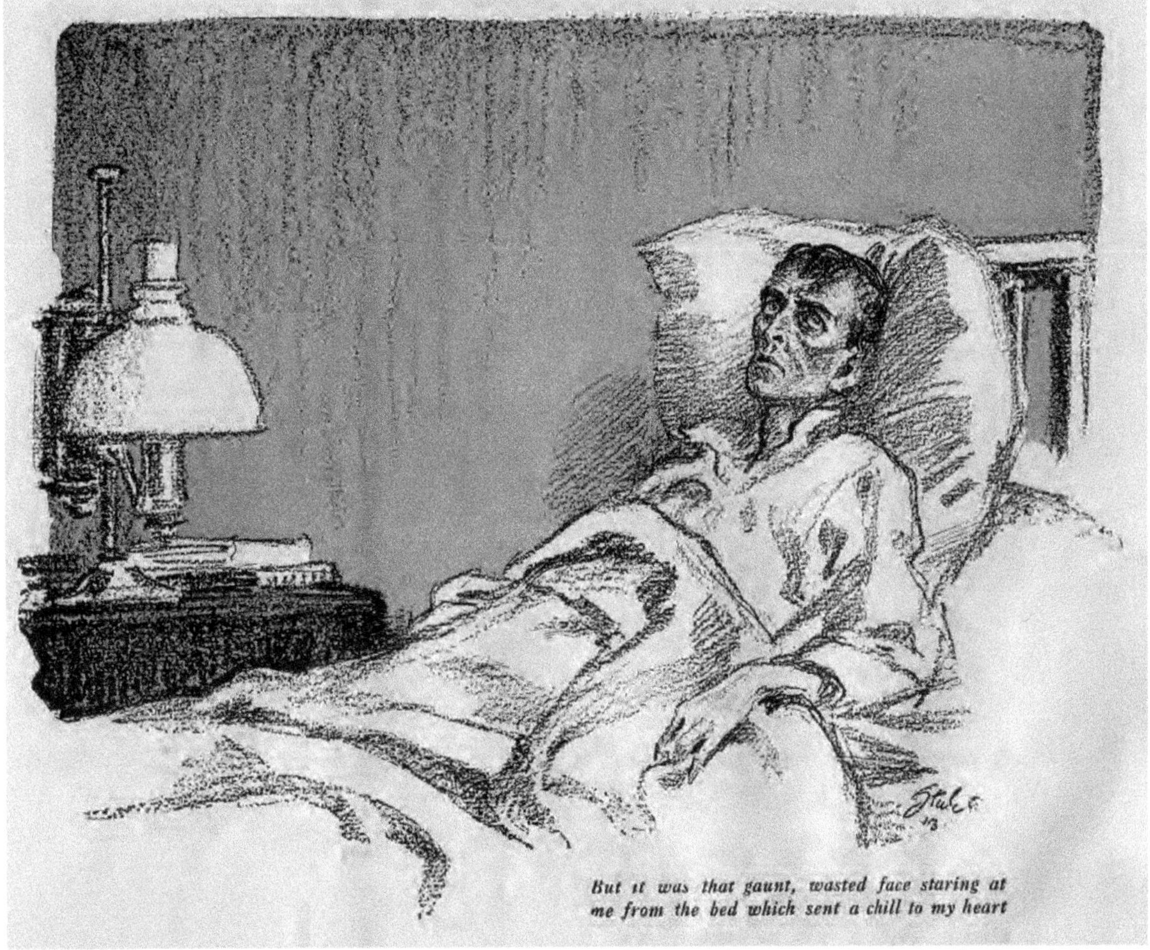

Images 2/5. Page 5. But it was that gaunt, wasted face staring at me from the bed which
sent a chill to my heart
Ref. SH-FDS131

Images 3/5. Page 6. "Put it down!"
Ref. SH-FDS132

Images 4/5. Page 7. (No Caption)
Ref. SH-FDS133

Images 5/5. Page 24. (No caption)
Ref. SH-FDS134

Images 1/5. Cover.
Ref. SH-FDS135

Images 2/5. Page 5 (Frontispiece). "I shall get level with you. If it takes all my life, I shall get level with you!"
Ref. SH-FDS136

Images 3/5. Page 6. "This quiet house is the center of half the mischief in England; the sporting squire the most astute secret-service man in Europe!"
Ref. SH-FDS137

Images 4/5. Page 7. A dear old ruddy-faced woman in a country cap, bending over her knitting
Ref. SH-FDS138

Images 5/5. Page 7. "If I didn't dare things, mister, I wouldn't be in your service"
Ref. SH-FDS139

Images 1/5. Unused sketch.
Ref. SH-FDS140

Images 2/5. Page 6. "Don't break it!" a voice commanded, and the would-be assassin turned from the clever effigy to confront Sherlock Holmes himself!
Ref. SH-FDS141

Images 3/5. Page 7. "Thank you." Cried an unexpected voice, and Holmes faced his startled guests, the jewel in one hand and a revolver in the other.
Ref. SH-FDS142

"The one thing I don't know about it, you're going to tell me now," Holmes announced calmly.

Images 4/5. Page 8. "The one thing I don't know about it. You're going to tell me now."
Holmes announced calmly.
Ref. SH-FDS143

Images 5/5. Page 64. "I want that yellow diamond!"
Ref. SH-FDS144

Images 1/10. Cover.
Ref. SH-FDS145

Images 2/10. Page 8. Above Title illustration
Ref. SH-FDS146

Images 3/10. Page 9. "Something was moving along the passage, something dark and crouching; then suddenly it emerged into the light and I saw that it was he."
Ref. SH-FDS147

Images 4/10. Page 10. "I dare say it was twenty seconds or so that I lay paralyzed and watched its face. Then it vanished and I lay cold and shivering till morning."
Ref. SH-FDS148

1

Images 5/10. Page 11. "Hardly enough, Mr. Holmes!" the old man cried in a high
screaming voice.
Ref. SH-FDS149

Images 6/10. Page 12. The hall door slowly opened and against the lamp-lit background Holmes and Watson saw the tall figure of Professor Presbury. As he stood outlined in the doorway he was erect but leaned forward with dangling arms.
Ref. SH-FDS150

Images 7/10. Page 13. With his dressing-gown flapping on each side of him he looked like some huge bat glued against. . . the moonlit wall.
Ref. SH-FDS151

Images 8/10. Page 2. To Sherlock Holmes the confidential secretary of the great Prof.
Presbury described the astounding scene . . . "The passage was dark save for one window. I
could see that something was coming along the passage, something dark and crouching.
The suddenly it emerged into the light, and I saw that it was he." . . . one of the greatest
men in England and creeping, yet moving with ease!
Ref. SH-FDS152

Images 9/10. Page 46. The passage was dark save for one window. I could see that something was coming along the passage, something dark and crouching. The suddenly it emerged into the light, and I saw that it was he."
Ref. SH-FDS153

Images 10/10. Page 48. "With his dressing-gown flapping on each side of him he looked
like some huge bat glued against the side of his own house."
Ref. SH-FDS154

Images 1/1. Sherlock Holmes, standing by the fireside watches, Ferguson, the father, takes the child into his arms and fondles it most tenderly, with evident devotion. "Fancy anyone having the heart to hurt him." He mutters.
Ref. SH-FDS155

Images 1/1. Page 4. "'But you have been in England for some time,' said Sherlock Holmes to Mr. Garrideb, of Kansas."
Ref. SH-FDS156

Images 1/1. Page 4. "Mr. Holmes, I beg that you will bring this interview to an end," said
the icy voice. "I have obeyed my father's wish in seeing you, but I am not compelled to
listen to the ravings of this person." – Drawn especially for The Courier-Journal by Frederic
Dorr Steele.
Ref. SH-FDS157

Images 1/8. Page 9. (No caption)
Ref. SH-FDS158

Images 2/8. Page 10. Holmes raised his pipe, languidly smiling.
Ref. SH-FDS159

Images 3/8. Page 11. "When I woke, one man was at the bedside and another was rising with a bundle in his hand."
Ref. SH-FDS160

Images 4/8. Page 12. Holmes flung open the door and dragged in a gaunt woman, whom he had seized by the shoulder.
Ref. SH-FDS161

Images 5/8. Sketch of next illustration
Ref. SH-FDS162

Images 6/8. Page 13. "Shall I give this back?" she asked.
Ref. SH-FDS163

Images 7/8. Page 14. (No Caption).
Ref. SH-FDS164

Images 8/8. Page 3. There was a calcined mass which she broke up with the poker. "Shall I give this back?" she asked.
Ref. SH-FDS165

Images 1/10. Initial sketch showing lamp and face at window.
Ref. SH-FDS166

Images 2/10. Refined sketch showing just the face at window.
Ref. SH-FDS167

Images 3/10. Similar sketch to first showing the lamp and face at window.
Ref. SH-FDS168

Images 4/10. Page 17. It was his face that held my gaze. He was deadly pale – never have I seen a man so white.
Ref. SH-FDS169

Images 5/10. Title Page. There was Godfrey Emsworth standing before me. He was outside the window.
Ref. SH-FDS170

Images 6/10. Page 18. There was a crack in the shutter so that I could see inside the room.
Ref. SH-FDS171

Images 7/10. Page 19. "I extend the same warning to you . . . take your reputed talents to some other field."
Ref. SH-FDS172

Images 8/10. Page 20. (No caption)
Ref. SH-FDS173

Images 9/10. Page 21. (No caption)
Ref. SH-FDS174

Images 10/10. Page 46. (No caption)
Ref. SH-FDS175

Images 1/9. Initial sketch for title page that was never used.
Ref. SH-FDS176

Images 2/9. Page 18. His back was covered with dark red lines, a though he had been terribly flogged.
Ref. SH-FDS177

**Frederic Dorr Steele – Lion's Mane, The
Liberty 27th November 1926**

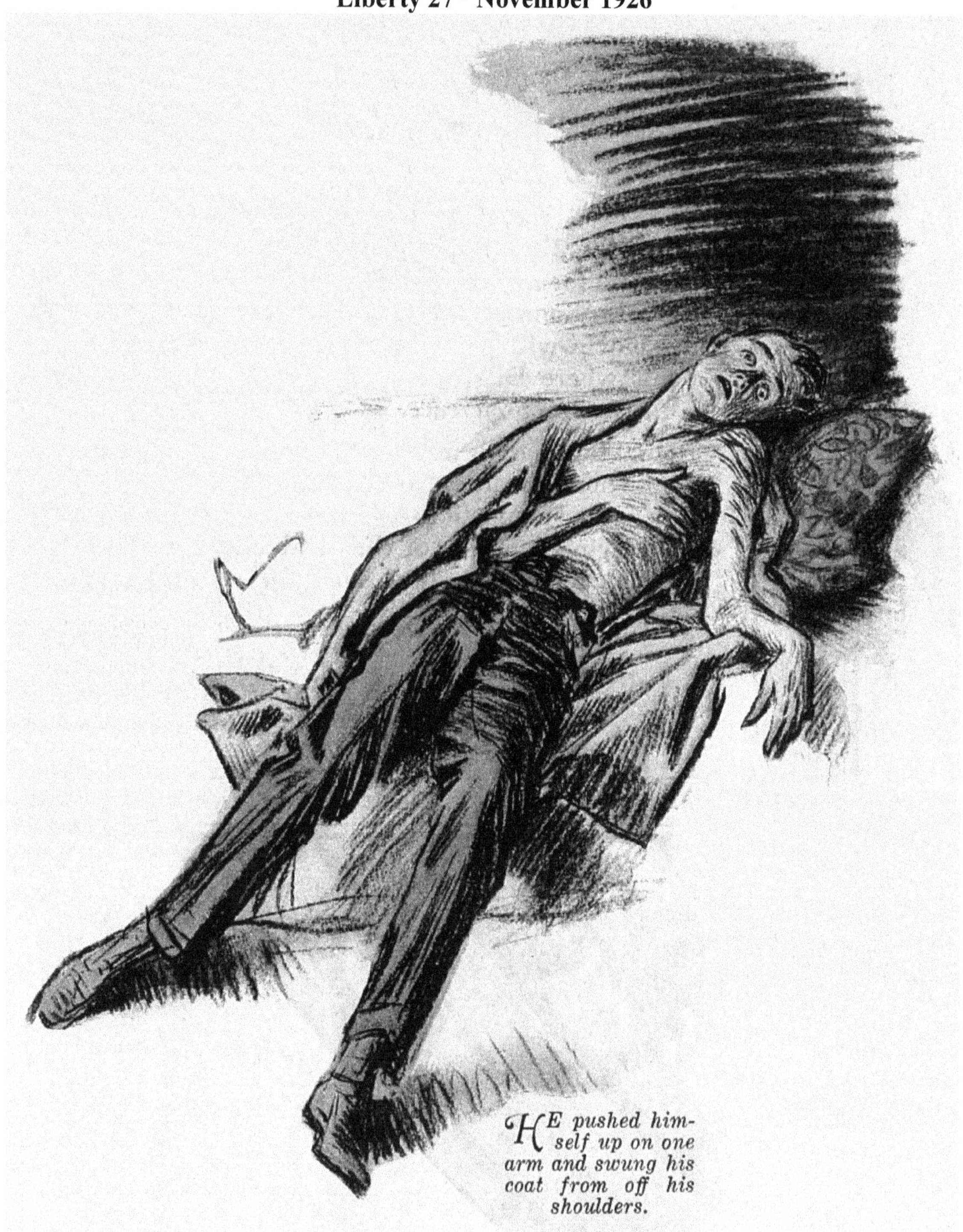

Images 3/9. Page 19. He pushed himself up on one arm and swung his coat from off his shoulders.
Ref. SH-FDS178

Images 4/9. Page 20. "The whole world will know the facts presently, so there can be no harm if I discuss them here."
Ref. SH-FDS179

Images 5/9. Page 21. "For a long time I stood in deep mediation while the shadows grew darker around me.
Ref. SH-FDS180

Images 6/9. Page 22. (No caption)
Ref. SH-FDS181

Images 7/9. Page 23. (No caption).
Ref. SH-FDS182

Images 8/9. Page 24. (No caption).
Ref. SH-FDS183

Images 9/9. Page 4. "I know already that Fitzroy is dead."
Ref. SH-FDS184

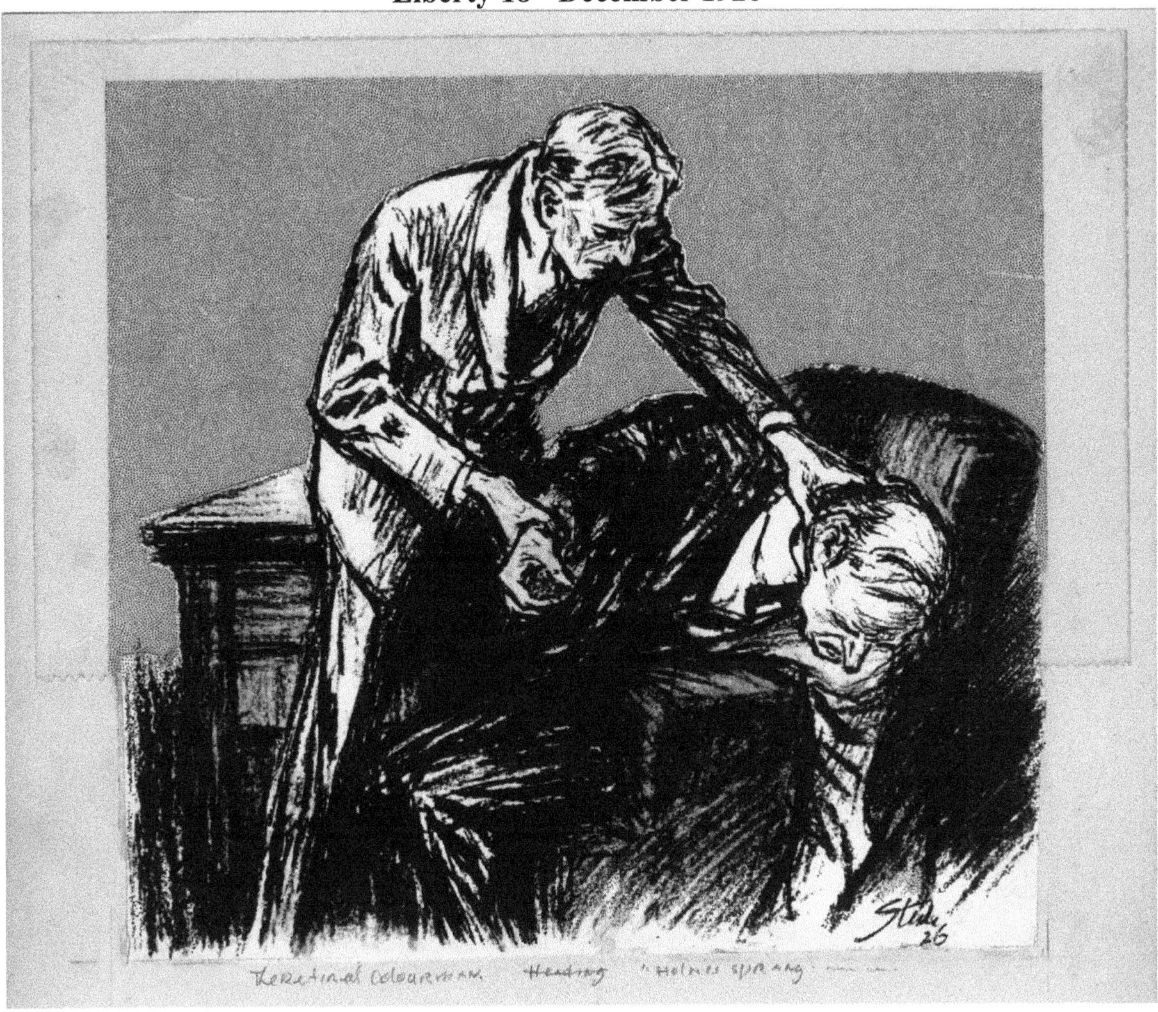

Images 1/7. Initial sketch for the next page.
Ref. SH-FDS185

Images 2/7. Page 7. Holmes sprang at him like a tiger, and twisted his face towards the floor.
Ref. SH-FDS186

Images 3/7. Page 8. He tore up one of his wife's photographs in my presence. "I never wish to see her damned face again!" he shrieked."
Ref. SH-FDS187

Images 4/7. Page 9. Holmes' eyelids drooped so lazily that he might almost have been asleep.
Ref. SH-FDS188

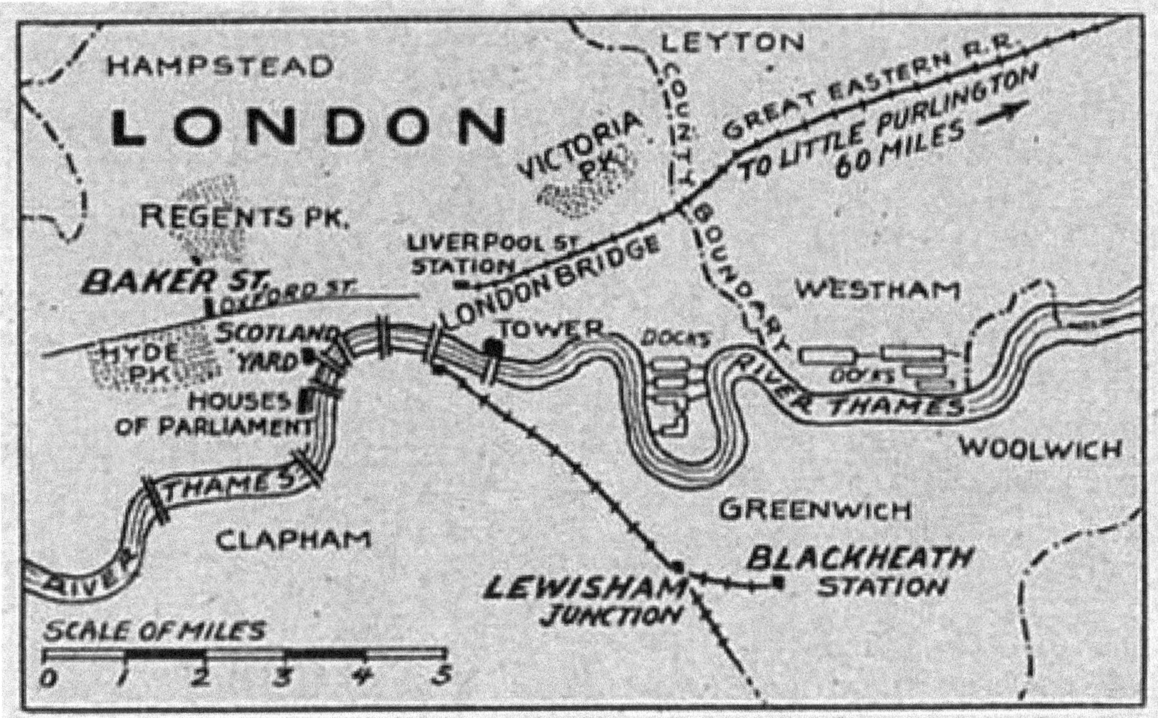

Images 5/7. Page 10. Map of London
Ref. SH-FDS189

Images 6/7. Page 11. "I was slipping through the pantry window in the early dawn when I felt a hand inside my collar."
Ref. SH-FDS190

Images 7/7. Page 16-17. "What is the question, Mr. Holmes?"
Ref. SH-FDS191

Images 1/7. Initial sketch for the next image.
Ref. SH-FDS192

Images 2/7. Page 7. "That is Leonardo", she said.
Ref. SH-FDS193

Images 3/7. Page 8. "One night my cries brought Leonardo to the door of our van."
Ref. SH-FDS194

Images 4/7. Page 9. "Close to the door of the cage lay Mrs. Ronder, with the creature squatting and snarling above her."
Ref. SH-FDS195

Images 5/7. Page 10. (Sahara King)
Ref. SH-FDS196

Images 6/7. Page 53. (No caption).
Ref. SH-FDS197

Images 7/7. Page 16-17. The woman's answer was a terrible one. She raised her veil and stepped forward into the light
Ref. SH-FDS198

Images 1/8. Page 39. "It was a head and a few bones of a mummy that must have been a thousand years old."
Ref. SH-FDS199

Images 2/8. Page 40. (No Caption)
Ref. SH-FDS200

Images 3/8. Page 41.
Ref. SH-FDS201

Images 4/8. Page 42.
Ref. SH-FDS202

Images 5/8. Page 43. "Who the devil are you and what are you doing upon my property?"
he asked, raising his heavy stick.
Ref. SH-FDS203

Images 6/8. Page 44. Holmes crouched behind the bush with the dog as the carriage approached.
Ref. SH-FDS204

Images 7/8. Page 45. (No Caption)
Ref. SH-FDS205

Images 8/8. Page 45. He turned and tore open the coffin behind him. In the glare of the lantern I saw a body swathed in a sheet from head to foot, with dreadful, witch-like features, all nose and chin, projecting at one end, the dim glazed eyes staring from a discolored and crumbling face.
Ref. SH-FDS206

Images 1/4. Page 155. "He was much saturniner than usual, and the others at once deduced there was something toward"
Ref. SH-FDS207

Images 2/4. Page 156. No caption
Ref. SH-FDS208

Images 3/4. Page 156. "The lady had dropped her slipper"
Ref. SH-FDS209

Images 4/4. Page 157. "'Marvelous! Holmes, marvelous!' said Watson"
Ref. SH-FDS210

Alexander Boguslavsky

The 1923 Cigarette card collection from Alexander Boguslavsky, Ltd.
They were a cigarette company founded in 1892 by Alexander and they produced the Piccadilly.
In 1913 they were bought out by Carreras, but clearly continued to advertise under their old name. The Turf cigarette brand was brought out by Carreras in 1921 and two years later they produced a set of 25 cards featuring Arthur Conan Doyle Characters, but only 18 were Sherlock Holmes related.

Each Card had an image of one of Doyle's characters on the front and a description of the character on the reverse. The Back of each card had

"TURF"
CIGARETTES
Series of Twenty-Five
Conan Doyle Characters

at the top of the card.

Followed by a description of the character and at the bottom

Alexander Boguslavsky, ltd.
55,PICCADILLY,LONDON,W.

The 25 Cards comprised

Card No.	Character
1	**Sherlock Holmes**
2	**Sherlock Holmes in Disguise.**
3	**Dr. Watson.**
4	**Lestrade.**
5	**Miss Mary Morstan.**
6	**Tonga.**
7	**Professor Moriarty.**
8	**Lucy Ferrier.**
9	**Jefferson Hope.**
10	Dame Ermyntrude Loring.
11	Sir Nigel Loring.
12	**Miss Helen Stoner.**
13	**Dr. Grimesby Roylott.**
14	Mother Superior.
15	Brigadier Gerard.
16	**The Hound of the Baskervilles.**
17	**"Miss Stapleton."**
18	**"The Man with the Twisted Lip."**
19	Polly Hinton.
20	**King of Bohemia**
21	**Mr. Jabez Wilson.**
22	**Irene Adler.**
23	**Miss Violet Hunter**
24	Rebecca Taylforth
25	**Miss Hatty Doran.**

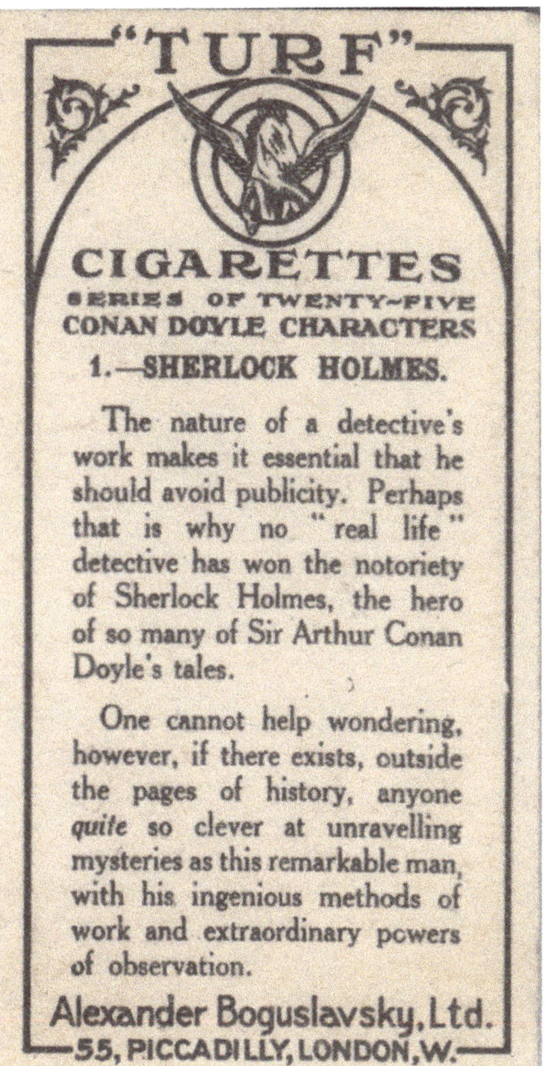

1.– Sherlock Holmes.

The nature of a detective's work makes it essential that he should avoid publicity. Perhaps that is why no "real life" detective has won the notoriety of Sherlock Holmes, the hero of so many of Sir Arthur Conan Doyle's tales.
One cannot help wondering. however, if there exists, outside the of history, anyone quite so clever at unravelling mysteries as this remarkable man, with his ingenious methods of work and extraordinary powers of observation.
SH-AB1

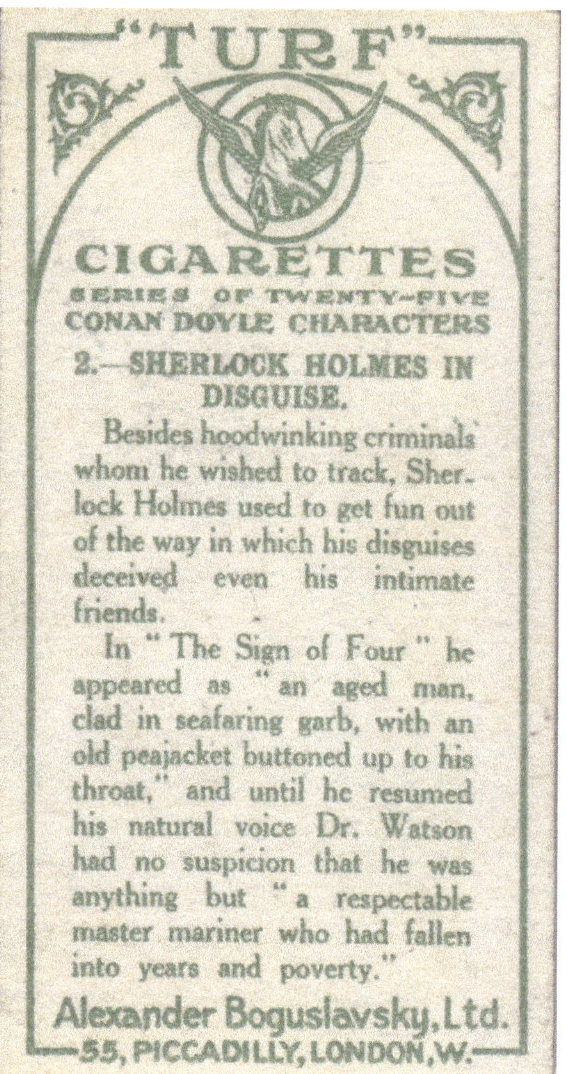

2. SHERLOCK HOLMES IN DISGUISE.

Besides hoodwinking criminals whom he wished to track, Sherlock Holmes used to get fun out of the way in which his disguises deceived even his intimate friends.
In "The Sign of Four" he appeared as "an aged man, clad in seafaring garb, with an old peajacket buttoned up to his throat," and until he resumed his natural voice Dr. Watson had no suspicion that he was anything but :a respectable master mariner who had fallen into years and poverty."
SH-AB2

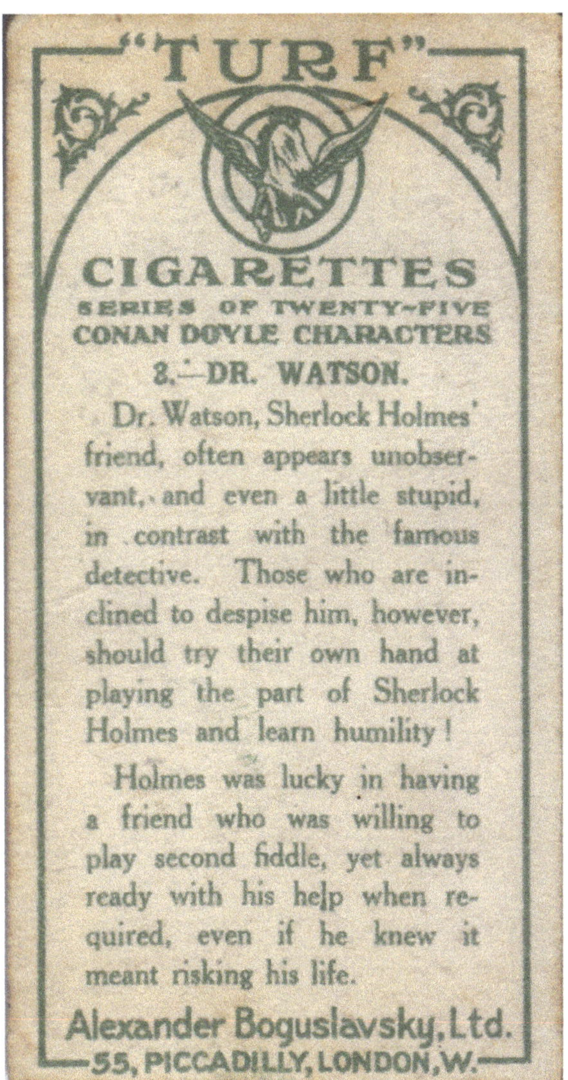

3. DR WATSON

Dr. Watson, Sherlock Holmes friend, often appears unobservant, and even a little stupid, in contrast with the famous detective. Those who are inclined to despise him, however, should try their own hand at playing the part of Sherlock Holmes and learn humility! Holmes was lucky in having a friend who was willing to play second fiddle, yet always ready with his help when required even if he knew it meant risking his life.
SH-AB3

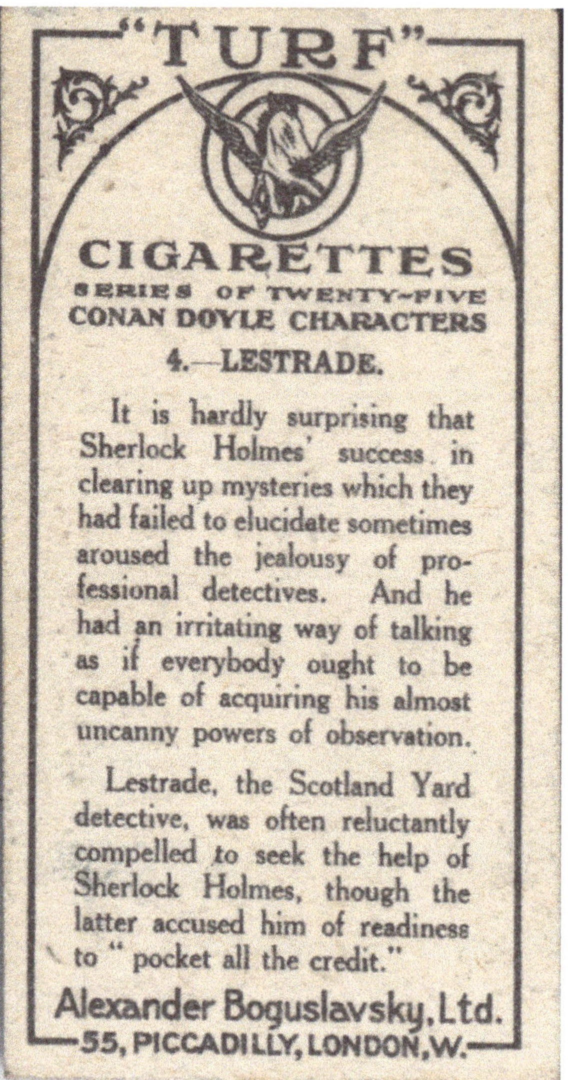

4. LESTRADE

It is hardly surprising that Sherlock Holmes' success in clearing up mysteries which they had failed to elucidate sometimes aroused the jealousy of professional detectives. And he had an irritating way of talking as if everybody ought to be capable of acquiring his almost uncanny powers of observation.

Lestrade, the Scotland Yard detective, was often reluctantly compelled to seek the help of Sherlock Holmes thought the latter accused him of readiness to "pocket all the credit."
SH-AB4

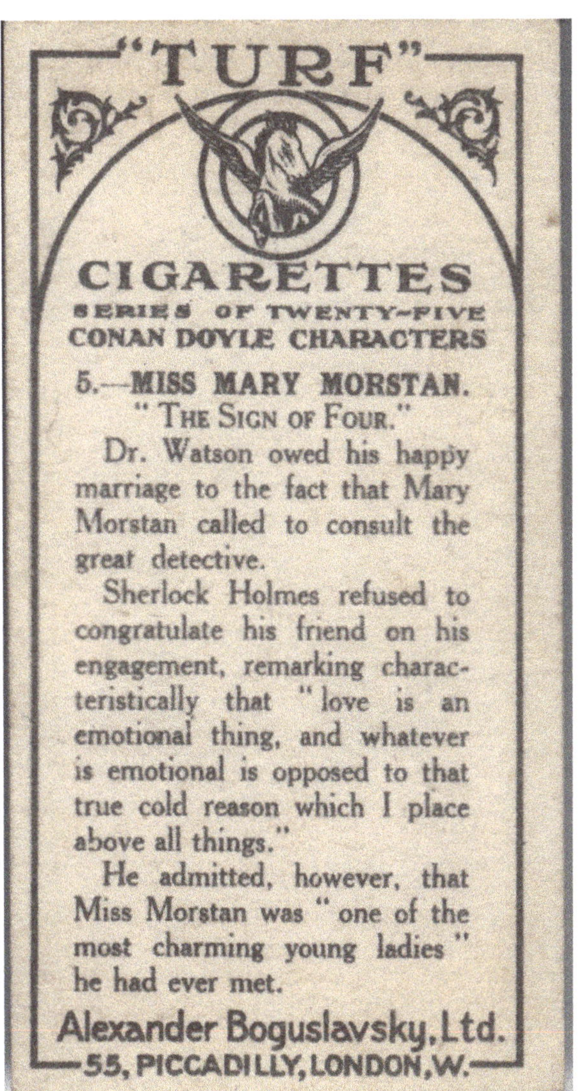

5. MISS MARY MORSTAN.
"The Sign of Four"

Dr. Watson owed his happy marriage to the fact that Mary Morstan called to consult the great detective.

Sherlock Holmes refused to congratulate his friend on his engagement, remarking characteristically that "love is an emotional thing, and whatever is emotional is opposed to that true cold reason which I place above all things."

He admitted, however that Miss Morstan was "one of the most charming young ladies" he had ever met.

SH-AB5

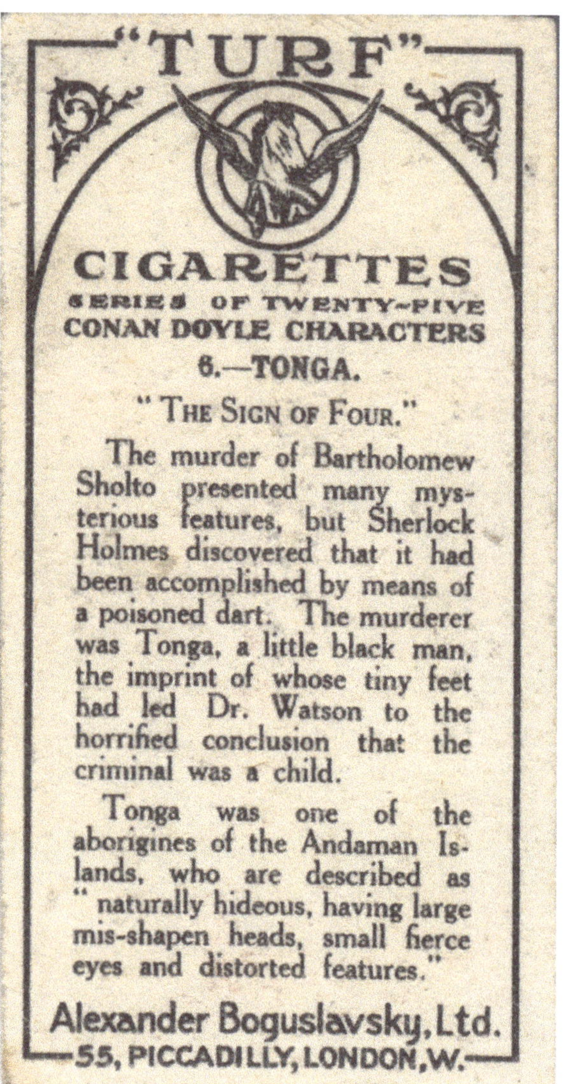

6. TONGA.
"The Sign of Four"

The murder of Bartholomew Sholto presented many mysterious features, but Sherlock Holmes discovered that it had been accomplished by means of a poisoned dart. The murderer was Tonga, a little black man, the imprint of whose tiny feet had led Dr. Watson to the horrified conclusion that the criminal was a child.

Tonga was one of the aborigines of the Andaman Islands, who are described as "naturally hideous, having large mis-shapen heads, small fierce eyes and distorted features."

SH-AB6

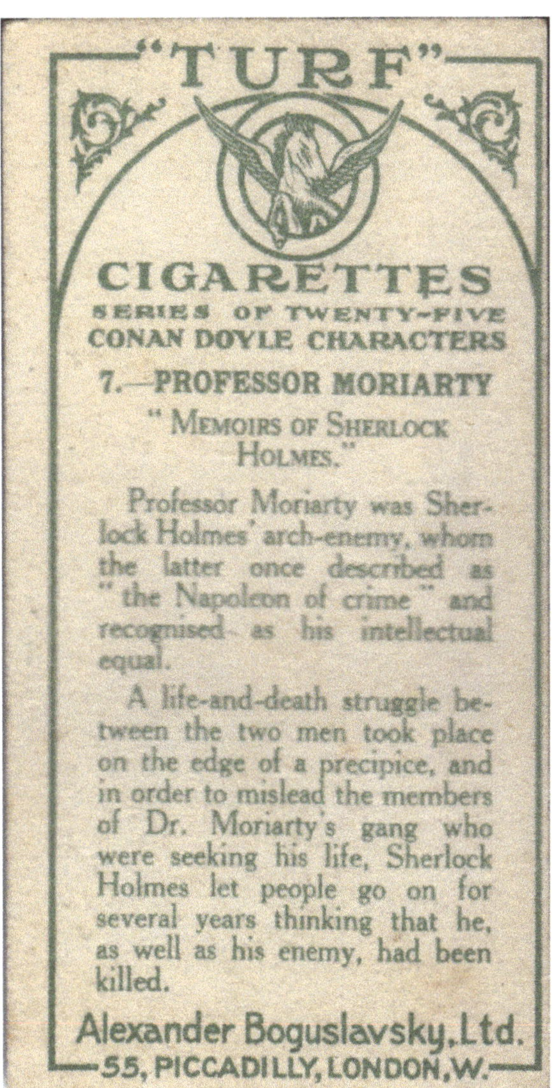

7. PROFESSOR MORIARTY

Professor Moriarty was Sherlock Holmes arch-enemy, whom the latter once described as "the Napoleon of crime" and recognised as his intellectual equal.

A life-and-death struggle between the two men took place on the edge of a precipice, and in order to mislead the members of Dr. [sic] Moriarty's gang who were seeking his life, Sherlock Holmes let people go on for several years thinking that he, as well as his enemy, had been killed.

SH-AB7

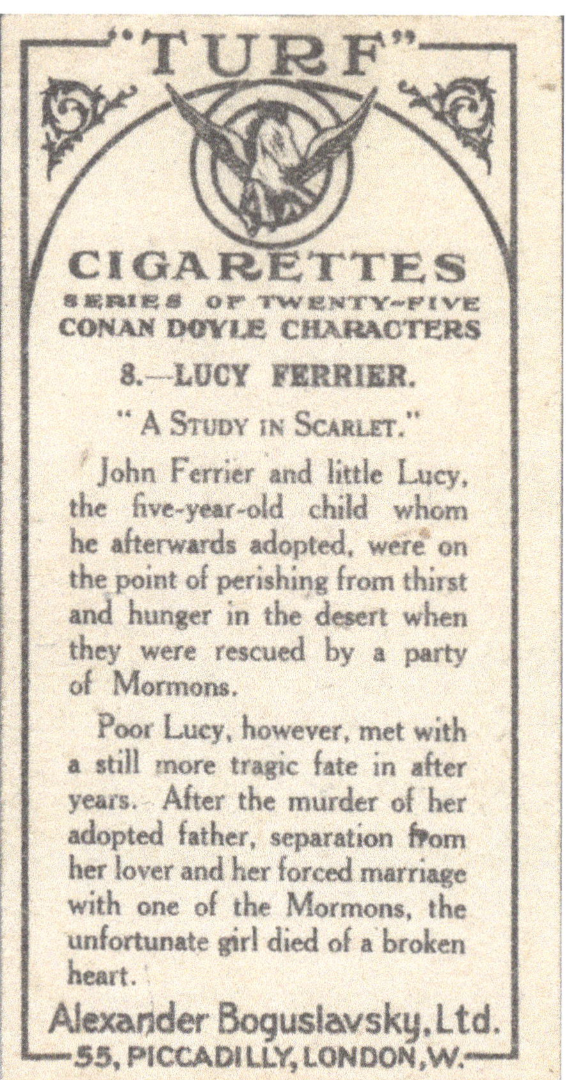

8. LUCY FERRIER
"A Study in Scarlet."

John Ferrier and little Lucy, the five-year-old child whom he afterwards adopted, were on the point of perishing from thirst and hunger in the desert when they were rescued by a party of Mormons.

Poor Lucy, however, met with a still more tragic fate in after years. After the murder of her adopted father, separation from her lover and her forced marriage with one of the Mormons, the unfortunate girl died of a broken heart.

SH-AB8

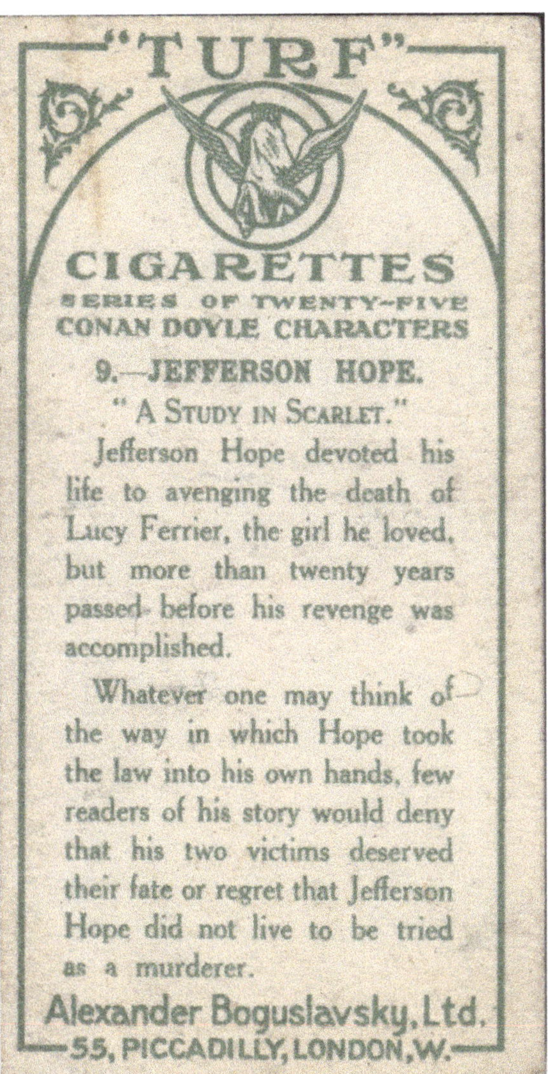

9. JEFFERSON HOPE.
"A Study in Scarlet."

Jefferson Hope devoted his life to avenging the death of Lucy Ferrier, the girl he loved, but more than twenty years passed before his revenge was accomplished.

Whatever one may think of the way in which Hope took the law into his own hands, few readers of his story would deny that his two victims deserved their fate or regret that Jefferson Hope did not live to be tried as a murderer.

SH-AB9

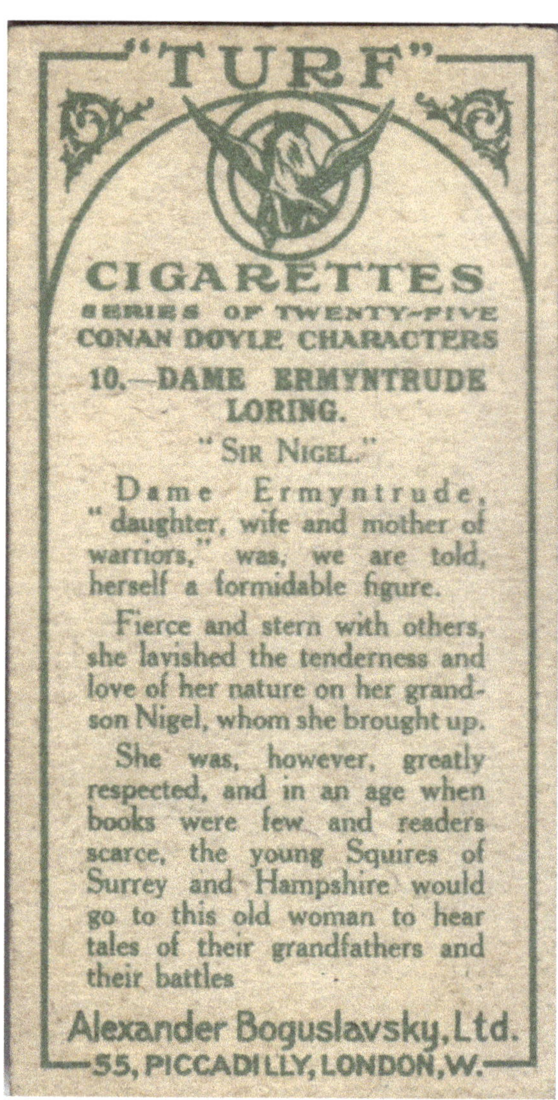

10. DAME ERMYNTRUDE LORING.
"Sir Nigel"

Dame Ermyntrude, "daughter, wife and mother of warriors," was we are told herself a formidable figure.

Fierce and stern with others, she lavished the tenderness and love of her nature on her Grandson Nigel, whom she brought up.

She was however greatly respected, and in an age when books were few and readers scarce, the young Squires of Surry and Hampshire would go to this old woman to hear tales of their grandfathers and their battles.

SH-AB10

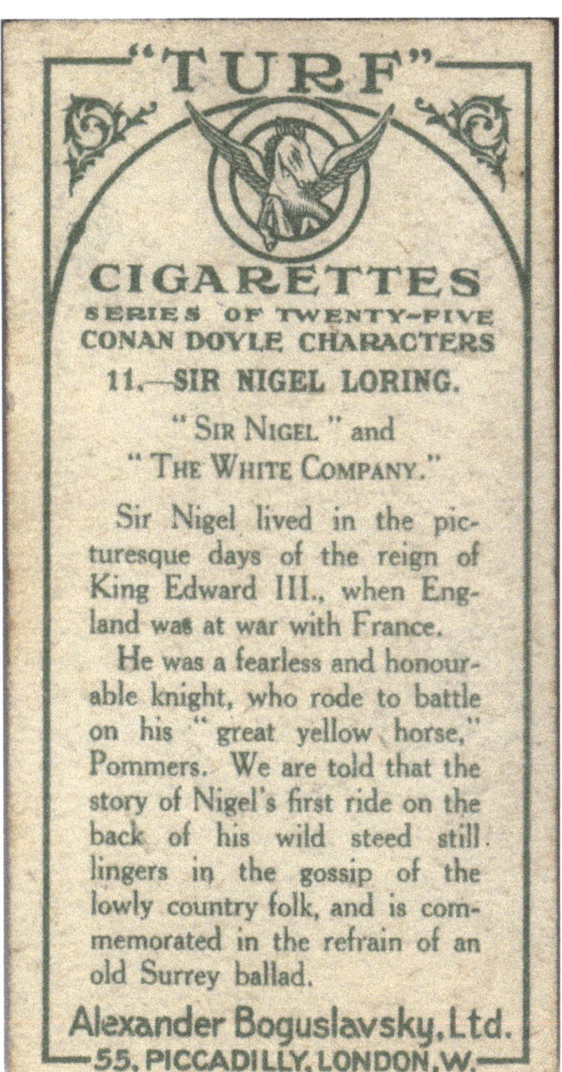

11. SIR NIGEL LORING.
"Sir Nigel" and "The White Company."

Sir Nigel lived in the picturesque days of the reign of King Edward lll., when England was at war with France.

He was a fearless and honourable knight, who rode to battle on his "great yellow horse. 'Pommers'. We are told that the story of Nigel's first ride on the back of his wild steed still lingers in the gossip of the lowly country fold and is commemorated in the refrain of an old Surry ballad.

SH-AB11

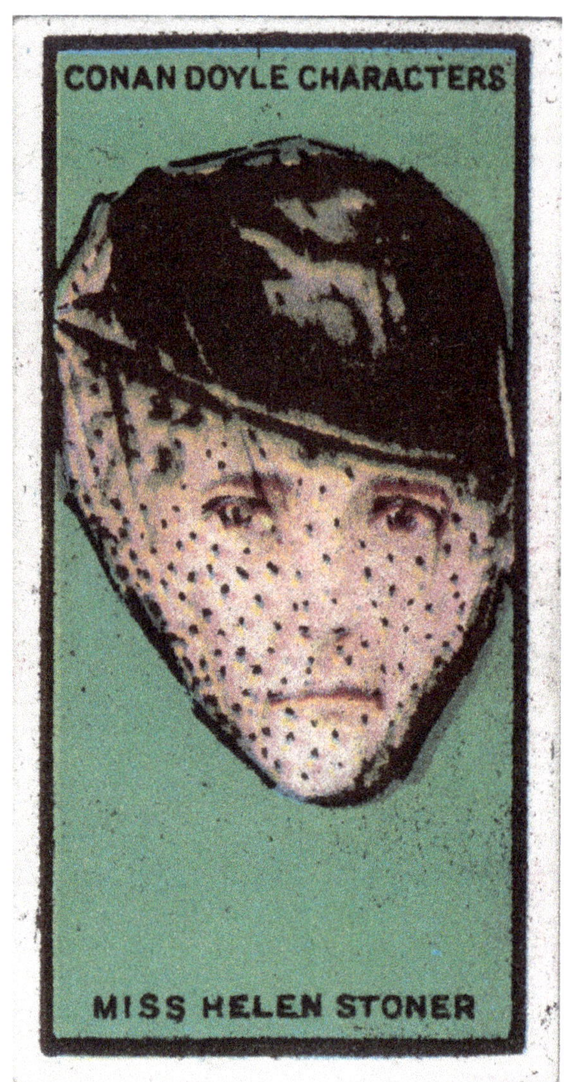

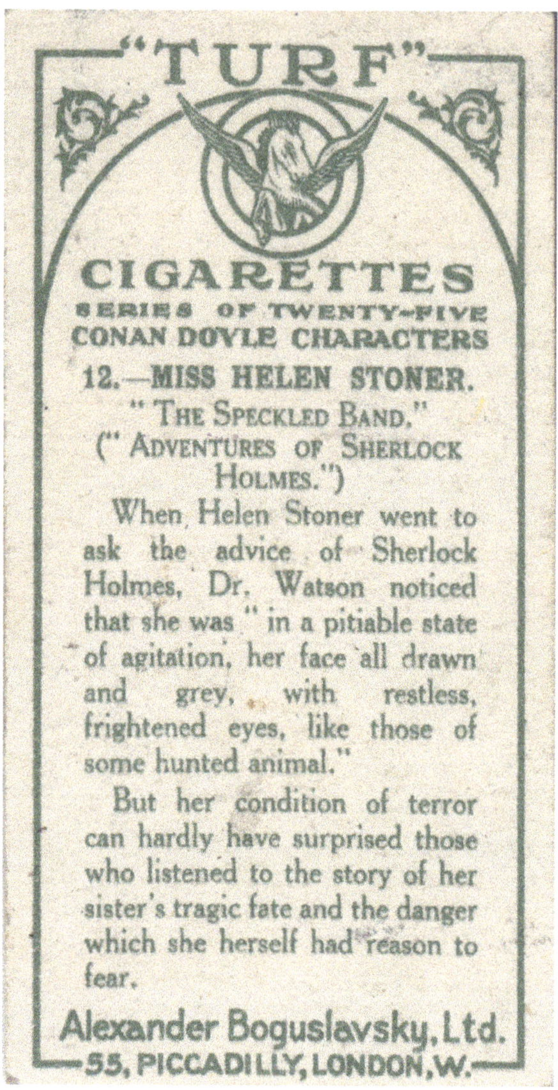

12. MISS HELEN STONER.

"The Speckled Band," ("Adventures of Sherlock Holmes.")"
When Helen Stoner went to ask the advice of Sherlock Holmes, Dr. Watson noticed that she was "in a pitiable state of agitation, her face all drawn and grey, with restless, frightened eyes, like those of some hunted animal."
But her condition of terror can hardly have surprised those who listened to the story of her sister's tragic fate and the danger which she herself had reason to fear.
SH-AB12

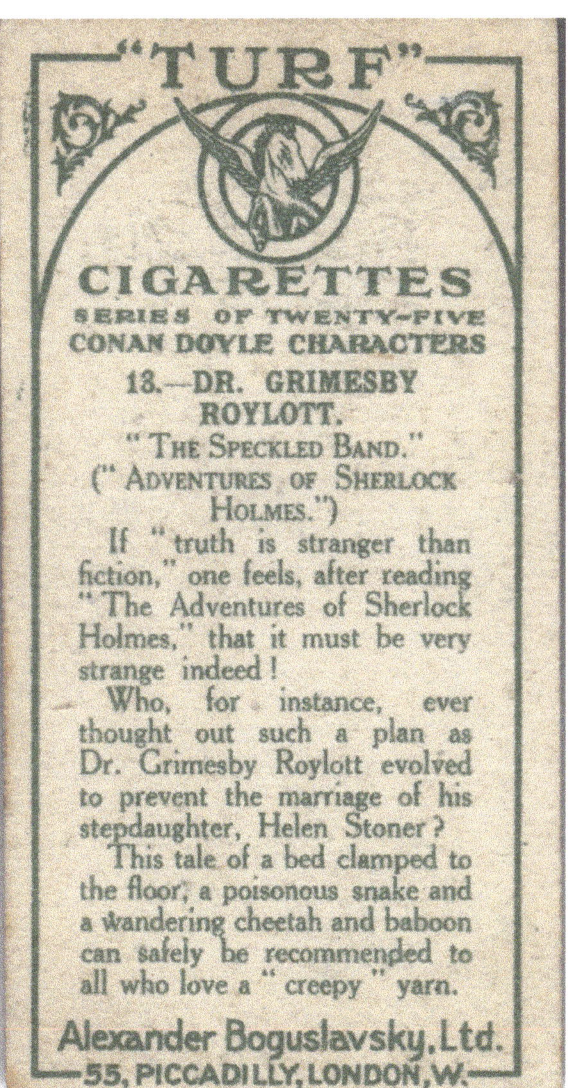

13. DR. GRIMESBY ROYLOTT.

"The Speckled Band." ("Adventures of Sherlock Holmes.")"

If "truth is stranger than fiction," one feels, after reading "The Adventures of Sherlock Holmes," that if must be very strange indeed!

Who, for instance, ever thought out such a plan as Dr. Grimsby Roylott evolved to prevent the marriage of his stepdaughter, Helen Stoner?

This tale of a bed clamped to the floor, a poisonous snake and a wandering cheetah and baboon can safely be recommended to all who love a "creepy" yarn.

SH-AB13

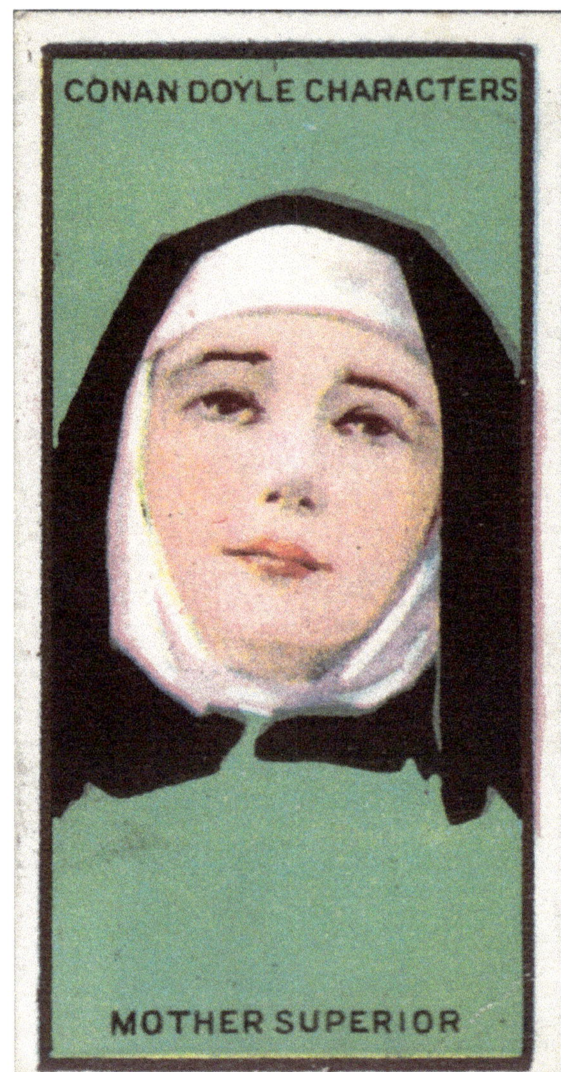

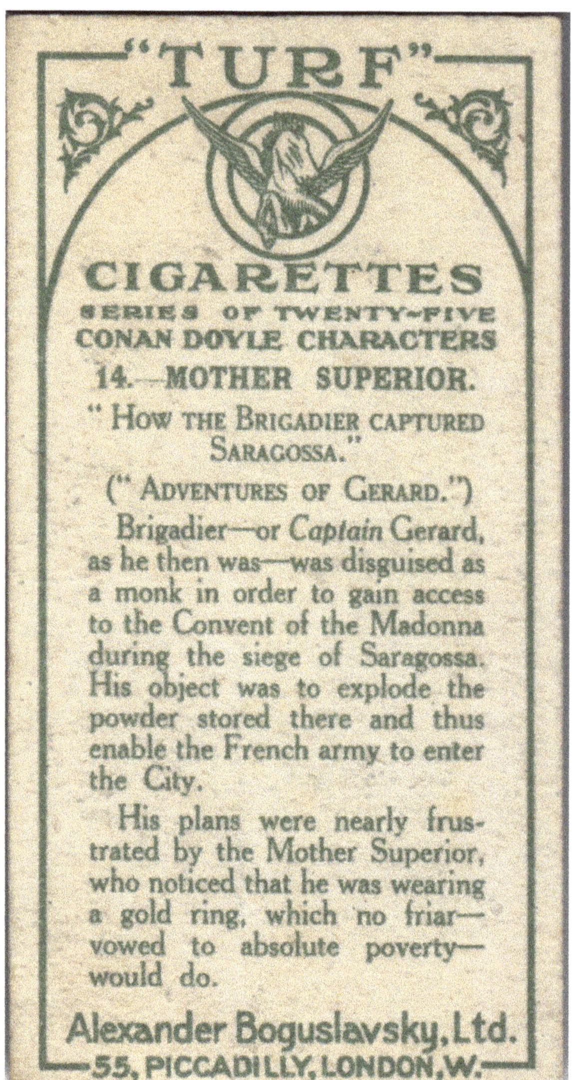

14. MOTHER SUPERIOR.
"How the Brigadier captured Saragossa" ("Adventures of Gerald.")

Brigadier – or Captain Gerald, as he then was- was disguised as a monk in order to gain access to the convert of the Madonna during the siege of Saragossa.
His object was to explode the powder stored there and thus enable the French army to enter the city.
His plans were nearly frustrated by the Mother Superior, who noticed that he was wearing a gold ring, which no friar – vowed to absolute poverty – would do.
SH-AB14

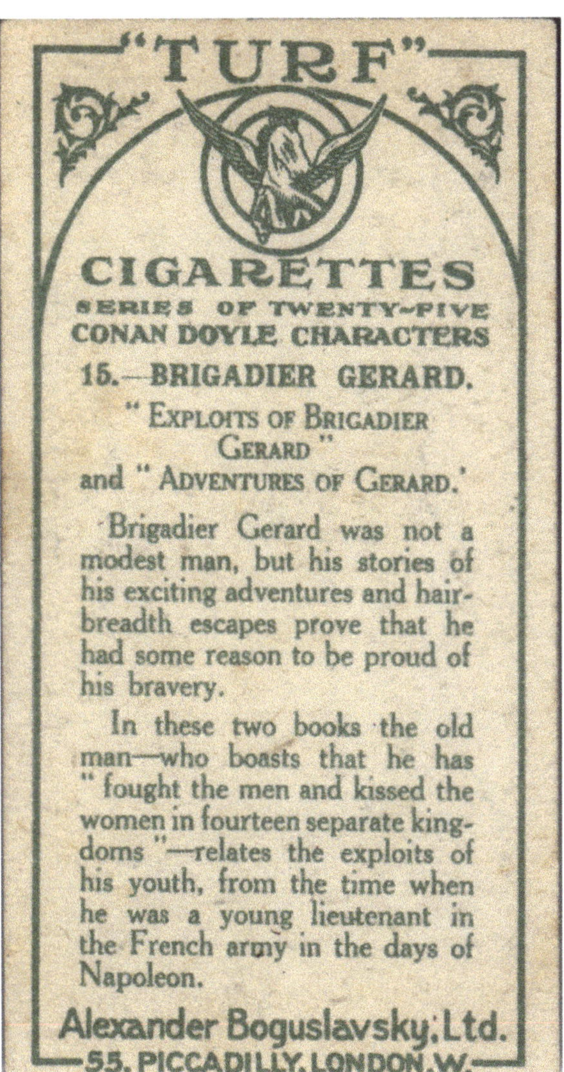

15. BRIGADIER GERARD.
"Exploits of Brigadier Gerald" and "Adventures of Gerald."

Brigadier Gerard was not a modest man, but his stories of his exciting adventures and hair-breadth escapes prove that he had some reason to be proud of his bravery.
In these two books the old man – who boasts that he has "fought the men and kissed the women in fourteen separate kingdoms" – relates the exploits of his youth, from the time when he was a young lieutenant in the French army in the days of Napoleon.
SH-AB15

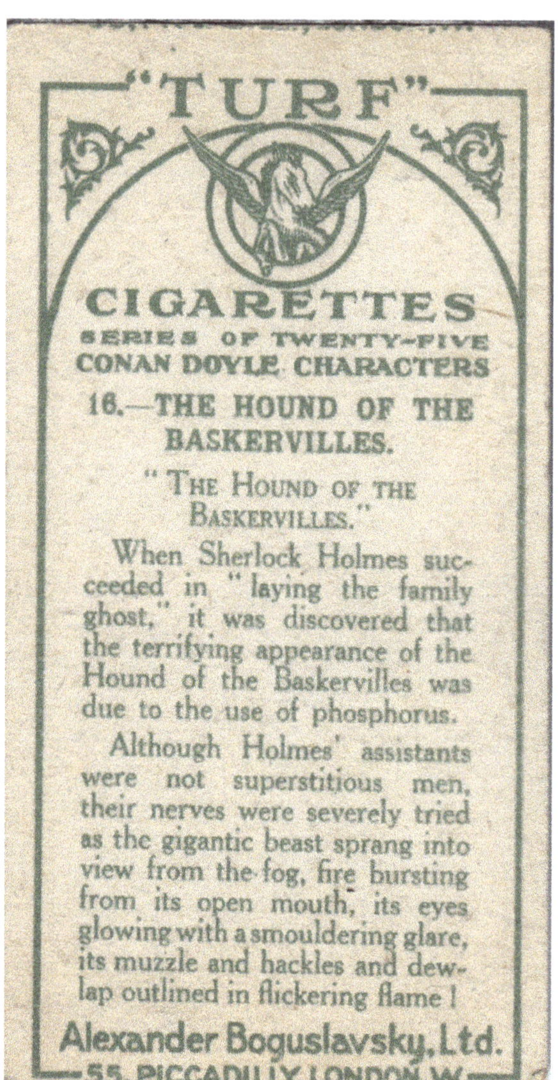

16. THE HOUND OF THE BASKERVILLES.
"The Hound of the Baskervilles."

When Sherlock Holmes succeeded in "Laying the family ghost," it was discovered that the terrifying appearance of the Hound of the Baskervilles was due to the use of phosphorus. Although Holmes' assistants were not superstitious men, their nerves were severely tried as the gigantic beast sprang into view from the fog, fire bursting from its open mouth, its eyes glowing with a smouldering glare, its muzzle and hackles and dewlap outlined in flickering flames!

SH-AB16

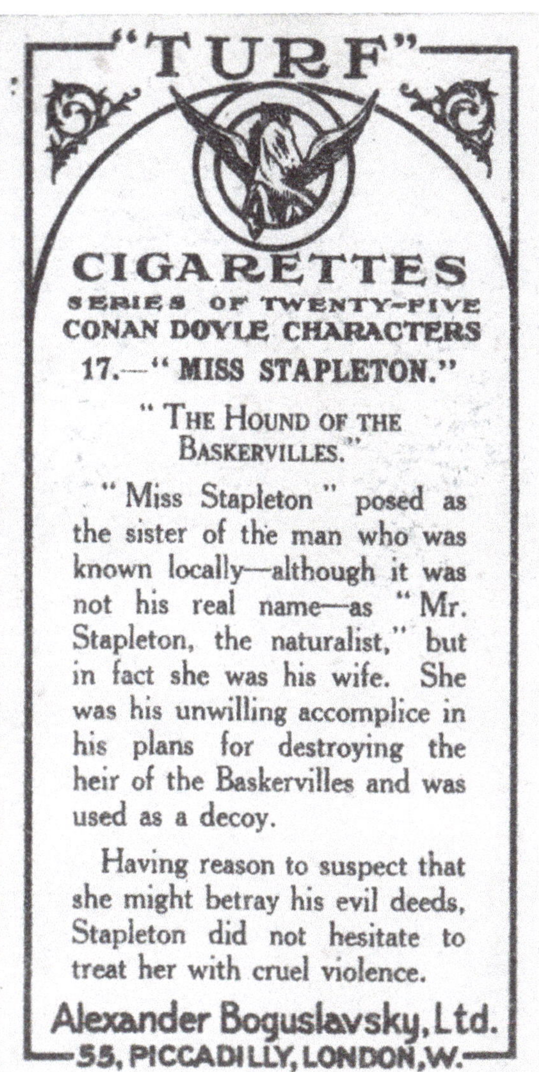

17. "MISS STAPLETON."
"The Hound of the Baskervilles."

"Miss Stapleton" posed as the sister of the man who was known locally – although it was not his real name - as "Mr. Stapleton, the naturalist," but in fact she was his wife. She was his unwilling accomplice in his plans for destroying the heir of the Baskervilles and was used as a decoy.

Having reason to suspect that she might betray his evil deeds, Stapleton did not hesitate to treat her with cruel violence.

SH-AB17

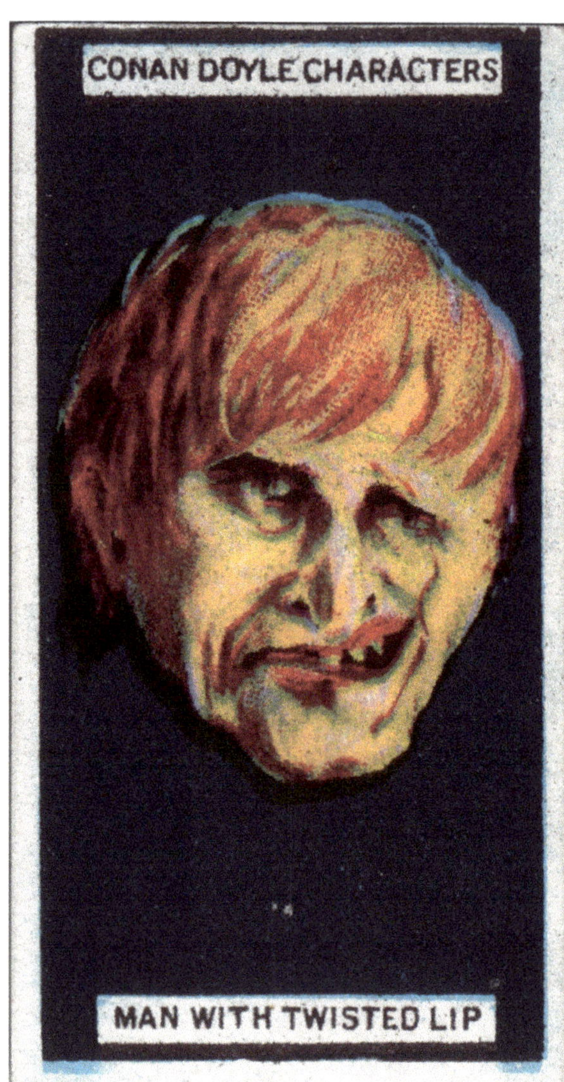

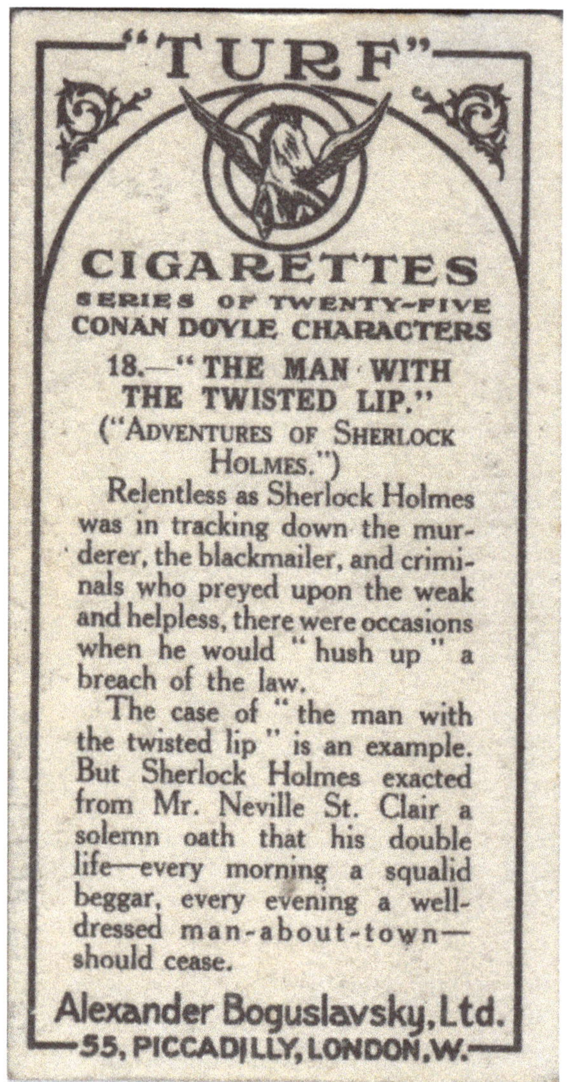

18. "THE MAN WITH THE TWISTED LIP."
"Adventures of Sherlock Holmes.")

Relentless as Sherlock Holmes was in tracking down the murderer, the blackmailer, and criminals who preyed upon the weak and helpless, there were occasions when he would "hush up" a breach of the law.

The case of "the man with the twisted lip" is an example/ But Sherlock Holmes exacted from Mr. Neville St. Clair a solemn oath that his double life- every morning a squalid beggar, every evening a well-dressed man-about-town= should cease.

SH-AB18

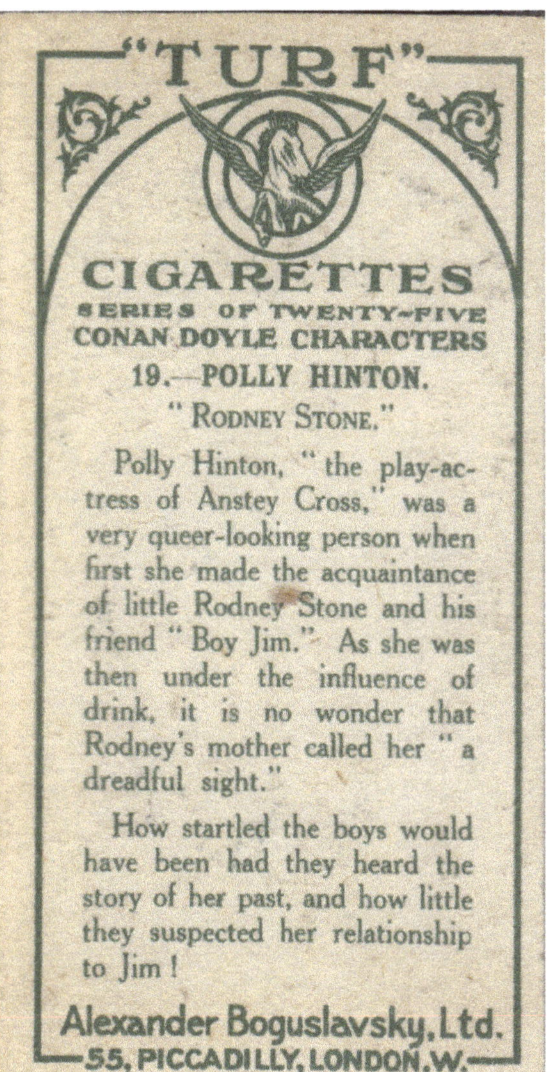

19. POLLY HINTON.
"Rodney Stone."

Polly Hinton. "the play-actress of Anstey Cross." Was a very queer-looking person when first she made the acquaintance of little Rodney Stone and his friend "Boy Jim." As she was then under the influence of drink, it is no wonder that Rodney's mother called her "a dreadful sight."

How startled the boys would have been had they heard the story of her past, and how little they suspected her relationship to Jim!

SH-AB19

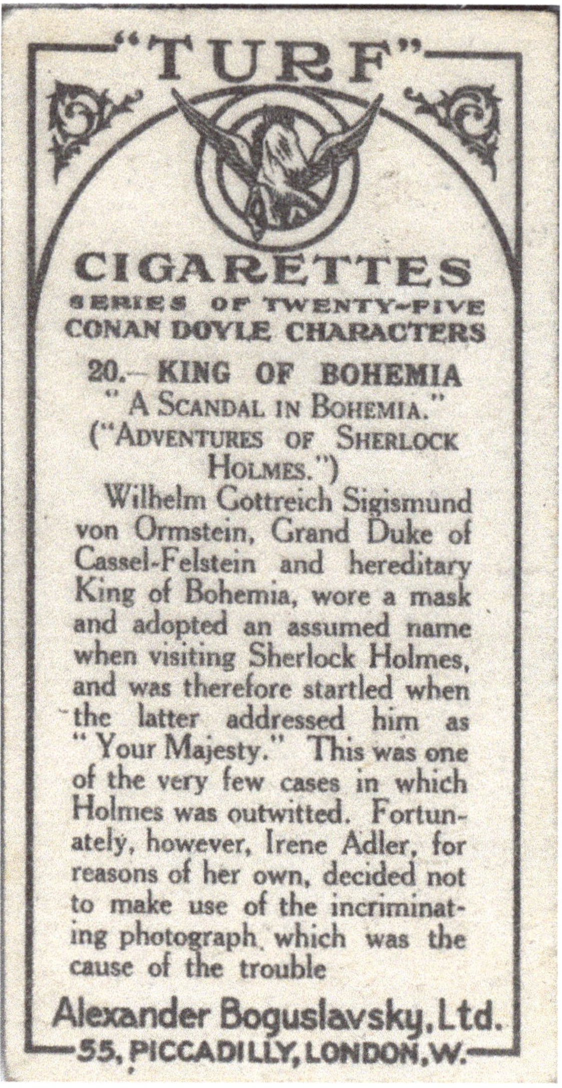

20. KING OF BOHEMIA.
"A Scandal in Bohemia." ("Adventures of Sherlock Holmes."

Wilhelm Gottreich Sigismund von Ormstein, Grand Duke of Cassel-Felstein and hereditary King of Bohemia, wore a mask and adopted an assumed name when visiting Sherlock Holmes, and was therefore started when the latter addressed him as "Your Majesty." This was one of the very few cases in which Holmes was outwitted. Fortunately, however, Irene Adler, for reasons of her own, decided not to make use of the incriminating photograph, which was the cause of the trouble
SH-AB20

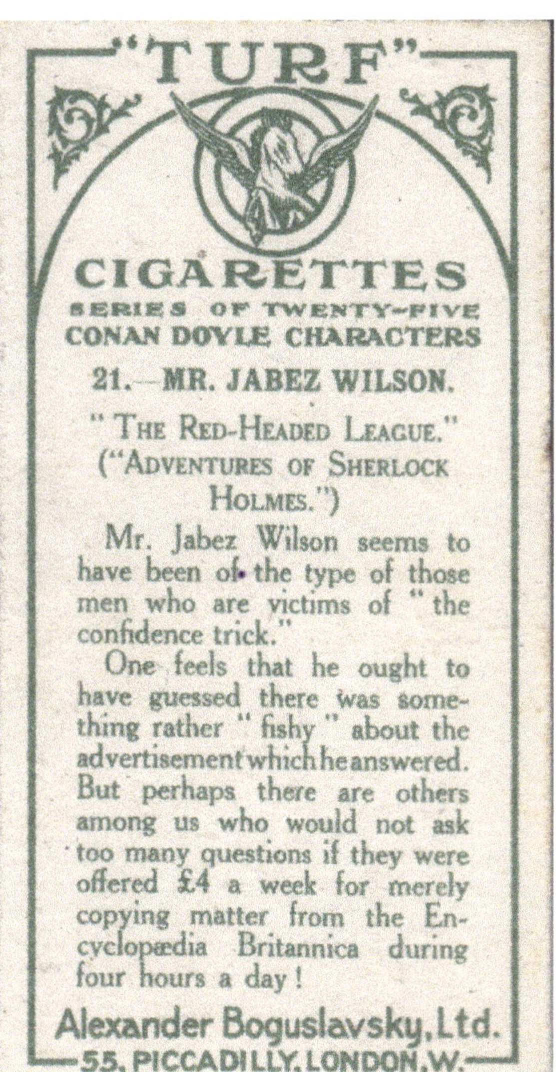

21. MR. JABEZ WILSON.
"The Red-Headed League." ("Adventures of Sherlock Holmes."

Mr. Jabez Wilson seems to have been of the type of those men who are victims of "the confidence trick."
One feels that he ought to have guessed there was something rather "fishy" about the advertisement which he answered/ But perhaps there are others among us who would not ask too many questions if they were offered £4 a week for merely copying matter from the Encyclopâedia Britannica during four hours a day!
SH-AB21

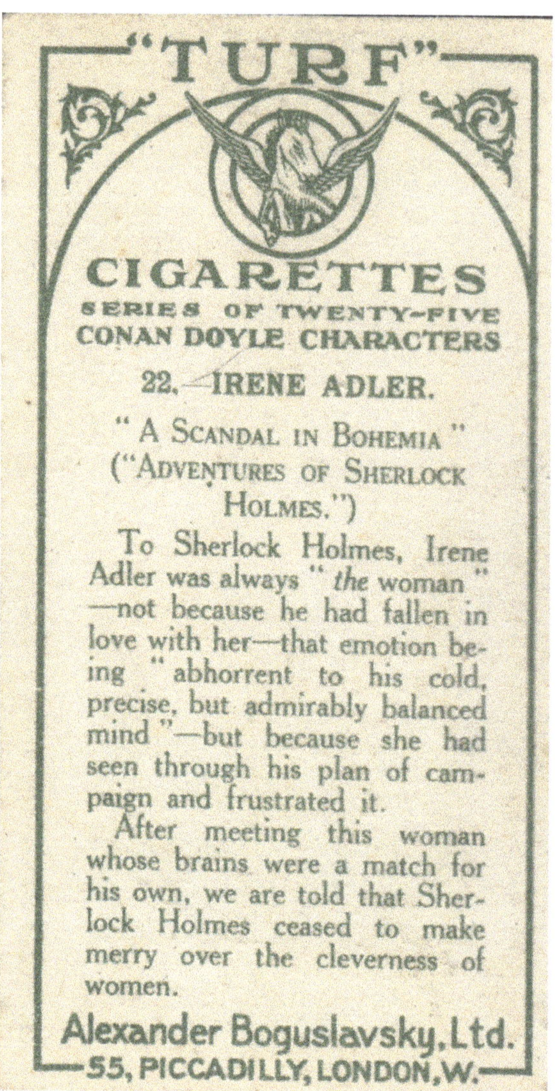

22. IRENE ADLER.
"A Scandal in Bohemia." ("Adventures of Sherlock Holmes."

To Sherlock Holmes, Irene Adler was always "*the* woman" – not because he had fallen in love with her – that emotion being "Abhorrent to his cold, precise, but admirably balanced mind" – but because she had seen through his plan of campaign and frustrated it.
After meeting this woman whose brains were a match for his own, we are told that Sherlock Holmes ceased to make merry over the cleverness of women.
SH-AB22

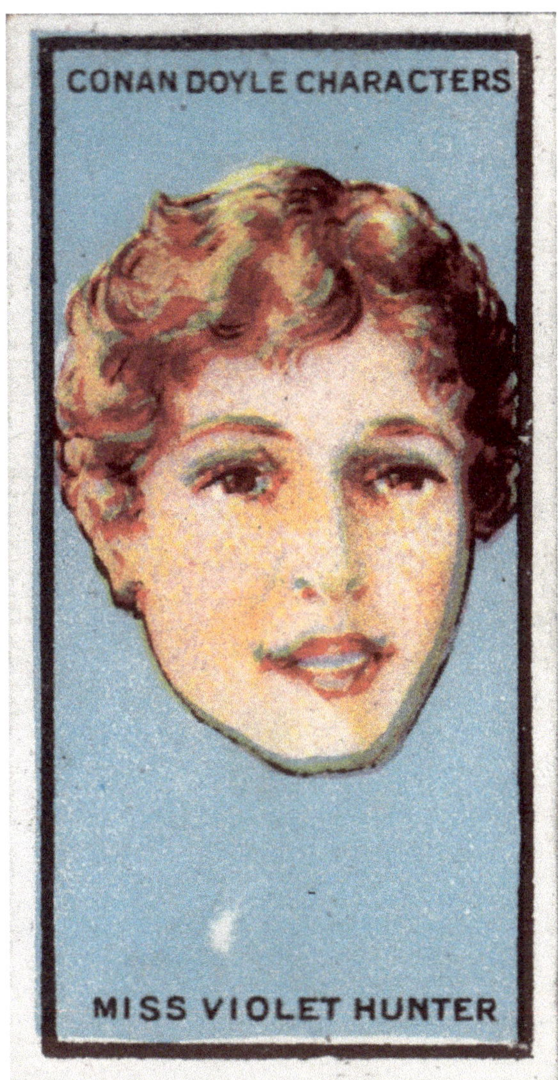

23. MISS VIOLET HUNTER.
"The Copper Beeches." ("Adventures of Sherlock Holmes."

Violet Hunter was engaged, nominally, to act as governess to Mr. Runcastle's little boy, but actually to impersonate his daughter, in order that it should not be suspected that he had the latter imprisoned.
Miss Hunter was selected owning to her striking likeness to the imprisoned girl, and went through some very painful experiences before Sherlock Holmes cleared up the mystery of the Copper Beeches and rescued the unhappy girl who had been shut up there.
SH-AB23

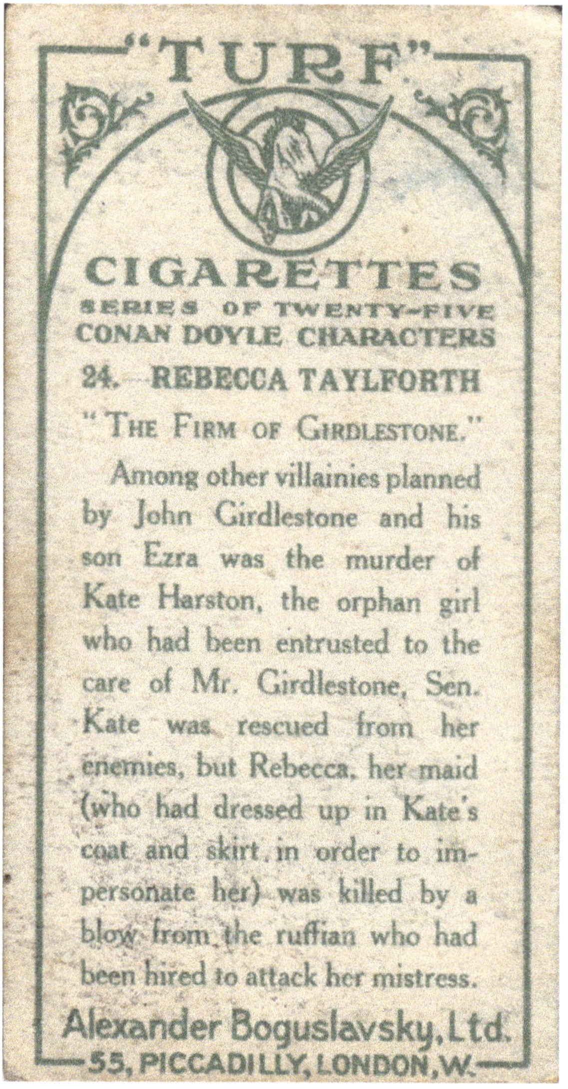

24. REBECCA TAYLFORTH
"The Firm of Girdlestone."

Among other villainies planned by John Girdlestone and his son Ezra was the murder of Kate Harston, the orphan girl who had been entrusted to the care of Mr. Girdlestone, Sen. Kate was rescued from her enemies, nut Rebecca, her maid (who had dressed up in Kate's coat amid skirt in order to impersonate her) was killed by a blow from the ruffian who had been hired to attack her mistress.
SH-AB24

25. MISS HATTY DORAN.
"The Noble Bachelor." ("Adventures of Sherlock Holmes."

Sherlock Holmes was certainly right in describing the disappearance of Lord St. Simon's bride as "quite dramatic." He added that "they often vanish before the ceremony and occasionally during the honeymoon, but I cannot call to mind anything quite so prompt as this."
For Miss Hatty Doran – the fascinating daughter of a Californian millionaire – disappeared while her wedding breakfast was in process!
SH-AB25

Joaquin Coll Salieti –

Active from 1898 to 1918
Spanish Artist, Painter, and printmaker. He participated in the Fine Art exhibition held in Barcelona in 1898.
Had workshops in Barcelona and developed the production of phototypes, trichrome and etchings and produced colour postcards.
Produced a number of card collections as well as children book illustrations.

1920's collection of 40 Spanish Sherlock Holmes Card

Three Sherlock Holmes Stories were covered in this series.
- The Musgrave Ritual was covered in 10 cards
- The Speckled Band in 10 cards
- The Sign of Four in 20 cards.

On the bottom of the back of each card, details were printed about where these cards came from, it reads

Collection of 40 drawings
GIFT TO THE CONSUMERS OF
Chocolate Jaime Boix HOSPITAL, 46 -BARCELONA
J. Horta, printer; Meddez nunez

I have played fast and loose with the English Translation of the back of the Cards, any Spanish speakers please forgive me.

Series A, Card 1.   ADVENTURE OF SHERLOCK HOLMES

Série A.—Núm. 1

Collection of 40 Cards

SH-JCS1

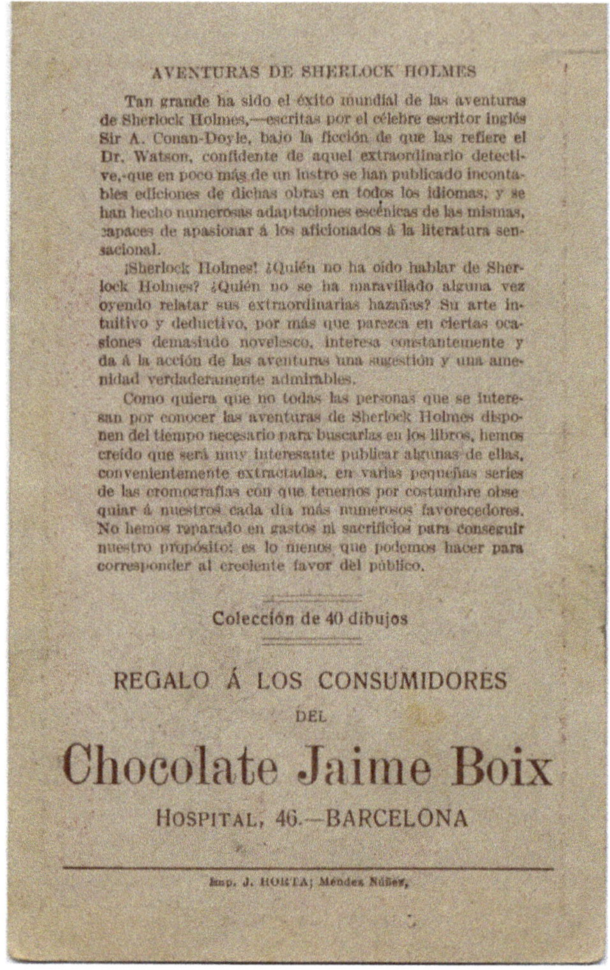

So great has been the worldwide success of the adventures by Sherlock Holmes, - written by the famous English writer Sir A. Conan-Doyle, under the fiction that he refers Dr. Watson. confidant of that extraordinary detective, -that in little more than five years countless editions of these works in all languages, as well as numerous stage adaptations of them, capable of enthralling fans of sensational literature.

Sherlock Holmes! Who hasn't heard of Sherlock Holmes? Who has not ever marvelled, hearing his extraordinary deeds recounted? His intuitive art of deductive, as much as it may seem on certain occasions too romantic, he is constantly interested and gives the action of the adventures a suggestion and an amenity truly admirable.

However, not all the people who are interested in knowing the adventures of Sherlock Holmes have the necessary time to look in the books, we have believed it will be very interesting to publish some of them conveniently extracted in several small series of the Colour prints with which we have the custom to give to our customer. most numerous days flattering. We have not spared expenses or sacrifices to achieve our purpose; it's the least we can do to correspond to the growing request from the public.

The Musgrave Ritual

SH-JCS2

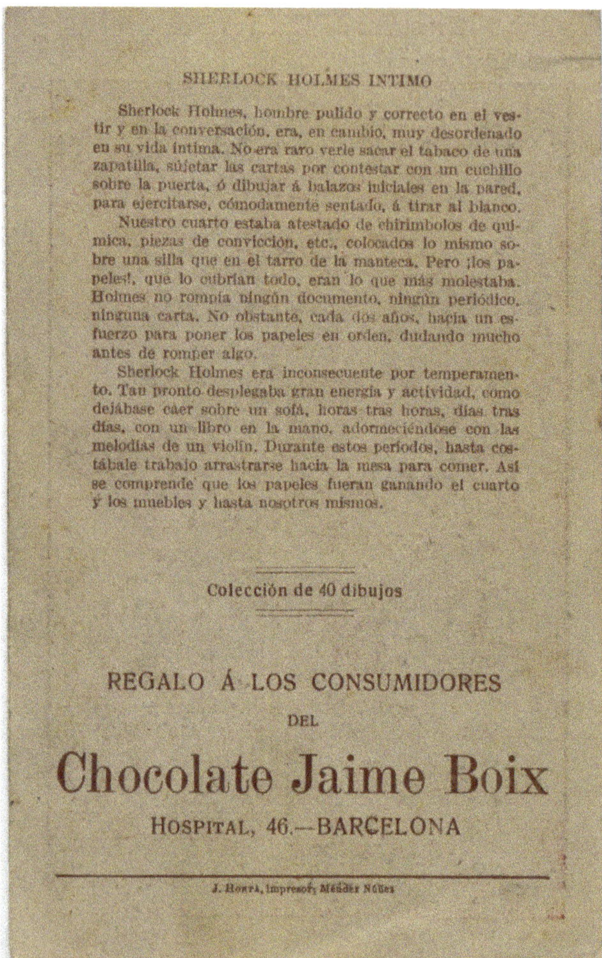

Sherlock Holmes, a polished and correct man in dress and conversation, was, on the other hand, very disorderly in his intimate life. It was not uncommon to see him take the tobacco out of a shoe, transfixed his unanswered letters with a knife to the mantlepiece, or fire bullets into initials on the wall. to exercise, comfortably seated, to shoot at the target.

Our room was crammed with chemistry experiments, pieces of conviction, etc., placed as likely on the chair as on the butter dish. But the papers, which covered everything, were what bothered me most. Holmes did not tear up any documents, no newspapers, no letters. However, around two years ago, I made an effort to put the papers in order, hesitating long before broaching the subject.

Sherlock Holmes was inconsistent by temperament. As soon as he displayed great energy and activity. like he flopped down on a sofa. hour after hour, day after day, with a book in hand. falling asleep to the melodies of a violin. During these periods, it was even difficult for him to crawl up to the tabletop to eat. Thus, it is understood that the papers were filling the room and the furniture and even ourselves.

One Winter afternoon…
SH-JCS3

THE WOODEN BOX

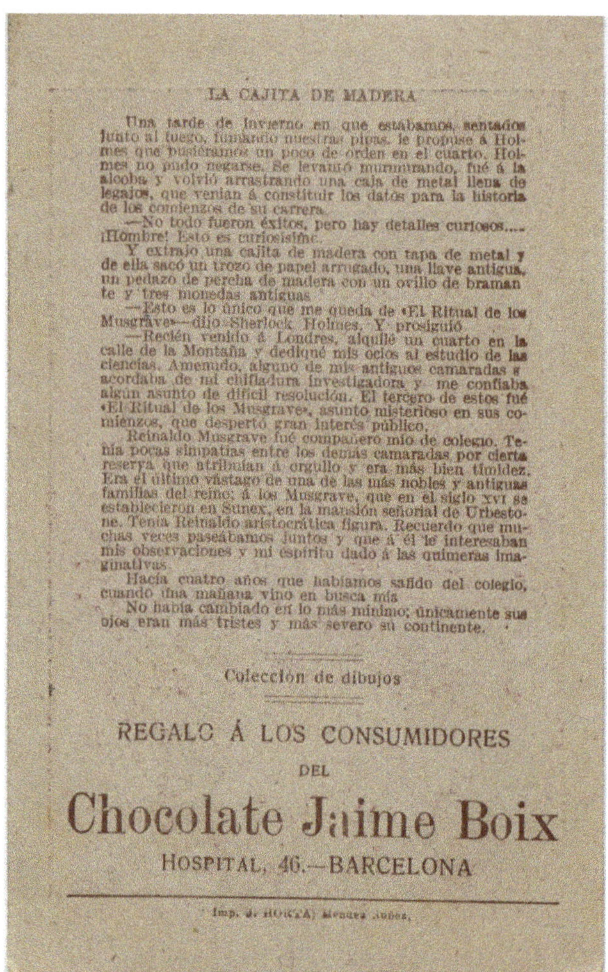

One winter afternoon we were sitting by the fire, smoking our pipes. I suggested to Holmes that we put a little order in the room. Holmes could not refuse. He got up, murmuring, went to the bedroom, and came back dragging a metal box full of files, which came to constitute the data for the history from the beginning of his career.

"Not all were successes, but there were curious details .- Old Chap! This is very curious", as he took out a little wooden box with a metal shank and from it, he took out a crumpled piece of paper, an old key, a piece wooden peg with a ball of twine and three old coins.

"This is the only thing I have left of 'The Ritual of the Musgrave'," Sherlock Holmes said. And he continued. "Having just come to London, I rented a room on Montana Street and devoted my time to the study of science. Often, some of my former comrades remembered my crazy Research and entrusted me with some matter that was difficult to resolve. The third of these was 'The-Ritual of the Musgrave', a mysterious matter in its beginnings, which aroused great interest in the public."

"Reginald Musgrave was my classmate at school. He had few friends among the other students, due to a certain reserve that they attributed to pride but was rather shyness. He was the last member of one of the noblest and oldest families in the kingdom; the Musgraves, who in the sixteenth century settled in Sussex, in the manor house at Hurlstone. He had an aristocratic figure. I remember that many times we walked together and that he was interested in my observations and my spirit, given to imaginative chimeras."

"We had been out of school for four years, when one morning he came looking for me."

"He has not changed in the slightest; only his eyes were sadder, and his continence was more severe."

I need your help…

SH-JCS4

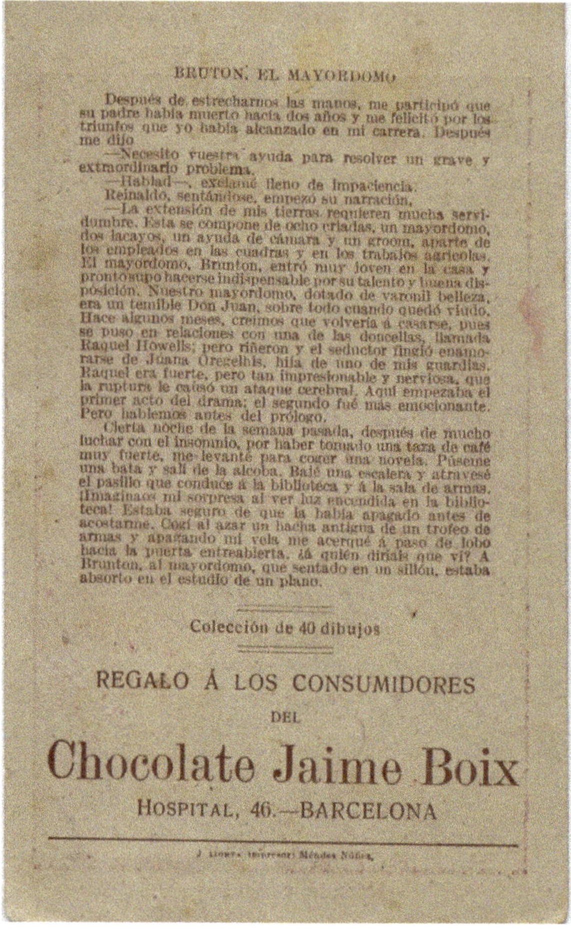

BRUTON, EL MAYORDOMO

Después de estrecharnos las manos, me participó que su padre había muerto hacía dos años y me felicitó por los triunfos que yo había alcanzado en mi carrera. Después me dijo

—Necesito vuestra ayuda para resolver un grave y extraordinario problema.

—Hablad—, exclamé lleno de impaciencia.

Reinaldo, sentándose, empezó su narración.

—La extensión de mis tierras requieren mucha servidumbre. Esta se compone de ocho criadas, un mayordomo, dos lacayos, un ayuda de cámara y un groom, aparte de los empleados en las cuadras y en los trabajos agrícolas. El mayordomo, Brunton, entró muy joven en la casa y pronto supo hacerse indispensable por su talento y buena disposición. Nuestro mayordomo, dotado de varonil belleza, era un temible Don Juan, sobre todo cuando quedó viudo. Hace algunos meses, creímos que volvería á casarse, pues se puso en relaciones con una de las doncellas, llamada Raquel Howells; pero riñeron y el seductor fingió enamorarse de Juana Oregelhis, hija de uno de mis guardias. Raquel era fuerte, pero tan impresionable y nerviosa, que la ruptura le causó un ataque cerebral. Aquí empezaba el primer acto del drama; el segundo fué más emocionante. Pero hablemos antes del prólogo.

Cierta noche de la semana pasada, después de mucho luchar con el insomnio, por haber tomado una taza de café muy fuerte, me levanté para coger una novela. Púseme una bata y salí de la alcoba. Bajé una escalera y atravesé el pasillo que conduce á la biblioteca y á la sala de armas. ¡Imaginaos mi sorpresa al ver luz encendida en la biblioteca! Estaba seguro de que la había apagado antes de acostarme. Cogí al azar un hacha antigua de un trofeo de armas y apagando mi vela me acerqué á paso de lobo hacia la puerta entreabierta. ¿á quién diríais que ví? A Brunton, al mayordomo, que sentado en un sillón, estaba absorto en el estudio de un plano.

Colección de 40 dibujos

REGALO Á LOS CONSUMIDORES

DEL

Chocolate Jaime Boix

HOSPITAL, 46.—BARCELONA

"After shaking hands, I was told that his father had died two years ago and he congratulated me on the triumphs that I had achieved in my career. He then said, 'I need your help to solve a grave and extraordinary problem.' "

"Tell me," I exclaimed impatiently.

Reginald, sitting down, began his narration. The extension of my lands requires a lot of servants, and these are made up of eight maids, a butler, two lackeys, a valet, and a groom, apart from employees on the stables and farm jobs. The butler, Brunton, entered the house when very young and he soon knew how to make himself indispensable because of his talent and good disposition. Our butler, endowed with manly beauty, was a fearsome Don Juan, especially when he was left a widower.

Some months ago, we believed that he would remarry, because he started dating one of our maids, called Raquel Howells; but they quarrelled and the seducer has now fallen in love with Janet Tregellis, daughter of the head gamekeeper.

Raquel was strong, but so impressionable and nervous, that her breakup caused her a touch of brain fever. Here began the first act of the drama; the second was more exciting. But let's talk before the prologue.

One night last week, after a long time struggling with insomnia, from having a cup of very strong coffee, I got up to get a novel. I put on my robe and left the bedroom. I went downstairs and went through the corridor that led to the library and the weapons room.

Imagine my surprise when I saw the light on in the. library! I was sure I had turned it off before going to bed. I randomly took an ancient axe from a trophy of weapons and putting out my candle I approached at a wolf's pace toward the half-open door. Who would you say I saw? It was Brunton, the butler, who was sitting in an armchair and was absorbed in the study of a document.

I was Dumbfounded…

SH-JCS5

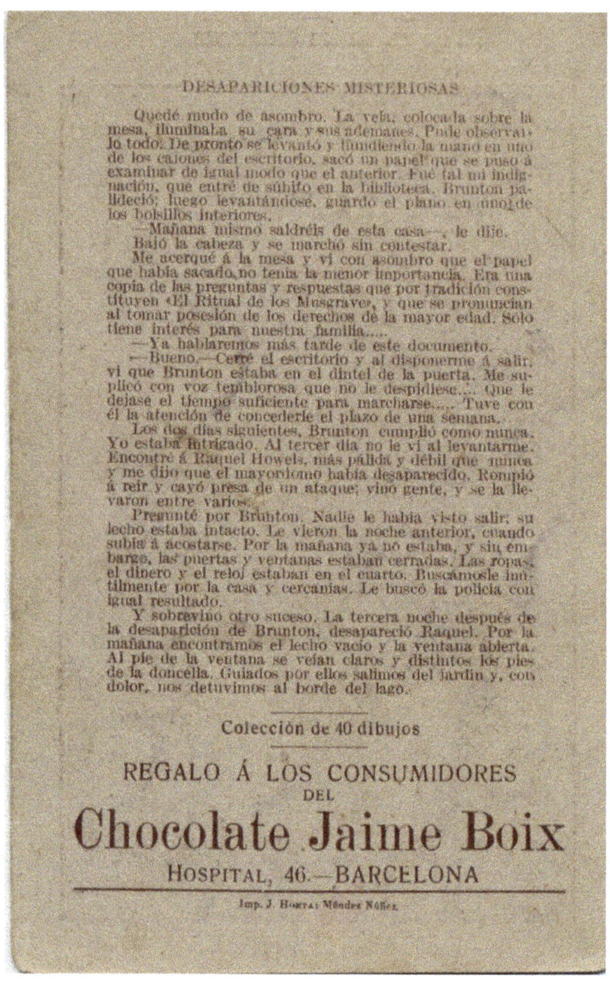

DESAPARICIONES MISTERIOSAS

Quedé modo de asombro. La vela, colocada sobre la mesa, iluminaba su cara y sus ademanes. Pude observarlo todo. De pronto se levantó y hundiendo la mano en uno de los cajones del escritorio, sacó un papel que se puso á examinar de igual modo que el anterior. Fué tal mi indignación, que entré de súbito en la biblioteca. Brunton palideció; luego levantándose, guardó el plano en uno de los bolsillos interiores.

—Mañana mismo saldréis de esta casa—, le dije.

Bajó la cabeza y se marchó sin contestar.

Me acerqué á la mesa y vi con asombro que el papel que había sacado, no tenía la menor importancia. Era una copia de las preguntas y respuestas que por tradición constituyen «El Ritual de los Musgrave», y que se pronuncian al tomar posesión de los derechos de la mayor edad. Sólo tiene interés para nuestra familia.....

—Ya hablaremos más tarde de este documento.

—Bueno.—Cerré el escritorio y al disponerme á salir, vi que Brunton estaba en el dintel de la puerta. Me suplicó con voz temblorosa que no le despidiese.... Que le dejase el tiempo suficiente para marcharse..... Tuve con él la atención de concederle el plazo de una semana.

Los dos días siguientes, Brunton cumplió como nunca. Yo estaba intrigado. Al tercer día no le vi al levantarme. Encontré á Raquel Howels, más pálida y débil que nunca y me dijo que el mayordomo había desaparecido. Rompió á reir y cayó presa de un ataque; vino gente, y se la llevaron entre varios.

Pregunté por Brunton. Nadie le había visto salir; su lecho estaba intacto. Le vieron la noche anterior, cuando subía á acostarse. Por la mañana ya no estaba, y sin embargo, las puertas y ventanas estaban cerradas. Las ropas, el dinero y el reloj estaban en el cuarto. Buscámosle inútilmente por la casa y cercanías. Le buscó la policía con igual resultado.

Y sobrevino otro suceso. La tercera noche después de la desaparición de Brunton, desapareció Raquel. Por la mañana encontramos el lecho vacío y la ventana abierta. Al pie de la ventana se veían claros y distintos los pies de la doncella. Guiados por ellos salimos del jardín y, con dolor, nos detuvimos al borde del lago.

Colección de 40 dibujos

REGALO Á LOS CONSUMIDORES

DEL

Chocolate Jaime Boix

HOSPITAL, 46.—BARCELONA

Imp. J. Horta: Méndez Núñez.

I was dumbfounded. The Candle placed on the table, illuminated his face and the gestures from him. I could see everything. Suddenly he got up and plunging his hand into one of the desk drawers, he took out a piece of paper and examine it in the same way as the previous one. Such was my indignation, that I burst into the library. Brunton paled; then getting up, he put the document into his inside pocket. Tomorrow you will get out of this house. I told him. He lowered his head and left without answering. I approached the table and I saw with amazement that the paper that he had taken out was not the least important, it was a copy of the questions and answers that by tradition constituted 'The Ritual of the Musgrave', and that they are recited upon taking possession of the rights of adulthood. exclusively of interest to our family. We will talk about this document later. Happier. I closed the desk and as I prepared to leave, I saw that Brunton was on the lintel of the door. He begged me with a trembling voice that I did not dismiss him straight away, please give me enough time to leave. I gave him a week.

The next two days. Brunton fulfilled his duties like never before. I was intrigued. On the third day, however, I didn't see him when I got up. I met Raquel Howells. she paler and weaker than she ever was and she told me that the butler had disappeared and burst out laughing and fell prey to an attack; other staff arrived, and they took her away. I asked about Brunton from others, but no one had seen him leave; his bed was intact. They saw him the night before when he went up to bed. In the morning he was gone, and yet the doors and windows were closed. The clothes, the money and his watch were in the room. We looked for him uselessly around the house and surroundings. The police looked for him with the same result.

Yet another event occurred. The third night after Brunton's disappearance, Raquel disappeared. In the morning we found the bed empty and the window open. At the foot of the window her footprints were clear and distinct. Guided by this we left the garden and, with worry, they stopped at the edge of the lake.

There the tracks stopped

SH-JCS6

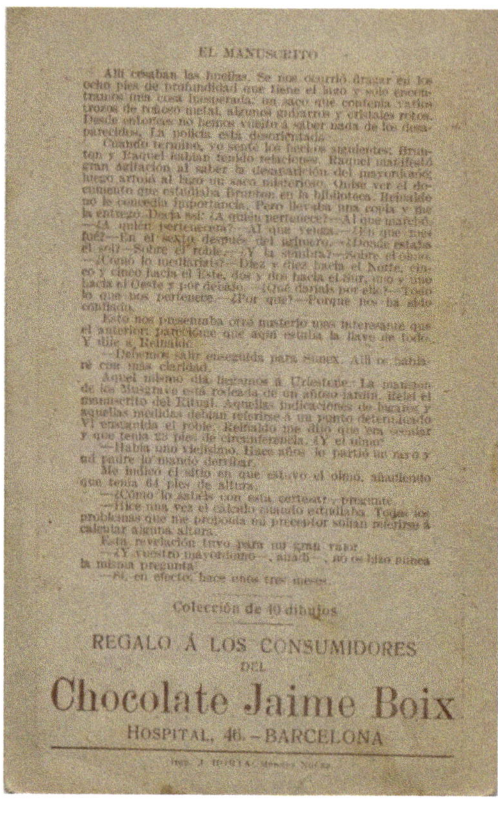

The tracks stopped there. It occurred to us to dredge the lake's eight feet depth and we only found one unexpected thing: a sack containing several pieces of roughened metal, some pebbles and broken glass. Since then, we have heard nothing. The police are Baffled.

When he finished, I recorded the following facts: Brunton and Raquel had had a relationship. Raquel expressed great agitation when she learned of the butler's disappearance; she then threw a mysterious sack into the lake. I wanted to see the document Brunton was studying in the library.

Reginald did not attach importance to it. But he carried a copy and gave it to me. It said the following.

'Whose was it?' - 'His who is gone.'

'Who shall have it?' - 'He who will come.'

'What was the month?' - 'The sixth from the first.'

'Where was the sun?' - 'Over the oak.'

'Where was the shadow?' - 'Under the elm.'

'How was it stepped?' - 'North by ten and by ten, east by five and by five, south by two and by two, west by one and by one, and so under.'

'What shall we give for it?' - 'All that is ours.'

'Why should we give it?' - 'For the sake of the trust.'

This presented us with another more interesting mystery than previous; It seemed to me that here it was, the key to everything. And I said to Reginald, we must leave immediately for Sussex. There I will speak more clearly. That same day we reached Hurlstone, the Musgrave mansion is surrounded by a centuries-old garden. I reread the Ritual manuscript. Those indications of places and measurements must have referred to a certain point. I immediately saw the oak. Reginald told me that it was magnificent and was 23 feet in circumference. And the elm?

There was one very old one, but years ago it was struck by lightning and my father had it cut down. He indicated to me the place where the elm had been. It was 64 feet tall.

"How do you know this with certainty?" ..... I asked.

"I did the calculation once when I was studying. All the problems my tutor proposed to me used to refer to calculating some height."

"This revelation was of great value to me,"

And your butler. I asked, "Did he ever asked you the same question?"

"Yes, indeed; about three months ago."

We went downstairs

SH-JCS7

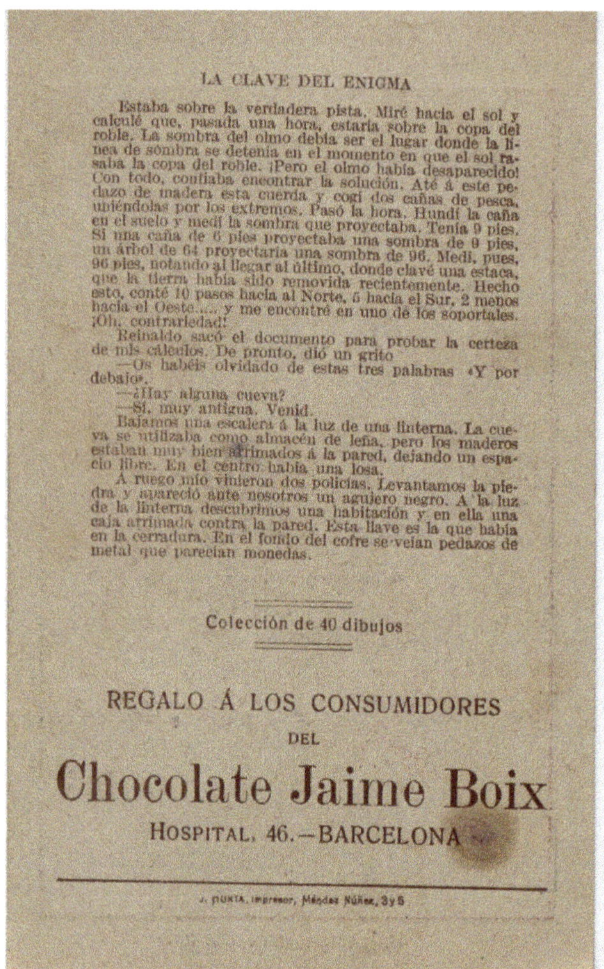

LA CLAVE DEL ENIGMA

Estaba sobre la verdadera pista. Miré hacia el sol y calculé que, pasada una hora, estaría sobre la copa del roble. La sombra del olmo debía ser el lugar donde la línea de sombra se detenía en el momento en que el sol rasaba la copa del roble. ¡Pero el olmo había desaparecido! Con todo, confiaba encontrar la solución. Até á este pedazo de madera esta cuerda y cogí dos cañas de pesca, uniéndolas por los extremos. Pasó la hora. Hundí la caña en el suelo y medí la sombra que proyectaba. Tenía 9 pies. Si una caña de 6 pies proyectaba una sombra de 9 pies, un árbol de 64 proyectaría una sombra de 96. Medí, pues, 96 pies, notando al llegar al último, donde clavé una estaca, que la tierra había sido removida recientemente. Hecho esto, conté 10 pasos hacia al Norte, 5 hacia el Sur, 2 menos hacia el Oeste..... y me encontré en uno de los soportales. ¡Oh, contrariedad!

Reinaldo sacó el documento para probar la certeza de mis cálculos. De pronto, dió un grito
—Os habéis olvidado de estas tres palabras «Y por debajo».
—¿Hay alguna cueva?
—Sí, muy antigua. Venid.

Bajamos una escalera á la luz de una linterna. La cueva se utilizaba como almacén de leña, pero los maderos estaban muy bien arrimados á la pared, dejando un espacio libre. En el centro había una losa.

A ruego mío vinieron dos policías. Levantamos la piedra y apareció ante nosotros un agujero negro. A la luz de la linterna descubrimos una habitación y en ella una caja arrimada contra la pared. Esta llave es la que había en la cerradura. En el fondo del cofre se veían pedazos de metal que parecían monedas.

Colección de 40 dibujos

REGALO Á LOS CONSUMIDORES

DEL

Chocolate Jaime Boix

HOSPITAL, 46.—BARCELONA

J. RONTA, impresor, Méndez Núñez, 3 y 5

He was on the real track. I looked up at the sun and figured that after an hour, it would be on the top of the oak tree. The shadow of the elm should be the place where the line of shadow stopped as the sun scraped the top of the oak. But the elm was gone! With everything. I was hoping to find the solution. I tied this rope to this piece of wood and took two fishing rods, joining them at the outer ends. The hour passed. I sank the cane into the ground and measured the shadow it cast. It was 9 feet. If a 6-foot reed cast a 9-foot shadow, a 64-foot tree would cast a 96-foot shadow. I measured out 96 feet, noticing when I got to the end, where I drove a stake. that the earth had recently been removed. This done, I counted 10 steps to the North, 5 to the East, 2 towards the South and 1 to the West ..... And I found myself in one of the arcades. Oh, disappointment! Reginald took out the document to test the accuracy of my calculations. Suddenly. he gave a yell

"You have forgotten these two words 'And under'."
"Is there a cellar?"
"Yes. very old. Come."
We descended a staircase by the light of a lantern. The cellar was used as a storage room for firewood, but the logs were very close to the wall, leaving a free space in the centre was a slab.
At my request, two policemen came. We lifted the stone and a black hole appeared before us. In the light of the flashlight, we discovered a room and in it a box nestled together. against the wall. This key is the one in the Lock. In the bottom of the chest there were pieces of metal that looked like coins.

SH-JCS8

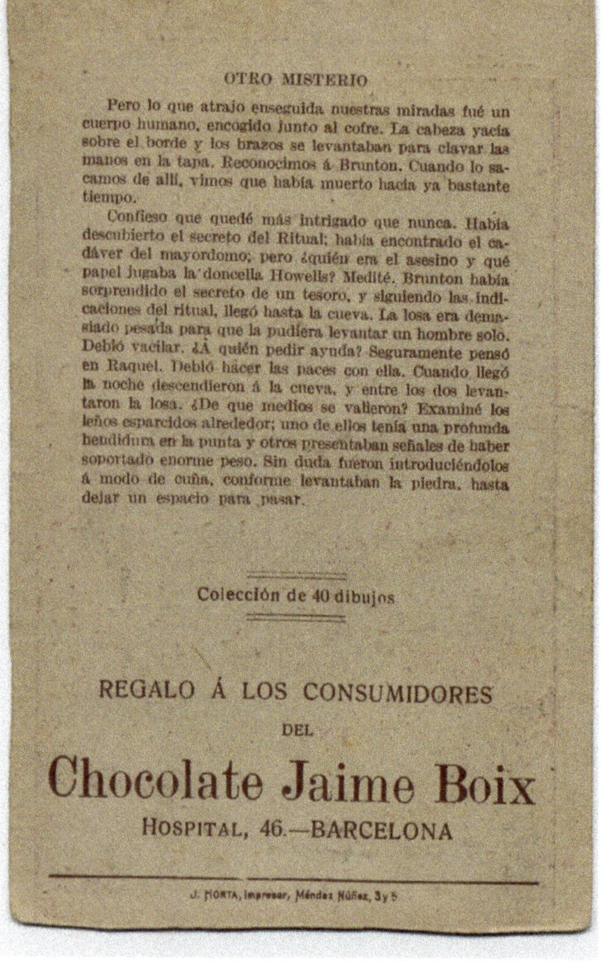

But what immediately attracted our eyes was a human body, huddled next to the chest. The head lay on the edge and the arms were raised to dig into the lid. We recognized Brunton. When we took him out of there, we saw that he had been dead for some time.

I confess that I was more intrigued than ever. We had discovered the secret of the Ritual; We had found the corpse of the butler; But who was the murderer, and what role did Maid Howells play? I meditated. Brunton had solved the secret of a treasure and following the indications of the ritual. he got to the cellar. The slab was too heavy to be lifted by one man alone. He must have hesitated. Who to ask for help? He surely must have thought of Raquel. He must have made peace with her. When night came, they went down to the cellar, and between the two of them they raised the stone. What means did they use? I examined the logs scattered around; one of them had one deep indentation at the tip and others showed signs of having supported enormous weight. No doubt they were being wedged in as they lifted the stone. until leaving a space to enter.

El Ritual de los Musgrave

Série A.—Núm. 9

Brunton was in her power.

SH-JCS9

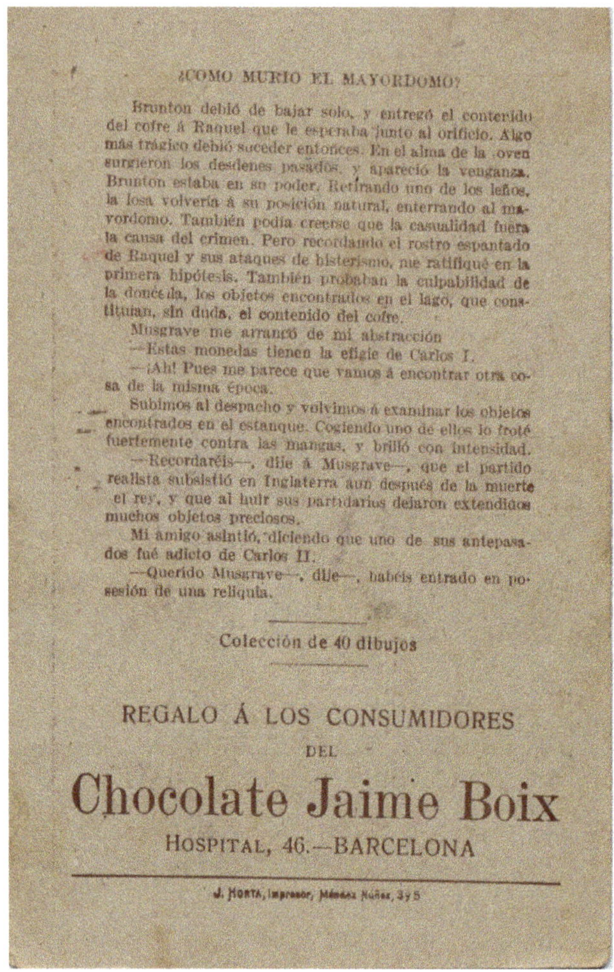

¿COMO MURIO EL MAYORDOMO?

Brunton debió de bajar solo, y entregó el contenido del cofre á Raquel que le esperaba junto al orificio. Algo más trágico debió suceder entonces. En el alma de la joven surgieron los desdenes pasados, y apareció la venganza. Brunton estaba en su poder. Retirando uno de los leños, la losa volvería á su posición natural, enterrando al mayordomo. También podía creerse que la casualidad fuera la causa del crimen. Pero recordando el rostro espantado de Raquel y sus ataques de histerismo, me ratifiqué en la primera hipótesis. También probaban la culpabilidad de la doncella, los objetos encontrados en el lago, que constituían, sin duda, el contenido del cofre.

Musgrave me arrancó de mi abstracción

—Estas monedas tienen la efigie de Cárlos I.

—¡Ah! Pues me parece que vamos á encontrar otra cosa de la misma época.

Subimos al despacho y volvimos á examinar los objetos encontrados en el estanque. Cogiendo uno de ellos lo froté fuertemente contra las mangas, y brilló con intensidad.

—Recordaréis—, dije á Musgrave—, que el partido realista subsistió en Inglaterra aun después de la muerte del rey, y que al huir sus partidarios dejaron extendidos muchos objetos preciosos.

Mi amigo asintió, diciendo que uno de sus antepasados fué adicto de Cárlos II.

—Querido Musgrave—, dije—, habéis entrado en posesión de una reliquia.

Colección de 40 dibujos

REGALO Á LOS CONSUMIDORES

DEL

Chocolate Jaime Boix

HOSPITAL, 46.—BARCELONA

J. Horta, Impresor, Mendez Nuñez, 3 y 5

Brunton must have gone in alone. and he gave the contents of the chest to Rachel who was waiting for him by the hole. Something most tragic must have happened then. In her soul from her youth arose past disdain, and revenge appeared, Brunton was in her power. Removing one of the logs. the slab would return to her natural position, burying the butler. Chance could have also been the cause of the crime. But remembering Raquel's scared face and her hysterical attacks, I believed the first hypothesis. What also proved the guilt of the maiden, the objects found in the lake, which undoubtedly constituted the contents of the chest.

Musgrave ripped me out of my abstraction

"These coins bear the effigy of Charles 1."

"Ah! Well, it seems to me that we are going to find other things from the same time."

We went up to the office and examined the objects found in the pond. Picking up one piece, I rubbed it lightly against my sleeve, and it glowed brightly.

"You will remember." I told Musgrave, "That the party royalist survived in England even after the king's death, and that when his party fled, they left widespread many precious objects."

My friend nodded, saying that one of his ancestors was a follower of Charles II.

"Dear Musgrave." I said, "You have come into possession of a relic."

El Ritual de los Musgrave

Série A.—Núm. 10

Aquí teneis la corona...

Here you have the crown ...

SH-JCS10

Back of Card 10.

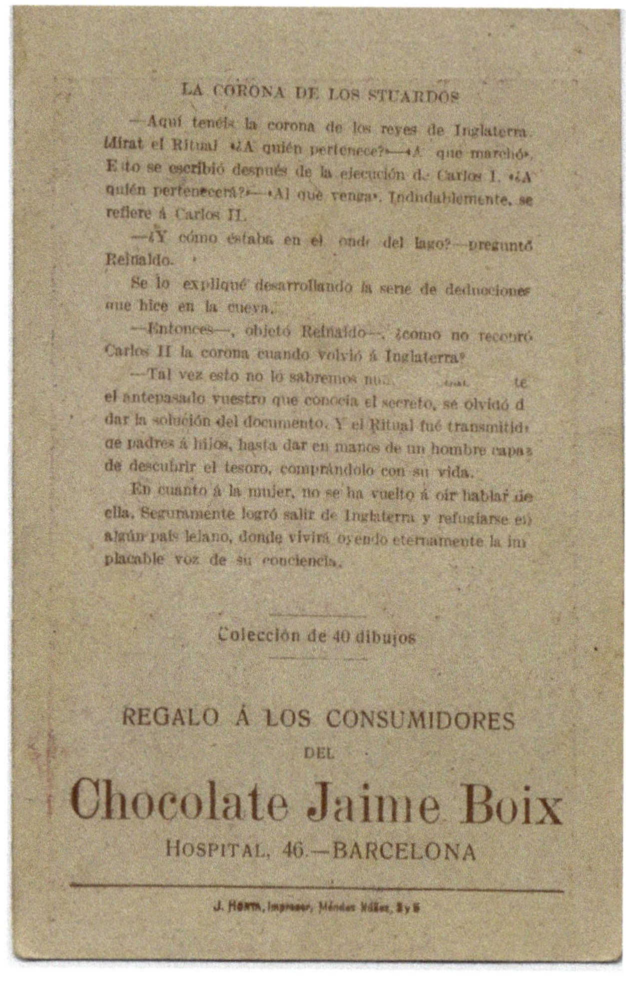

LA CORONA DE LOS STUARDOS

—Aquí tenéis la corona de los reyes de Inglaterra. Mirat el Ritual ¿A quién pertenece?—«A que marchó». Esto se escribió después de la ejecución de Carlos I. «¿A quién pertenecerá?»—«Al que venga». Indudablemente, se refiere á Carlos II.

—¿Y cómo estaba en el onde del lago?—preguntó Reinaldo.

Se lo expliqué desarrollando la serie de deducciones que hice en la cueva.

—Entonces—, objetó Reinaldo—, ¿cómo no recobró Carlos II la corona cuando volvió á Inglaterra?

—Tal vez esto no lo sabremos nun... ... te el antepasado vuestro que conocía el secreto, se olvidó de dar la solución del documento. Y el Ritual fué transmitid de padres á hijos, hasta dar en manos de un hombre capaz de descubrir el tesoro, comprándolo con su vida.

En cuanto á la mujer, no se ha vuelto á oir hablar de ella. Seguramente logró salir de Inglaterra y refugiarse en algún país lejano, donde vivirá oyendo eternamente la implacable voz de su conciencia.

Colección de 40 dibujos

REGALO Á LOS CONSUMIDORES

DEL

Chocolate Jaime Boix

HOSPITAL, 46.—BARCELONA

J. Horta, Impresor, Méndez Núñez, 3 y 5

Here you have the crown of the kings of England.
Look at the Ritual
Whose was it?
Who shall have it?
This was written after the execution of Charles 1
Who shall have it?
He who will come.
Undoubtedly, this refers to Charles II.
And how are you, on the wave of the lake?
Reginald-
Explain it by developing the series of deductions that I did in the cellar.
Then Reginald objected. "I do not understand why Charles II did not recover his crown when he returned to England?"
We won't know why it remained hidden; your Ancestors who knew the secret forgot to give the solution of the document. And the ritual was transmitted from father to son until it came into the hands of a capable man who discovered it's secret and the treasure and paid for it with his life.

As for the woman. she was never heard of again. She surely managed to leave England and take refuge in some distant country. where she will live eternally hearing the implacable voice of her conscience.

Joaquin Coll Salieti – Series B, The Speckled Band 10 card set.

Series B, Card 11.   THE SPECKLED BAND

SH-JCS11

Back of Card 11.

LA BANDÁ MOTEADA

Hojeando los infinitos apuntes referentes á más de setenta casos en los cuales pude estudiar los procedimientos analíticos y deductivos de Sherlock Holmes, no he hallado uno solo que fuera vulgar. Y es que Holmes no emprendía ningún asunto sin cerciorarse antes muy bien de su importancia y excentricidad; y de entre todos estos casos curiosísimos, ninguno tan original ni tan emocionador como el referente á la familia Roylott, de Stoke Moran.

Hubiera podido hablar antes de este asunto, á no ser por la promesa de guardar silencio que le hice á Holmes, y que la reciente muerte de este querido amigo ha destruido. Creo también muy oportuno este relato como refutación y destrucción de ciertos rumores que corrieron acerca de la muerte del Doctor Grimesby Roylott.

Colección de 40 dibujos

REGALO Á LOS CONSUMIDORES

DEL

Chocolate Jaime Boix

HOSPITAL, 46.—BARCELONA

Imp. J. HORTA; Méndez Núñez,

Leafing through the infinite reference notes. more than seventy cases in which I was able to study the procedures of Sherlock Holmes analytics and deductions. I have not found just one that was commonplace. Holmes did not undertake a case without first ascertaining very well its importance and eccentricity; and among all these cases some curious, but none are as original or as exciting as that concerning the Roylott family, at Stoke Moran. I could have spoken on this matter earlier, but for the promise of silence I made to the lady involved. And with the recent death of this dear lady, I also think this story is very appropriate as a refutation and destruction of certain rumours that concerned the death of Doctor Grimesby Roylott.

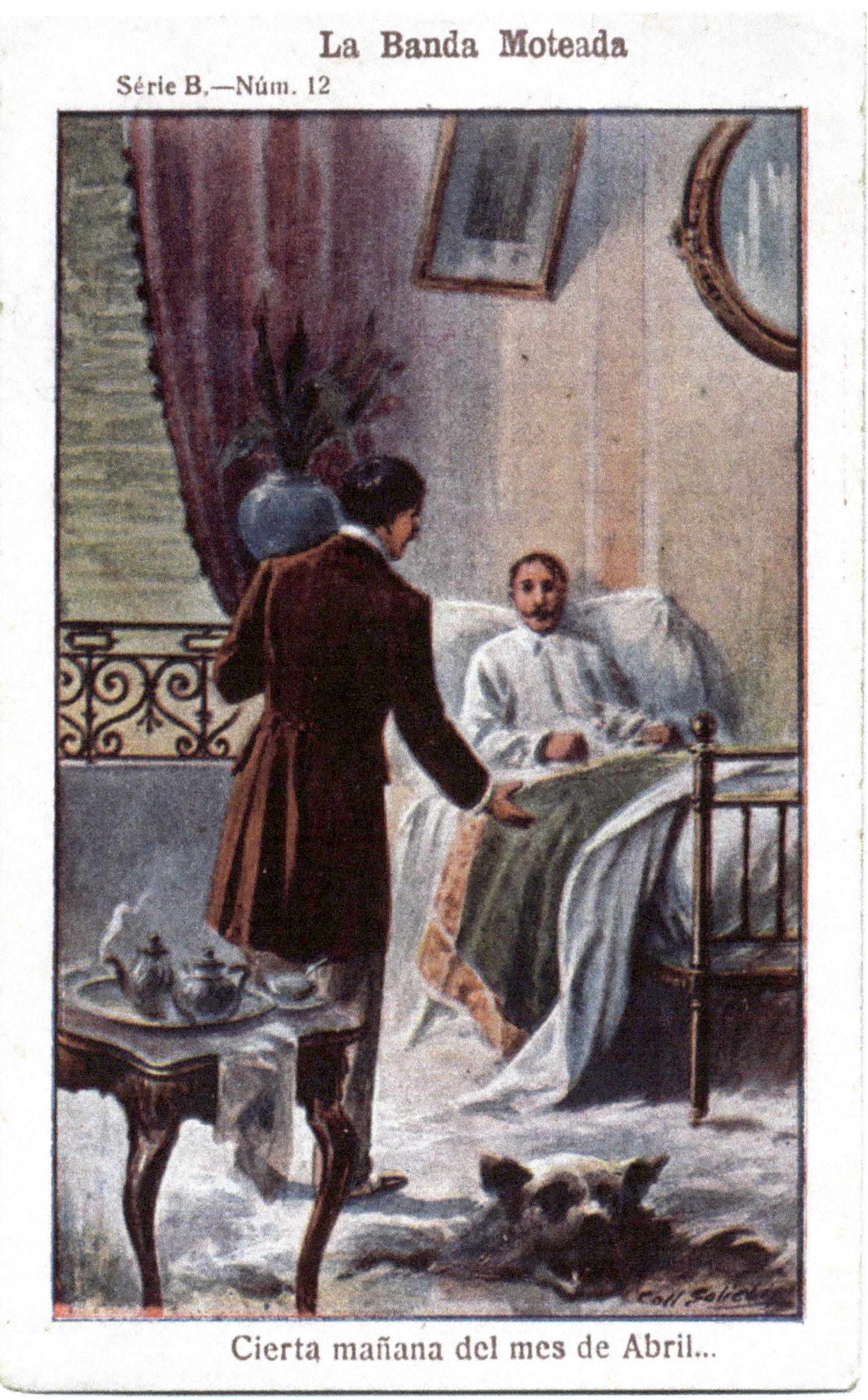

A certain morning in April…

SH-JCS12

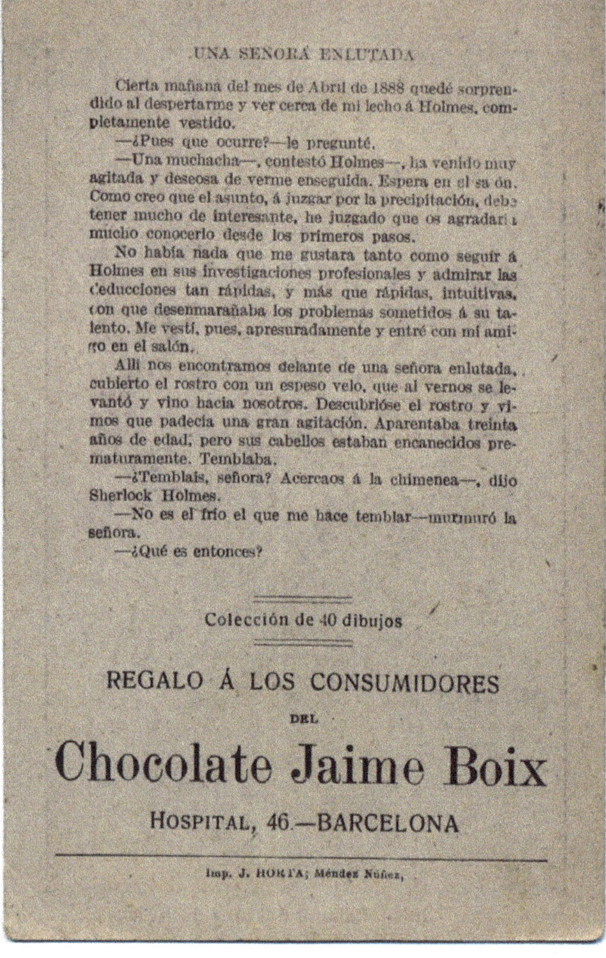

UNA SEÑORA ENLUTADA

Cierta mañana del mes de Abril de 1888 quedé sorprendido al despertarme y ver cerca de mi lecho á Holmes, completamente vestido.

—¿Pues que ocurre?—le pregunté.

—Una muchacha—, contestó Holmes—, ha venido muy agitada y deseosa de verme enseguida. Espera en el salón. Como creo que el asunto, á juzgar por la precipitación, debe tener mucho de interesante, he juzgado que os agradaría mucho conocerlo desde los primeros pasos.

No había nada que me gustara tanto como seguir á Holmes en sus investigaciones profesionales y admirar las deducciones tan rápidas, y más que rápidas, intuitivas, con que desenmarañaba los problemas sometidos á su talento. Me vestí, pues, apresuradamente y entré con mi amigo en el salón.

Allí nos encontramos delante de una señora enlutada, cubierto el rostro con un espeso velo, que al vernos se levantó y vino hacia nosotros. Descubrióse el rostro y vimos que padecía una gran agitación. Aparentaba treinta años de edad, pero sus cabellos estaban encanecidos prematuramente. Temblaba.

—¿Tembláis, señora? Acercaos á la chimenea—, dijo Sherlock Holmes.

—No es el frío el que me hace temblar—murmuró la señora.

—¿Qué es entonces?

———————

Colección de 40 dibujos

———————

REGALO Á LOS CONSUMIDORES

DEL

Chocolate Jaime Boix

HOSPITAL, 46.—BARCELONA

Imp. J. HORTA; Méndez Núñez,

One morning in April 1888 I was surprised when I woke up and saw Holmes near my bed, completely dress. "Well, what is it?" I asked him.

"A Lady," Holmes replied, "has come very agitated and eager to see me right away. She waits in the room."

As I believe that the matter, judging by the haste, must have a lot of interest. I have judged that you would like to know a lot from the first steps.

I cannot think of anything that I liked as much as following Holmes on his professional investigations and admire the deductions so fast, and more than fast, intuitive. with which he unravelled the problems submitted to his talent. So, I dressed hastily and went in with my friend into the study.

There we found ourselves in front of a mourning lady, covered her face with a thick veil, and when she saw us, she got up and she came towards us. She uncovered her face and we saw that she was in great agitation. She looked thirty-year-old. but her hair was prematurely grey. She was Shivering.

"Shivering, madam? Come closer to the fireplace." said Sherlock Holmes.

"It's not the cold that makes me shiver", murmured the lady.

"What is it then?"

My name is Helen Stoner

SH-JCS13

THE STOKE MORAN

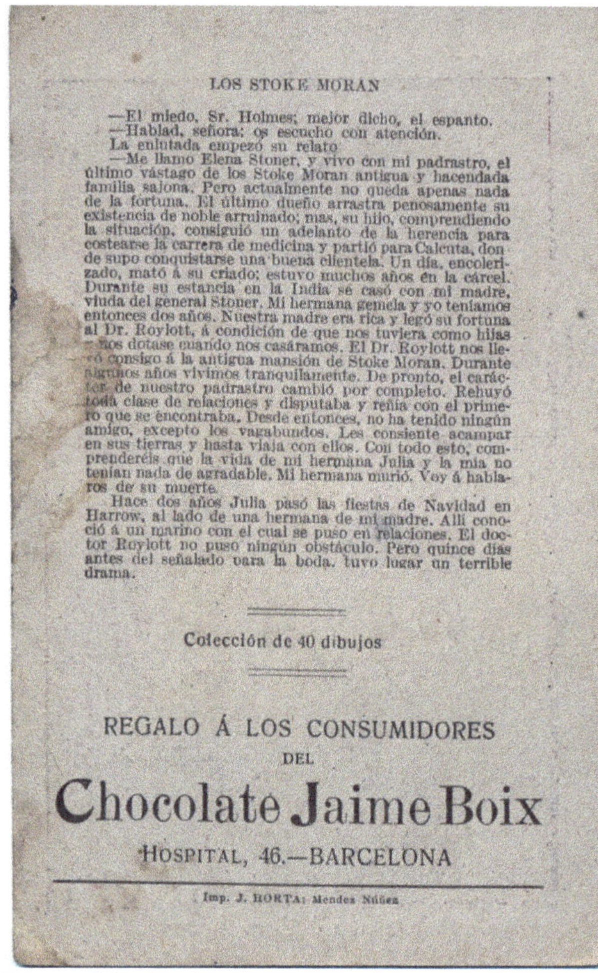

“The fear, Mr. Holmes; rather, the Horror.”

“Speak, ma'am;” as I listened carefully.

The woman in mourning began her story.

“My name is Helen Stoner, and I live with my stepfather, Last Scion of the Old Stoke Moran Saxon family. Currently there is hardly anything left of the fortune. The last owner painfully dragged his ruined noble existence. But his son, understanding the situation, got an advance on his inheritance to pay for a medical career and left for Calcutta, where he knew how to succeed and get good clientele. One day however, angry, he killed his servant and spent many years in jail. During his stay in India, he fell in love with my mother, the widow of General Stoner. My twin sister and I were then two years old. Our mother was rich, and she bequeathed her fortune to Dr. Roylott. on condition that he had us as daughters and give us our inheritance when we got married. Dr. Roylott took us with him to the old mansion at Stoke Moran. We lived quietly for a few years.

But suddenly the character of our stepfather changed completely. He shunned all kind of relationships and he disputed and quarrelled with everyone he met. Since then, he has not had any friends, except the gypsies. Allowing them to camp in his lands and even travels with them. With all this, you can understand that my sister Julia's life and mine were not pleasant at all. My sister died. I'm going to tell you about her death.

Two years ago, Julia passed the Christmas at a party in Harrow, with the sister of my mother. There she met a sailor with whom she got engaged. Doctor Roylott did not put up any obstacles. But fifteen days before the appointed time for the wedding there took place a terrible event.

I saw her appear with a livid face…

SH-JCS14

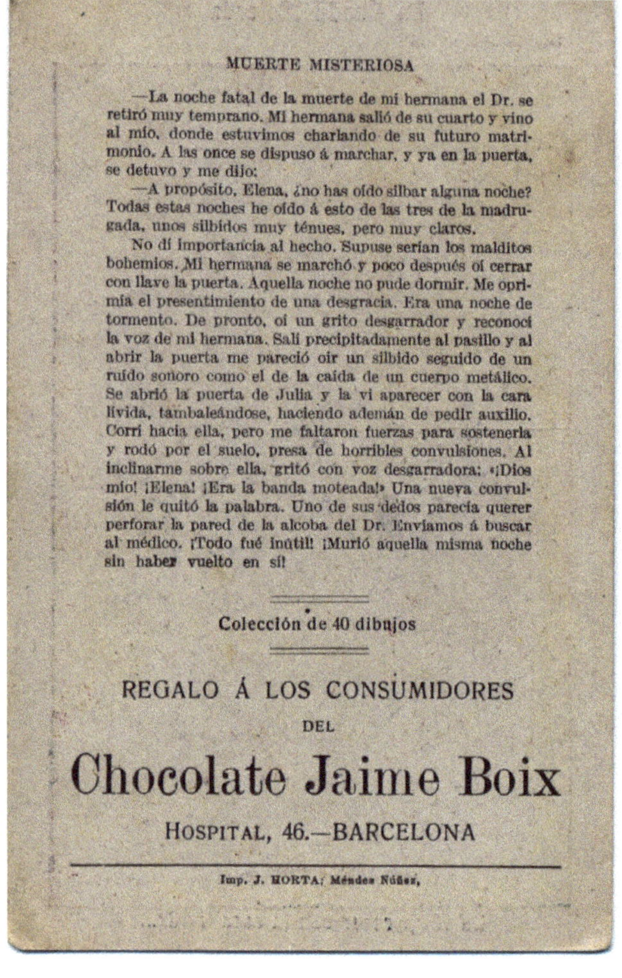

MUERTE MISTERIOSA

—La noche fatal de la muerte de mi hermana el Dr. se retiró muy temprano. Mi hermana salió de su cuarto y vino al mío, donde estuvimos charlando de su futuro matrimonio. A las once se dispuso á marchar, y ya en la puerta, se detuvo y me dijo:

—A propósito, Elena, ¿no has oído silbar alguna noche? Todas estas noches he oído á esto de las tres de la madrugada, unos silbidos muy ténues, pero muy claros.

No dí importancia al hecho. Supuse serían los malditos bohemios. Mi hermana se marchó y poco después oí cerrar con llave la puerta. Aquella noche no pude dormir. Me oprimía el presentimiento de una desgracia. Era una noche de tormento. De pronto, oí un grito desgarrador y reconocí la voz de mi hermana. Salí precipitadamente al pasillo y al abrir la puerta me pareció oir un silbido seguido de un ruido sonoro como el de la caída de un cuerpo metálico. Se abrió la puerta de Julia y la vi aparecer con la cara lívida, tambaleándose, haciendo ademán de pedir auxilio. Corrí hacia ella, pero me faltaron fuerzas para sostenerla y rodó por el suelo, presa de horribles convulsiones. Al inclinarme sobre ella, grité con voz desgarradora: ¡Dios mío! ¡Elena! ¡Era la banda moteada! Una nueva convulsión le quitó la palabra. Uno de sus dedos parecía querer perforar la pared de la alcoba del Dr. Enviamos á buscar al médico. ¡Todo fué inútil! ¡Murió aquella misma noche sin haber vuelto en sí!

Colección de 40 dibujos

REGALO Á LOS CONSUMIDORES

DEL

Chocolate Jaime Boix

HOSPITAL, 46.—BARCELONA

Imp. J. HORTA; Méndez Núñez,

The fatal night of my sister's death, The Doctor had retired very early. My sister left her room and came into mine, where we were chatting about her future marriage. At eleven o'clock she prepared to leave. and already at the door. she stopped and said to me:

"By the way, Helen, have you heard a whistle during the night? I have heard this at three in the morning, very low whistles. but very clear."

I did not give importance to the fact. I assumed they would be the damned bohemians.

My sister left and shortly after I heard her close and lock her door. That night I couldn't sleep due to a feeling of a coming misfortune. It was a night of torment. Suddenly, I heard a heart-breaking scream and recognized my sister's voice. I rushed out into the hall and into the opening of the door, I thought I heard a hiss followed by a sort of noise like that of the fall of a metallic body. Julia's door opened and I saw her appear with her face, livid, staggering, making a request for help.

I ran towards her, but I lacked the strength to hold her, and she rolled on the floor in horrible convulsions. As I leant over her, she cried in a heart-breaking voice.

"O, my God! Helen! It was the Speckled band!"

A new convulsion took the word out of her. One of her fingers seemed to stab in the direction of the Doctor's bedroom. Calling out for my stepfather, but everything was useless! She! She died that very night, without having recovered consciousness.

I thought maybe it was a delusion…

SH-JCS15

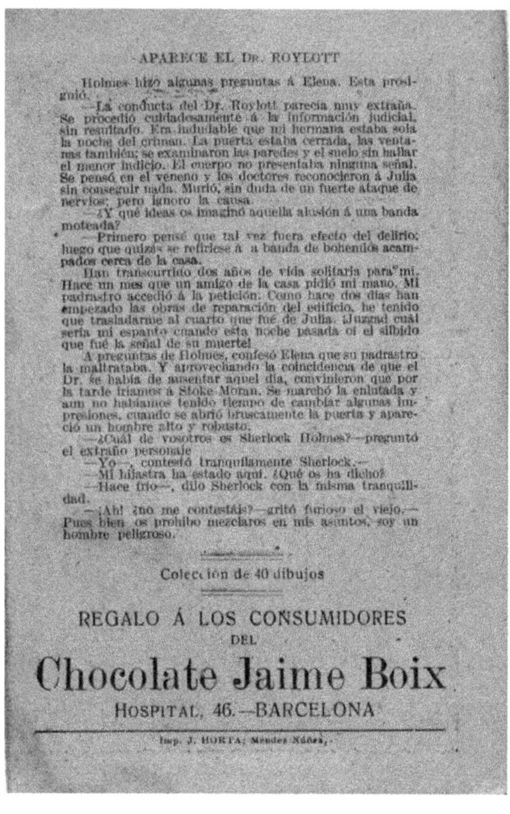

Holmes asked some questions of Helen. She continued. Dr. Roylott's behaviour seemed very strange, he carefully proceeded to the judicial information, without result. It was undoubtedly that my sister was alone the night of the crime. The door was locked, the windows too; the walls and the floor were examined without finding the slightest clue. The body showed no signs of poison and the doctors examined Julia without finding anything. She died; no doubt from a strong attack of nerves; but I do not know the cause.

"And what ideas did that allusion to a speckled band?"

"At first, I thought that maybe it was the effect of delirium; then perhaps it was referring to a band of bohemians camped out near the house.

Two years of lonely life have since passed for me. A month ago, a friend of the house asked for my hand. My stepfather agreed to the request: But two days ago, they started repair work in the building. I have had to move to the room that belonged to Julia. Imagine my horror when last night I heard the whistle that was the sign of her death!"

When asked by Holmes, Helen confided that her stepfather mistreated her and taking advantage of the coincidence that the Doctor was to be absent that day, we agreed that in the afternoon we would go to Stoke Moran_ she left the study and we had not yet had time to exchange some impressions, when the door was opened abruptly, and a tall and robust man appeared.

"Which one of you is Sherlock Holmes?" asked the strange character.

"I" Sherlock replied calmly.

"My stepdaughter has been here. What did she tell you?"

"It's cold," said Sherlock with the same calmness.

"Ah! You do not answer me?" - the man yelled furious. "Well, I forbid you to mix in my business. I am a dangerous man."

And taking the tongs from the fireplace…

SH-JCS16

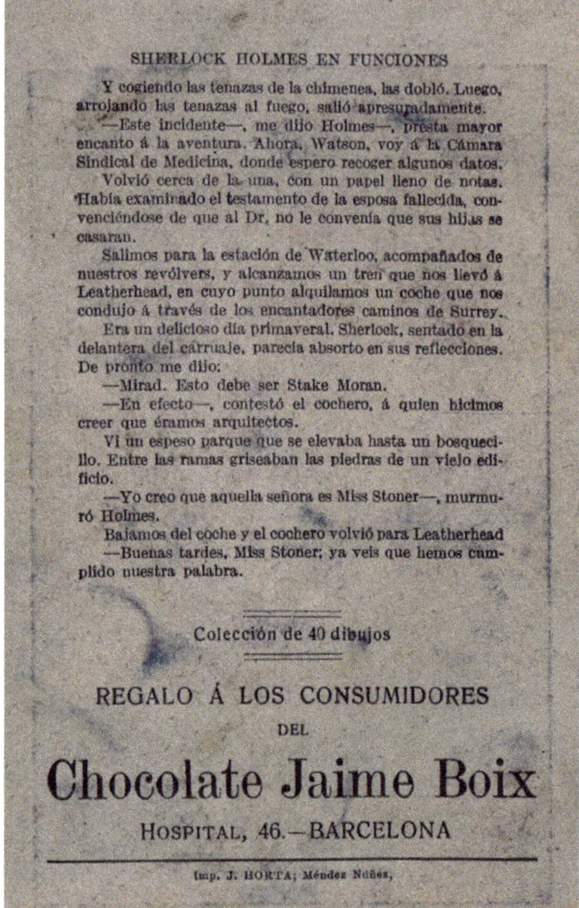

SHERLOCK HOLMES EN FUNCIONES

Y cogiendo las tenazas de la chimenea, las dobló. Luego, arrojando las tenazas al fuego, salió apresuradamente.

—Este incidente—, me dijo Holmes—, presta mayor encanto á la aventura. Ahora, Watson, voy á la Cámara Sindical de Medicina, donde espero recoger algunos datos.

Volvió cerca de la una, con un papel lleno de notas. Había examinado el testamento de la esposa fallecida, convenciéndose de que al Dr, no le convenía que sus hijas se casaran.

Salimos para la estación de Waterloo, acompañados de nuestros revólvers, y alcanzamos un tren que nos llevó á Leatherhead, en cuyo punto alquilamos un coche que nos condujo á través de los encantadores caminos de Surrey.

Era un delicioso día primaveral. Sherlock, sentado en la delantera del carruaje, parecía absorto en sus reflecciones. De pronto me dijo:

—Mirad. Esto debe ser Stake Moran.

—En efecto—, contestó el cochero, á quien hicimos creer que éramos arquitectos.

Vi un espeso parque que se elevaba hasta un bosquecillo. Entre las ramas griseaban las piedras de un viejo edificio.

—Yo creo que aquella señora es Miss Stoner—, murmuró Holmes.

Bajamos del coche y el cochero volvió para Leatherhead

—Buenas tardes, Miss Stoner; ya veis que hemos cumplido nuestra palabra.

Colección de 40 dibujos

REGALO Á LOS CONSUMIDORES

DEL

Chocolate Jaime Boix

HOSPITAL, 46.—BARCELONA

Imp. J. HORTA; Méndez Núñez,

And taking the tongs from the fireplace. he bent them. throwing the tongs back into the fireplace, he hurried out.

"This incident", said Holmes, "gives zest to our investigations. Now. Watson, I'm going to the Doctors' Commons where I hope to collect some data."

He came back around one o'clock, with a paper full of notes. He had examined the will of the deceased wife. Finding that it was not in the Doctor's interest if his daughters were to marry.

We left for Waterloo station, accompanied by our revolvers, and we caught a train that took us to Leatherhead, at which point we hired a cab to drive through the enchanted Surrey roads.

It was a delicious spring day. Sherlock, sitting on the front of the carriage. he seemed engrossed in reflections. Suddenly he told me:

"Behold. This must be Stoke Moran."

"Indeed, " answered the coachman, to whom we had made believe that we were architects. I saw a thick park that rose to a grove. Between the branches, the stones of an old building gleamed.

"I think that lady is Miss Stoner." murmured Holmes.

We got out of the car and the coachman returned to Leatherhead.

"Good afternoon, Miss Stoner; you see that we have kept to our word."

I was waiting for you with so much impatience…

SH-JCS17

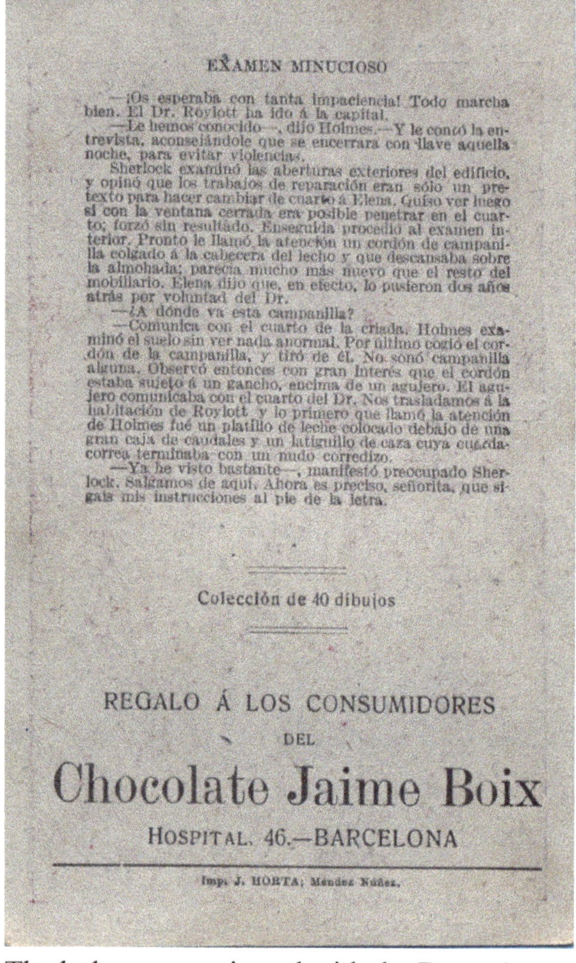

EXAMEN MINUCIOSO

—¡Os esperaba con tanta impaciencia! Todo marcha bien. El Dr. Roylott ha ido á la capital.

—Le hemos conocido—, dijo Holmes.—Y le concó la entrevista, aconsejándole que se encerrara con llave aquella noche, para evitar violencias.

Sherlock examinó las aberturas exteriores del edificio, y opinó que los trabajos de reparación eran sólo un pretexto para hacer cambiar de cuarto á Elena. Quiso ver luego si con la ventana cerrada era posible penetrar en el cuarto; forzó sin resultado. Enseguida procedió al examen interior. Pronto le llamó la atención un cordón de campanilla colgado á la cabecera del lecho y que descansaba sobre la almohada; parecía mucho más nuevo que el resto del mobiliario. Elena dijo que, en efecto, lo pusieron dos años atrás por voluntad del Dr.

—¿A dónde va esta campanilla?

—Comunica con el cuarto de la criada. Holmes examinó el suelo sin ver nada anormal. Por último cogió el cordón de la campanilla, y tiró de él. No sonó campanilla alguna. Observó entonces con gran interés que el cordón estaba sujeto á un gancho, encima de un agujero. El agujero comunicaba con el cuarto del Dr. Nos trasladamos á la habitación de Roylott y lo primero que llamó la atención de Holmes fué un platillo de leche colocado debajo de una gran caja de caudales y un latiguillo de caza cuya cuerda correa terminaba con un nudo corredizo.

—Ya he visto bastante—, manifestó preocupado Sherlock. Salgamos de aquí. Ahora es preciso, señorita, que sigáis mis instrucciones al pie de la letra.

Colección de 40 dibujos

REGALO Á LOS CONSUMIDORES
DEL

Chocolate Jaime Boix

HOSPITAL. 46.—BARCELONA

Imp. J. HORTA; Méndez Núñez.

"I was waiting for you, with so much impatience! Everything worked out, Dr. Roylott has gone to the capital."

"We have met him", said Holmes. And he told her about the interview, advising her to lock herself up that night. to avoid violence. Sherlock examined the exterior openings of the building and he thought that the repair works were just a pretext to make Helen change rooms. He wanted to see later, with the window closed. If it was possible to enter the room; he tried without result. He then proceeded to the internal examination. Soon a bell cord caught his eye hanging at the head of the bed and resting on Pillow; It seemed much newer than the rest of the furniture. Helen said that. indeed. they had been put it two years back at the will of doctor.

"Where is this bell going?"

"It communicates with the maid's room." Holmes scanned the floor, seeing nothing of his own. At last, he took the cord of the bell, and tugged it. No bell rang, he then observed with great interest that the cord was attached to a hook, and above was a hole.

The hole communicated with the Doctor's room. In Doctor Roylott's room the first thing that caught my eye was a saucer of milk placed under a big safe and a hunting rope belt which ended with a slip knot.

"I've seen enough," Sherlock said worriedly.

"Let's get out of here. It is now important. Miss, that you follow my instructions to the letter."

Silently we climbed in through the window…
SH-JCS18

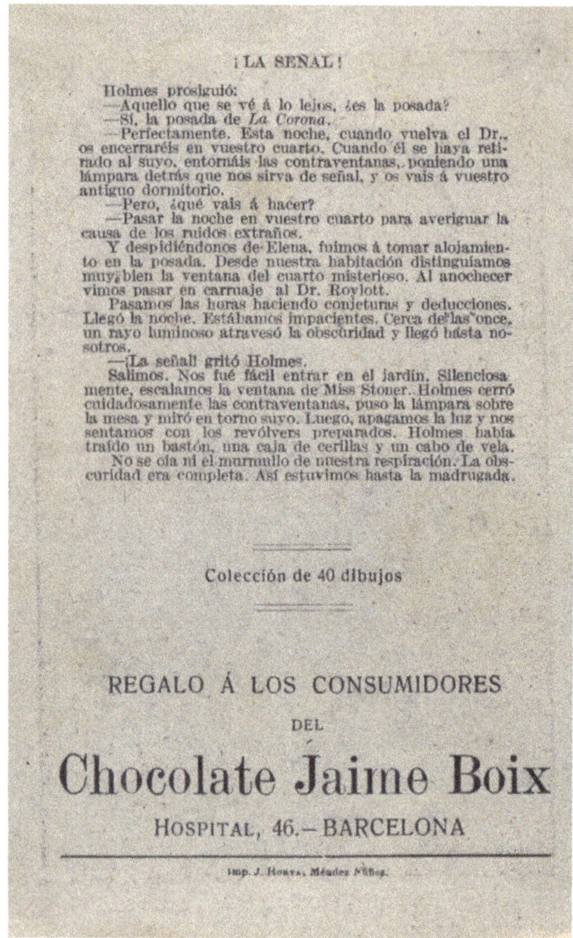

¡LA SEÑAL!

Holmes prosiguió:
—Aquello que se vé á lo lejos, ¿es la posada?
—Sí, la posada de *La Corona*.
—Perfectamente. Esta noche, cuando vuelva el Dr.. os encerraréis en vuestro cuarto. Cuando él se haya retirado al suyo, entornáis las contraventanas, poniendo una lámpara detrás que nos sirva de señal, y os vais á vuestro antiguo dormitorio.
—Pero, ¿qué vais á hacer?
—Pasar la noche en vuestro cuarto para averiguar la causa de los ruidos extraños.
Y despidiéndonos de Elena, fuimos á tomar alojamiento en la posada. Desde nuestra habitación distinguíamos muy bien la ventana del cuarto misterioso. Al anochecer vimos pasar en carruaje al Dr. Roylott.
Pasamos las horas haciendo conjeturas y deducciones. Llegó la noche. Estábamos impacientes. Cerca de las once, un rayo luminoso atravesó la obscuridad y llegó hasta nosotros.
—¡La señal! gritó Holmes.
Salimos. Nos fué fácil entrar en el jardín. Silenciosamente, escalamos la ventana de Miss Stoner. Holmes cerró cuidadosamente las contraventanas, puso la lámpara sobre la mesa y miró en torno suyo. Luego, apagamos la luz y nos sentamos con los revólvers preparados. Holmes había traído un bastón, una caja de cerillas y un cabo de vela.
No se oía ni el murmullo de nuestra respiración. La obscuridad era completa. Así estuvimos hasta la madrugada.

Colección de 40 dibujos

REGALO Á LOS CONSUMIDORES

DEL

Chocolate Jaime Boix

HOSPITAL, 46.—BARCELONA

Imp. J. Horta, Méndez Núñez.

Holmes continued:
"Is that an inn I see in the distance?"
"Yes, the inn is called the Crown."
"Perfect. Tonight. when the Dr. returns home, you will lock yourself in your room until he retires. Then open the shutters of your window. putting a lamp to serve as a signal. and then go to your old bedroom."
"But what are you going to do?"
"Spend the night in your room to find out the cause of the strange noises.
And saying goodbye to Helen, we went to take lodging at the inn.
From our room we had a commanding view out of the window of the mysterious room. At dusk, we saw Dr. Roylott go by in his carriage.
We spend the next few hours making guesses and deductions. The night has come. We were impatient. About eleven o'clock. a bright ray pierced the darkness and reached us.
"The signal!" yelled Holmes. We went out. It was easy for us to enter the Garden.

Silently. We climbed through Miss Stoner's window. Holmes carefully closed the shutters, he put the lamp on the table and looked around him. Then he turned off the light and we sat down with revolvers ready. Holmes had brought a cane, a box of matches and a candle stub. Not even the murmur of our breathing was heard. The darkness was complete. So, we waited until dawn.

He began to beat loudly…
SH-JCS19

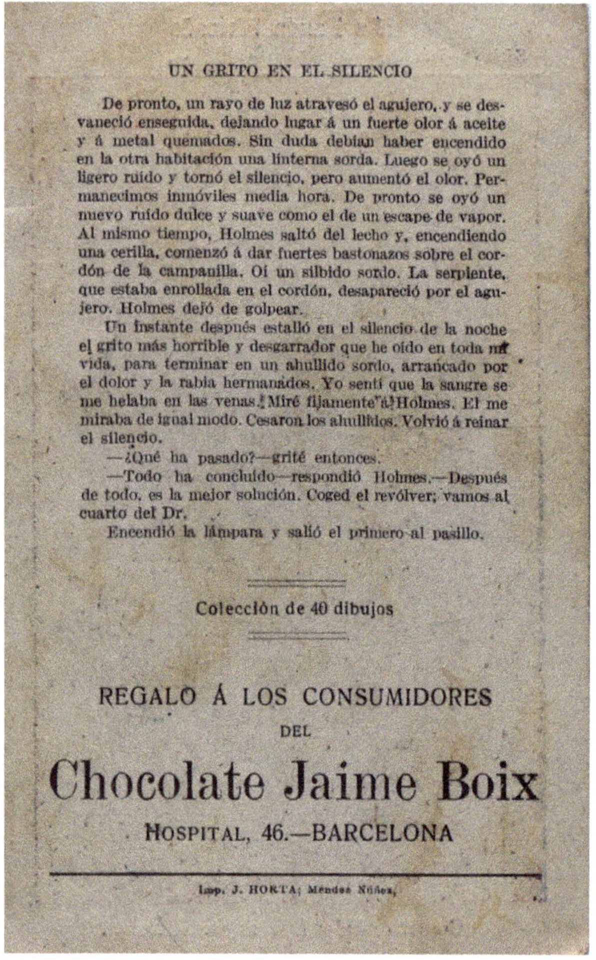

UN GRITO EN EL SILENCIO

De pronto, un rayo de luz atravesó el agujero, y se desvaneció enseguida, dejando lugar á un fuerte olor á aceite y á metal quemados. Sin duda debían haber encendido en la otra habitación una linterna sorda. Luego se oyó un ligero ruido y tornó el silencio, pero aumentó el olor. Permanecimos inmóviles media hora. De pronto se oyó un nuevo ruido dulce y suave como el de un escape de vapor. Al mismo tiempo, Holmes saltó del lecho y, encendiendo una cerilla, comenzó á dar fuertes bastonazos sobre el cordón de la campanilla. Oí un silbido sordo. La serpiente, que estaba enrollada en el cordón, desapareció por el agujero. Holmes dejó de golpear.

Un instante después estalló en el silencio de la noche el grito más horrible y desgarrador que he oído en toda mi vida, para terminar en un ahullido sordo, arrancado por el dolor y la rabia hermanados. Yo sentí que la sangre se me helaba en las venas. Miré fijamente á Holmes. El me miraba de igual modo. Cesaron los ahullidos. Volvió á reinar el silencio.

—¿Qué ha pasado?—grité entonces.

—Todo ha concluido—respondió Holmes.—Después de todo, es la mejor solución. Coged el revólver; vamos al cuarto del Dr.

Encendió la lámpara y salió el primero al pasillo.

Colección de 40 dibujos

REGALO Á LOS CONSUMIDORES

DEL

Chocolate Jaime Boix

HOSPITAL, 46.—BARCELONA

Imp. J. HORTA; Méndez Núñez,

Suddenly. a ray of light pierced the darkness, and faded immediately, leaving room for a strong smell of oil, and burned metal. Surely, they should have lit in the other room a dark lantern. Then a slight noise and silence, but the smell increased. We stayed motionless for half an hour Suddenly we heard a new, sweet, and soft noise like that of steam escaping.

At the same time Holmes jumped onto the bed and, lighting a match, he began to beat boldly on the bell cord. I heard a dull hiss. The snake, which was wrapped around the cord, disappeared through the hole.

Holmes stopped striking.

An instant later it exploded into the silence of the night, the most horrible and heart-breaking scream I've ever heard in my entire life, ending in a howling, torn by pain and rage. twinned. I felt that my blood was frozen in my veins. I looked at Holmes. He looked the same way. The howling stopped. The silence reigned again.

"What happened? " I shouted.

"Everything is over" Holmes answered. "It is the best solution. Take the revolver; let's go to the Doctor's room.

He lit the lamp, and we went first into the hall.

The speckled band …

SH-JCS20

EYE FOR EYE! TOOTH FOR TOOTH!

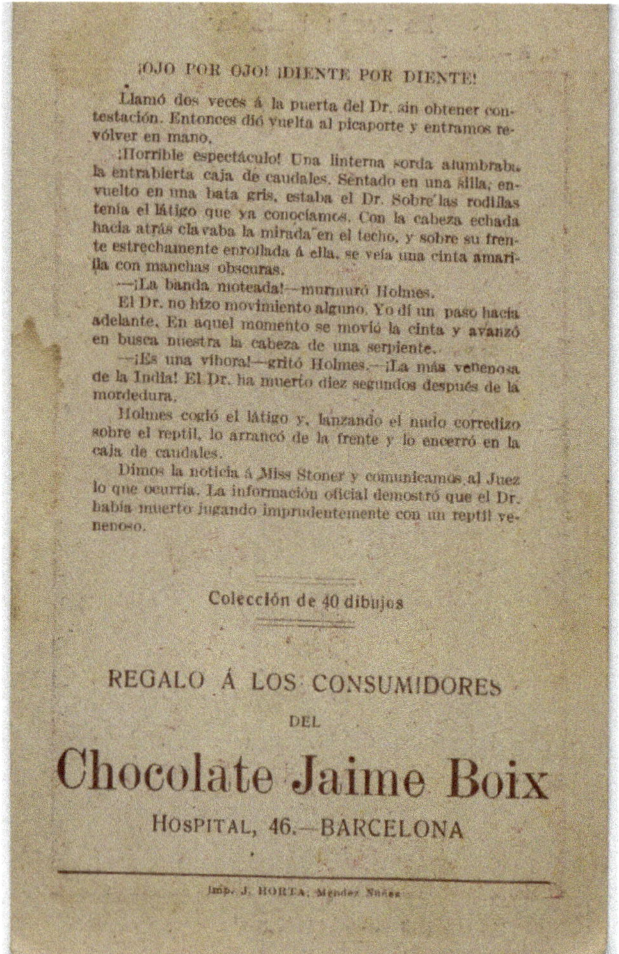

He knocked twice on the Doctor's door without obtaining a reply, then he turned the doorknob and I put my revolver in my hand .

Horrible show! A dark lantern illuminated the safe that was ajar. Sitting in a chair; wrapped in a grey dressing gown, was the Doctor. He held the whip we already knew. He was staring at the ceiling, and on his forehead closely wrapped around it was a yellow tape with dark spots. ·

"The Speckled band!" Holmes muttered. The Doctor made no move. I took a step towards him, instantly the band moved and advanced looking at us, the head of a serpent .

"It's a snake!" Holmes shouted. "The most poisonous from India! The doctor. has died ten seconds after the bite.

Holmes took the whip and, tossing the noose over the reptile, he tore it from his forehead and locked it in the safe.

We gave the news to Miss Stoner and communicated to the Judge what had happened. The Official information showed that the Doctor had died playing recklessly with a poisonous reptile.

Joaquin Coll Salieti – Series C, The Sign of four.

Collection of 40 cards

SH-JCS21

Back of Card 21.

Aventuras de Sherlock Holmes

Colección de 40 dibujos

Serie C

La Marca de los Cuatro

REGALO Á LOS CONSUMIDORES
del CHOCOLATE JAIME BOIX
HOSPITAL, 46.—BARCELONA

Imp. J. HORTA; Méndes Núñes,

THE SIGN OF THE FOUR

Sherlock Holmes Adventures

Collection of 40 drawings

C SERIES

The Sign of Four

GIFT TO CONSUMERS
CHOCOLATE JAIME BOIX
HOSPITAL, 46.-BARCELONA
Printer. J. Horta; Méndes Núnes,

He gave himself the injection.

SH-JCS22

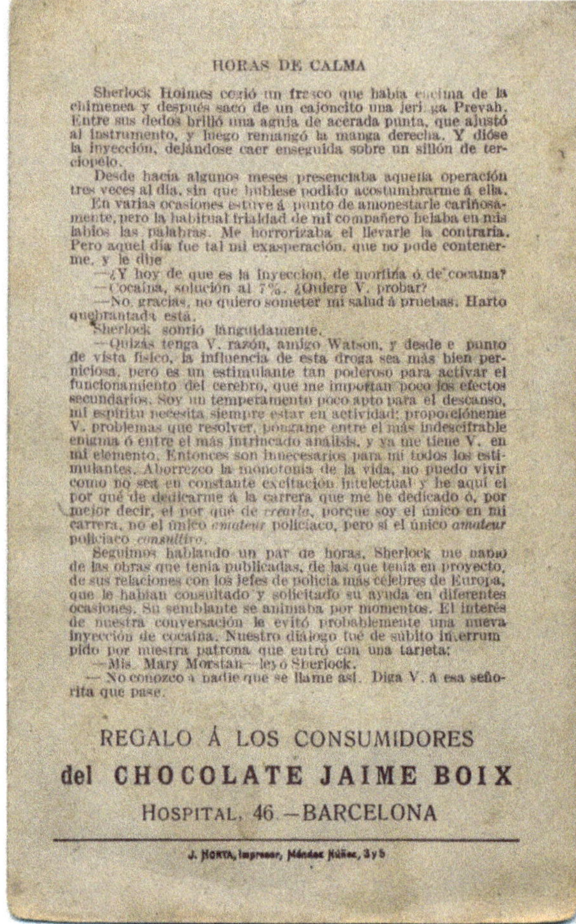

Sherlock Holmes picked up a bottle from on top of the fireplace and then took a hypodermic syringe out of a drawer. A steely pointed needle glinted between his fingers. while he adjusted the instrument, and then rolled up the right sleeve, and gave the injection, immediately collapsing onto a velvet chair.

For some months I had witnessed that operation three times a day, without being able to get used to it. On various occasions I was on the point of delivering my soul to him, but the usual coldness of my companion froze my words on my lips. I was horrified to contradict him. But that day was such my exasperation. I could not contain myself and I told him

"Which is it today, what is the injection, morphine, or cocaine?"

"Cocaine, 7% solution, do you want to try?"

"No thank you, I do not want to put my health to tests. It is still frail."

Sherlock smiled languidly, maybe you are right, friend Watson,

and from the point, from a physical point of view, the influence of this drug is rather pernicious. but it is such a powerful stimulant to activate the functioning of my brain, I do not care much about the secondary effects. I have a temperament unfit for rest, my spirit always needs to be active; provide me with problems to solve, put me among the most indecipherable enigma or among the most intricate analysis and you already have me in my element and stimulants would be unnecessary. I abhor the monotony of life, I cannot live except in constant intellectual excitement and here is the reason I dedicate myself to the career that I have chosen for myself or, better to say, why I created it, because I am the only one with this career, not the only amateur policeman, but the only Consulting Detective.

We kept talking for a couple of hours. Sherlock spoke to me of the works that I had published, of those cases that he worked on, of his relations with the most famous police chiefs in Europe, who had consulted him and requested his help in different occasions. His face brightened by the moment. The interest of our conventions probably spared him a new injection of cocaine.

Our dialogue was suddenly interrupted by our landlady, who came in with a card; "Miss. Mary Morstan"- Sherlock read.

I don't know anyone with that name. Tell that lady to come in.

A carefully dressed young woman.

SH-JCS22

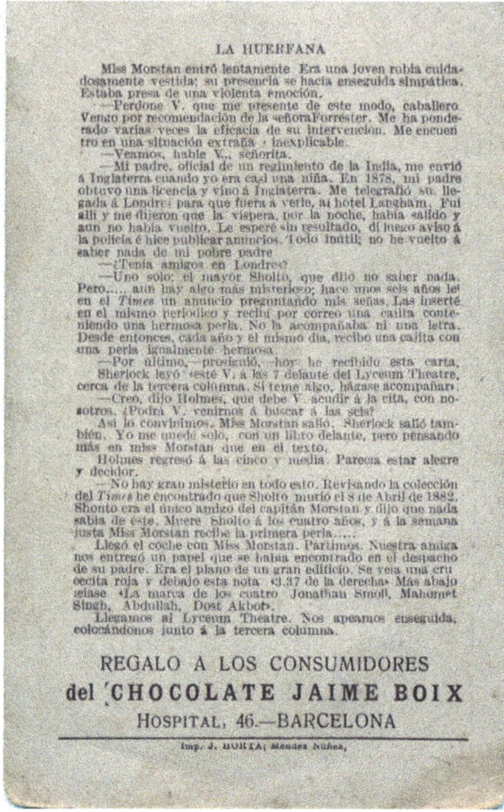

LA HUERFANA

Miss Morstan entró lentamente Era una joven rubia cuidadosamente vestida; su presencia se hacía enseguida simpática. Estaba presa de una violenta emoción.

—Perdone V. que me presente de este modo, caballero Vengo por recomendación de la señora Forrester. Me ha ponderado varias veces la eficacia de su intervención. Me encuentro en una situación extraña é inexplicable.

—Veamos, hable V., señorita.

—Mi padre, oficial de un regimiento de la India, me envió á Inglaterra cuando yo era casi una niña. En 1878, mi padre obtuvo una licencia y vino á Inglaterra. Me telegrafió su llegada á Londres para que fuera a verle, al hotel Langham. Fui allí y me dijeron que la víspera, por la noche, había salido y aún no había vuelto. Le esperé sin resultado, di luego aviso á la policía é hice publicar anuncios. Todo inútil; no he vuelto á saber nada de mi pobre padre

—¿Tenía amigos en Londres?

—Uno solo: el mayor Sholto, que dijo no saber nada. Pero..... aún hay algo más misterioso; hace unos seis años leí en el *Times* un anuncio preguntando mis señas. Las inserté en el mismo periódico y recibí por correo una cajita conteniendo una hermosa perla. No la acompañaba ni una letra. Desde entonces, cada año y el mismo día, recibo una cajita con una perla igualmente hermosa.

—Por último,—prosiguió,—hoy he recibido esta carta, Sherlock leyó «esté V. a las 7 delante del Lyceum Theatre, cerca de la tercera columna. Si teme algo, hágase acompañar».

—Creo, dijo Holmes, que debe V. acudir á la cita, con nosotros. ¿Podrá V. venirnos á buscar á las seis?

Así lo convinimos. Miss Morstan salió. Sherlock salió también. Yo me quedé solo, con un libro delante, pero pensando más en miss Morstan que en el texto.

Holmes regresó á las cinco y media. Parecía estar alegre y decidor.

—No hay gran misterio en todo esto. Revisando la colección del *Times* he encontrado que Sholto murió el 8 de Abril de 1882. Shonto era el único amigo del capitán Morstan y dijo que nada sabía de éste. Muere Sholto á los cuatro años, y á la semana justa Miss Morstan recibe la primera perla.....

Llegó el coche con Miss Morstan. Partimos. Nuestra amiga nos entregó un papel que se había encontrado en el despacho de su padre. Era el plano de un gran edificio. Se veía una crucecita roja y debajo esta nota «3.37 de la derecha» Más abajo leíase «La marca de los cuatro Jonathan Smoll, Mahomet Singh, Abdullah, Dost Akbot».

Llegamos al Lyceum Theatre. Nos apeamos enseguida, colocándonos junto á la tercera columna.

REGALO A LOS CONSUMIDORES
del 'CHOCOLATE JAIME BOIX
HOSPITAL, 46.—BARCELONA

Imp. J. HORTA; Mendez Núñez,

Miss Morstan entered slowly. She was one young blonde carefully dressed: her presence was immediately sympathetic. She was seized with a violent emotion.

"Excuse me as I introduce myself in this way, gentleman. I come on the recommendation of Mrs. Forrester. She has urged me several times to tell you about my inexplicable strange situation."

"Tell me more, miss."

"My father, an officer in a regiment in India, sent me to England as a child. In 1878, my father obtained leave to come to England. He telegraphed his arrival in London and asked me to go and see him. at the Langham Hotel. I arrived but they told me that the previous evening he had gone out and he still hadn't come back. I waited for him without result, then I gave notice to the police, and I had ads posted. All useless: nobody knew anything about my poor father"

"Did he have any friends in London?"

"Only one; a Major Sholto, who said he did not know anything. But there is still something more mysterious; about six years ago I read in the *Times* an advertisement asking my address. I inserted it in the same newspaper, and I received by mail a small box containing a beautiful pearl, without an accompanying letter. Since then, every year and on the same day, I receive a box with an equally beautiful pearl. Finally," she continued, "I received this letter today." Sherlock read this, "At 7 be in front of the Lyceum Theatre. near the third column. If you are afraid of something, have two friends accompany you."

"I believe," said Holmes, "that you must go to the appointment with us. Will you be able to come and pick us up at six o'clock?"

So, we agreed. Miss Morstan left. Sherlock left too and I was left alone, with a book in front of me. but thinking more of Miss Morstan than in the text.

Holmes returned at half past five. He seemed to be happy and resolved.

"There is no great mystery in all this. Checking the back issues of the *Times* I have found that Sholto died on April 8, 1882. Sholto was the only friend of Captain Morstan. Sholto died and within a week of his death, Miss Morstan receives the first pearl ...."

We got the cab with Miss Morstan, and she shows us a paper that had been found in her father's hotel room. It was the plan of a large building. There was a little red cross and below this note, 3.37 from the right lower corner, it Read 'The Sign of Four Jonathan Small, Mahomet Singh, Abdullah Khan, Dost Akbar'.

We arrived at the Lyceum Theatre and got out right away, standing next to the third column.

…A poorly dressed man approached us….

SH-JCS24

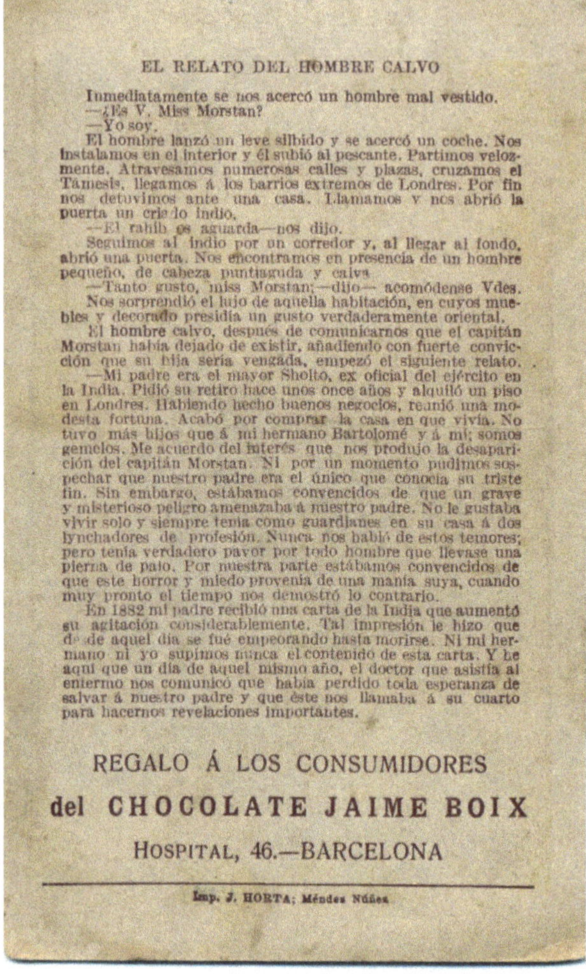

EL RELATO DEL HOMBRE CALVO

Inmediatamente se nos acercó un hombre mal vestido.

—¿Es V. Miss Morstan?

—Yo soy.

El hombre lanzó un leve silbido y se acercó un coche. Nos instalamos en el interior y él subió al pescante. Partimos velozmente. Atravesamos numerosas calles y plazas, cruzamos el Támesis, llegamos á los barrios extremos de Londres. Por fin nos detuvimos ante una casa. Llamamos y nos abrió la puerta un criado indio.

—El rahíb os aguarda—nos dijo.

Seguimos al indio por un corredor y, al llegar al fondo, abrió una puerta. Nos encontramos en presencia de un hombre pequeño, de cabeza puntiaguda y calva.

—Tanto gusto, miss Morstan;—dijo— acomódense Vdes.

Nos sorprendió el lujo de aquella habitación, en cuyos muebles y decorado presidía un gusto verdaderamente oriental.

El hombre calvo, después de comunicarnos que el capitán Morstan había dejado de existir, añadiendo con fuerte convicción que su hija sería vengada, empezó el siguiente relato.

—Mi padre era el mayor Sholto, ex oficial del ejército en la India. Pidió su retiro hace unos once años y alquiló un piso en Londres. Habiendo hecho buenos negocios, reunió una modesta fortuna. Acabó por comprar la casa en que vivía. No tuvo más hijos que á mi hermano Bartolomé y á mí; somos gemelos. Me acuerdo del interés que nos produjo la desaparición del capitán Morstan. Ni por un momento pudimos sospechar que nuestro padre era el único que conocía su triste fin. Sin embargo, estábamos convencidos de que un grave y misterioso peligro amenazaba á nuestro padre. No le gustaba vivir solo y siempre tenía como guardianes en su casa á dos lynchadores de profesión. Nunca nos habló de estos temores; pero tenía verdadero pavor por todo hombre que llevase una pierna de palo. Por nuestra parte estábamos convencidos de que este horror y miedo provenía de una manía suya, cuando muy pronto el tiempo nos demostró lo contrario.

En 1882 mi padre recibió una carta de la India que aumentó su agitación considerablemente. Tal impresión le hizo que desde aquel día se fué empeorando hasta morirse. Ni mi hermano ni yo supimos nunca el contenido de esta carta. Y he aquí que un día de aquel mismo año, el doctor que asistía al enfermo nos comunicó que había perdido toda esperanza de salvar á nuestro padre y que éste nos llamaba á su cuarto para hacernos revelaciones importantes.

REGALO Á LOS CONSUMIDORES

del CHOCOLATE JAIME BOIX

HOSPITAL, 46.—BARCELONA

Imp. J. HORTA; Méndez Núñez

We were immediately approached by a poorly dressed man.

"Are you Miss Morstan?"

"I am."

The man whistled slightly, and a cab pulled up. We went inside and he got on the box. We set off quickly. We crossed numerous streets and squares, we crossed the Thames, we reached the extreme suburbs of London. Finally, we stopped in front of a house. He called out and the door was opened by an Indian servant.

"The Sahib awaits you," he said.

We followed the Indian through a corridor and when we reach the back. he opened a door. We found ourselves in the presence of a small, pointed headed bald man.

"Nice to meet you, Miss Morstan," he said, "make yourself comfortable."

We were surprised by the luxury of that room, in whose furniture and decorated presided over a truly oriental taste.

The bald man told us that Captain Morstan was dead and adding with strong conviction that his daughter would be avenged.

He began the following story

"My father was Major Sholto, a former army officer in India. He received his retirement about eleven years ago and rented a flat in London. Having done good business. He had a great fortune. He ended up buying the house for us to live in. He had two children, my twin brother Bartolomé(sic) and me. I remember with interest the disappearance of Captain Morstan, not for a moment did we suspect that our father was the only one who knew about his sad end. However, we were convinced that a serious and mysterious danger threatened our father. He didn't like to be alone and always had two guards in his house, Boxers by profession. He never told us about these fears; but he had a real dread for any man who had a wooden leg. For our part we were convinced that this horror and fear came from a mania of his, but very soon we were shown otherwise.

In 1882 my father received a letter from India which shocked him considerably and from that day until he died, he was a worried man. Not my brother nor I ever knew the content of this letter. The doctor told us we needed to attend our father as he had lost all hope of him recovering

As we gathered around our dying father, he made an important revelation.

…The sick man was sunk in bed…

SH-JCS25

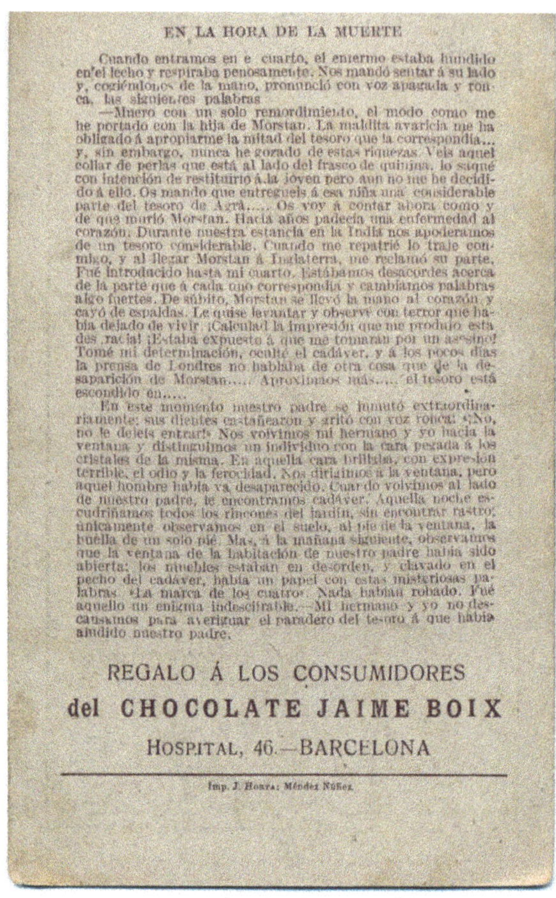

When we entered the room, our father was sunk in the bed, He was not asleep, but breathing heavily. He ordered us to sit by his side and, holding hands, he spoke in a muffled, husky voice. the following words
"I die with a single regret, the way I treated Morstan's daughter. Damn greed. I was obliged to give her half of the treasure, but I held onto it although I have never enjoyed these riches. You see that pearl necklace that is next to the quinine bottle, I took it out with the intention of restitution to the young woman, but I never got around to sending it, therefore. I command you to give that girl this lovely necklace, part of the Agra treasure ...... I am going to tell you about how and why Morstan died. For years he suffered from heart disease. During our stay in India. we seized this considerable treasure. When I repatriated, I brought it with me and when Morstan came to England, he claimed his share from me.
He was ushered into my room. We were at odds about which part was for whom and we exchanged words somewhat strong.
Suddenly. Morstan put his hand to his heart, and he fell backwards. I lifted him up and saw with terror that he had died. Imagine the situation I was in; I could be charged with his murder. I made my determination, to hide the corpse, and a few days later, when I looked in the London press, they did not speak of anything other than the disappearance of Morstan ...."
"Come closer .... the treasure is hidden in ...."
At this moment our father flinched extraordinarily: his teeth chattered, and he shouted in a hoarse voice: "No, do not let him in!" We turned, my brother and I, to the window and saw an individual with his face stuck to it. The glass of the pane distorted his face, but it had a terrible expression, hatred, and ferocity. We headed to the window, but the man had disappeared, so we went back to our father's side, but we found him dead. That night we searched all the corners of the garden, without finding a trace. we only found on the floor, at the foot of the window, the single footprint. But the next morning, we observe that the window in our father's room had been opened: the furniture was in disarray and nailed to the chest of the corpse there was a paper with these mysterious words 'The Sign of the Four'. Nothing had been stolen. That was an enigma. indescribable. My brother and I did not rest to find out the whereabouts of the treasure, that was alluded to by our father.

… we searched every corner of the garden...

SH-JCS26

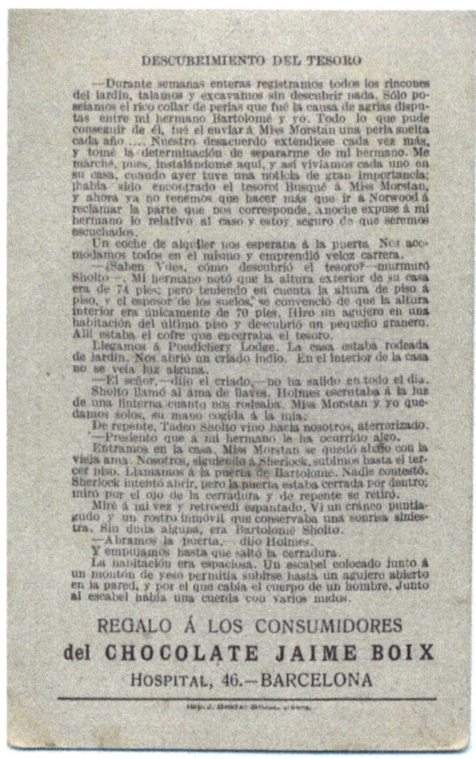

DESCUBRIMIENTO DEL TESORO

—Durante semanas enteras registramos todos los rincones del jardín, talamos y excavamos sin descubrir nada. Sólo poseíamos el rico collar de perlas que fué la causa de agrias disputas entre mi hermano Bartolomé y yo. Todo lo que pude conseguir de él, fué el enviar á Miss Morstan una perla suelta cada año..... Nuestro desacuerdo extendíose cada vez más, y tomé la determinación de separarme de mi hermano. Me marché, pues, instalándome aquí, y así vivíamos cada uno en su casa, cuando ayer tuve una noticia de gran importancia; ¡había sido encontrado el tesoro! Busqué á Miss Morstan, y ahora ya no tenemos que hacer más que ir á Norwood á reclamar la parte que nos corresponde. Anoche expuse á mi hermano lo relativo al caso y estoy seguro de que seremos escuchados.

Un coche de alquiler nos esperaba á la puerta. Nos acomodamos todos en el mismo y emprendió veloz carrera.

—¿Saben Vdes., cómo descubrió el tesoro?—murmuró Sholto—. Mi hermano notó que la altura exterior de su casa era de 74 piés; pero teniendo en cuenta la altura de piso á piso, y el espesor de los suelos, se convenció de que la altura interior era únicamente de 70 piés. Hizo un agujero en una habitación del último piso y descubrió un pequeño granero. Allí estaba el cofre que encerraba el tesoro.

Llegamos á Pondichery Lodge. La casa estaba rodeada de jardín. Nos abrió un criado indio. En el interior de la casa no se veía luz alguna.

—El señor,—dijo el criado,—no ha salido en todo el día. Sholto llamó al ama de llaves. Holmes escrutaba á la luz de una linterna cuanto nos rodeaba. Miss Morstan y yo quedamos solos, su mano cogida á la mía.

De repente, Tadeo Sholto vino hacia nosotros, aterrorizado.

—Presiento que á mi hermano le ha ocurrido algo.

Entramos en la casa. Miss Morstan se quedó abajo con la vieja ama. Nosotros, siguiendo á Sherlock, subimos hasta el tercer piso. Llamamos á la puerta de Bartolomé. Nadie contestó. Sherlock intentó abrir, pero la puerta estaba cerrada por dentro; miró por el ojo de la cerradura y de repente se retiró.

Miré á mi vez y retrocedí espantado. Vi un cráneo puntiagudo y un rostro inmóvil que conservaba una sonrisa siniestra. Sin duda alguna, era Bartolomé Sholto.

—Abramos la puerta,—dijo Holmes.

Y empujamos hasta que saltó la cerradura.

La habitación era espaciosa. Un escabel colocado junto á un montón de yeso permitía subirse hasta un agujero abierto en la pared, y por el que cabía el cuerpo de un hombre. Junto al escabel había una cuerda con varios nudos.

REGALO Á LOS CONSUMIDORES
del CHOCOLATE JAIME BOIX
HOSPITAL, 46.—BARCELONA

"For whole weeks we searched every corner of the garden, cut down and excavated without discovering anything. We only possessed the rich pearl necklace that was the cause of bitter disputes between my brother Bartolomé and myself. The only thing I could get from him. was sending Miss Morstan a loose pearl every year .... Our disagreement grew more and more. And I made the determination to separate from my brother. So, I left, settling here, and that's how each of us lived with him in his house, until yesterday I had news. of great importance, the treasure had been found!" I looked for Miss Morstan, and now we have nothing to do but go to Norwood to claim our share. Last night I explained all this to my brother about the case and I am sure that we will be heard.

A rental cab was waiting for us at the door. We all settled into it, and we started at a fast race.

"Do you know how he discovered the treasure?" Sholto murmured.

"My brother noticed that the exterior height of his house was 74 feet; but taking into account the height from floor to floor, and the thickness of the floors, he was convinced that the interior height was only 70 ft. He made a hole in a ceiling on the top floor and discovered a small attic. There was the chest that contained the treasure.

We arrive at Pondicherry Lodge. The house was surrounded by a garden. The door was opened by an Indian servant. There was no light inside the house.

"The Master," said the servant, "he has not gone out all day."

Sholto called the housekeeper. Holmes scrutinized by the light of a lantern all around us. Miss Morstan and I were left alone, her hand in mine.

Suddenly, Thaddeus Sholto came towards us, terrified. I have a feeling that something has happened to my brother.

We went into the house. Miss Morstan stayed downstairs with the old mistress, I followed Sherlock, as we went up to the third floor. We knocked on Bartolomé's door. No one answered. Sherlock tried to open it, but the door was locked. locked from the inside; he looked through the keyhole and suddenly withdrew.

I looked in my turn and backed away in terror. I saw a pointed skull and a motionless face with a sinister smile. Without a doubt, it was Bartolomé Sholto.

"Let's open the Door," said Holmes.

And we pushed until the lock clicked.

The room was spacious. A footstool placed next to a heap of plaster made it possible to climb up to a hole in the ceiling, and through which the body of a man could fit. Next to the footstool was a rope with several knots.

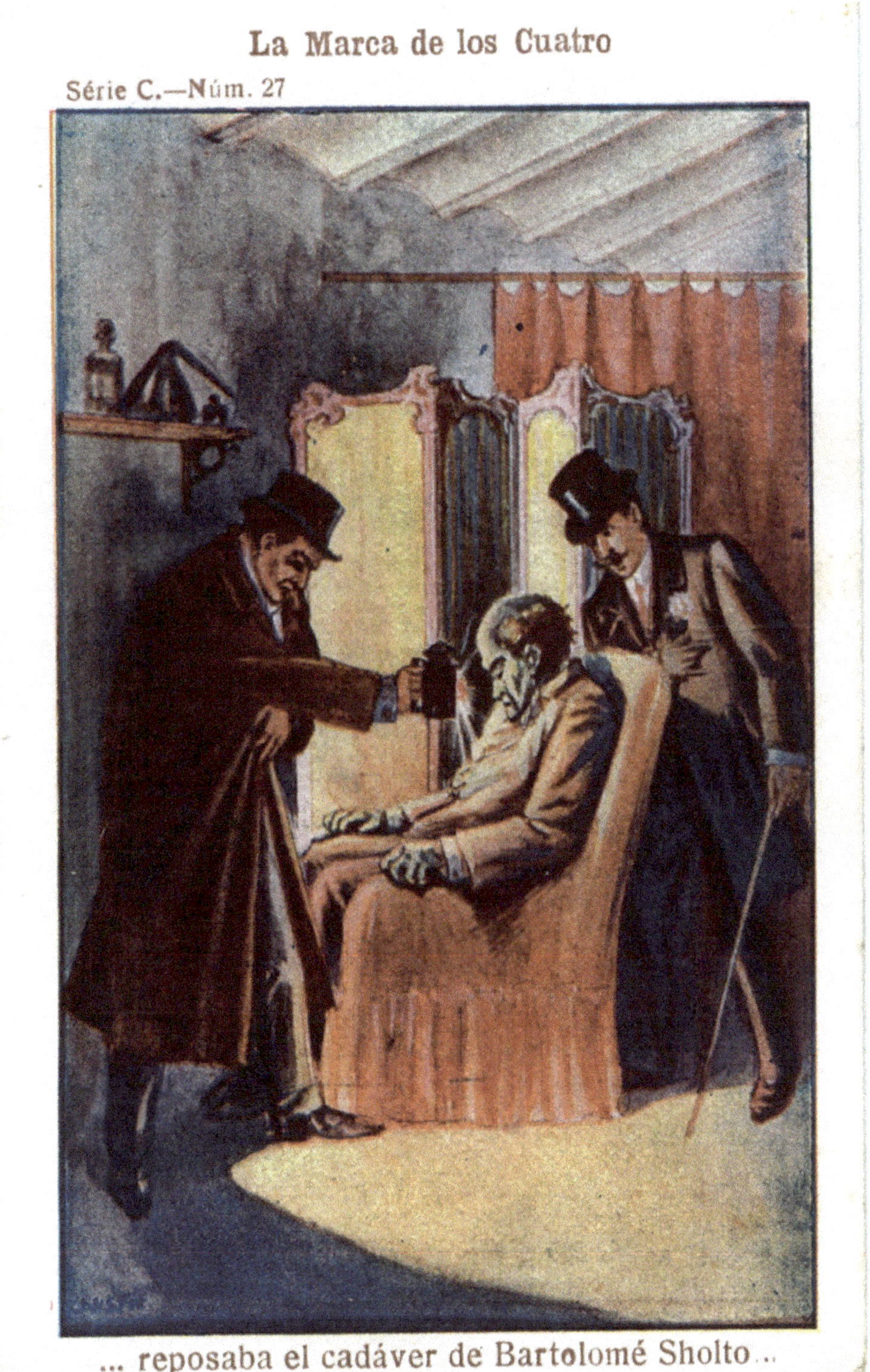

… the corpse of Bartolomé(sic) Sholto rested…

SH-JCS27

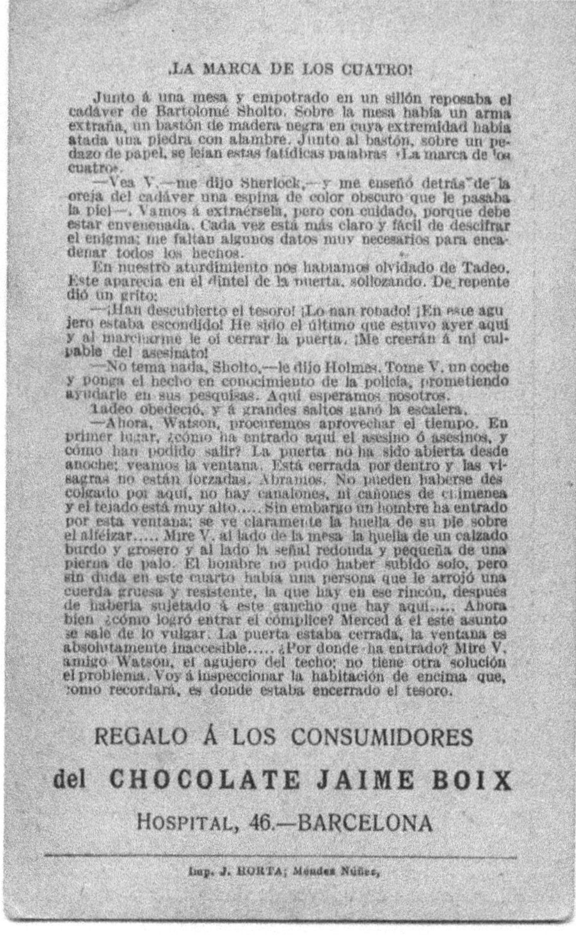

¡LA MARCA DE LOS CUATRO!

Junto á una mesa y empotrado en un sillón reposaba el cadáver de Bartolomé Sholto. Sobre la mesa había un arma extraña, un bastón de madera negra en cuya extremidad había atada una piedra con alambre. Junto al bastón, sobre un pedazo de papel, se leían estas fatídicas palabras «La marca de los cuatro».

—Vea V.—me dijo Sherlock,—y me enseñó detrás de la oreja del cadáver una espina de color obscuro que le pasaba la piel—. Vamos á extraérsela, pero con cuidado, porque debe estar envenenada. Cada vez está más claro y fácil de descifrar el enigma; me faltan algunos datos muy necesarios para encadenar todos los hechos.

En nuestro aturdimiento nos habíamos olvidado de Tadeo. Este aparecía en el dintel de la puerta, sollozando. De repente dió un grito:

—¡Han descubierto el tesoro! ¡Lo han robado! ¡En este agujero estaba escondido! He sido el último que estuvo ayer aquí y al marcharme le oí cerrar la puerta. ¡Me creerán á mí culpable del asesinato!

—No tema nada, Sholto,—le dijo Holmes. Tome V. un coche y ponga el hecho en conocimiento de la policía, prometiendo ayudarle en sus pesquisas. Aquí esperamos nosotros.

Tadeo obedeció, y á grandes saltos ganó la escalera.

—Ahora, Watson, procuremos aprovechar el tiempo. En primer lugar, ¿cómo ha entrado aquí el asesino ó asesinos, y cómo han podido salir? La puerta no ha sido abierta desde anoche; veamos la ventana. Está cerrada por dentro y las visagras no están forzadas. Abramos. No pueden haberse descolgado por aquí, no hay canalones, ni cañones de chimenea y el tejado está muy alto.... Sin embargo un hombre ha entrado por esta ventana; se ve claramente la huella de su pie sobre el alféizar..... Mire V. al lado de la mesa la huella de un calzado burdo y grosero y al lado la señal redonda y pequeña de una pierna de palo. El hombre no pudo haber subido solo, pero sin duda en este cuarto había una persona que le arrojó una cuerda gruesa y resistente, la que hay en ese rincón, después de haberla sujetado á este gancho que hay aquí..... Ahora bien ¿cómo logró entrar el cómplice? Merced á él este asunto se sale de lo vulgar. La puerta estaba cerrada, la ventana es absolutamente inaccesible..... ¿Por donde ha entrado? Mire V. amigo Watson, el agujero del techo; no tiene otra solución el problema. Voy á inspeccionar la habitación de encima que, como recordará, es donde estaba encerrado el tesoro.

REGALO Á LOS CONSUMIDORES

del CHOCOLATE JAIME BOIX

HOSPITAL, 46.—BARCELONA

Imp. J. HORTA; Méndez Núñez,

Next to a table and embedded in an armchair lay the corpse of Bartolomé Sholto. On the table was a strange weapon, a black wooden staff, at the end of which a stone had been tied with wire. Next to the cane, on a piece of paper, these fateful words we read. 'The Sign of the four.'

"Look!" Sherlock told me, and he showed me behind the corpse's ear a dark coloured thorn that passed through his skin. I am going to extract it, but carefully, because it must be poisoned. It is becoming clearer and easier to decipher the enigma; I am missing some very necessary data to link all the facts.

In our daze we had forgotten about Thaddeus. He appeared on the lintel of the door. sobbing. Suddenly he gave a cry!

"They have discovered the treasure! They have stolen it! In this hole it was hidden! I was the last one who was here yesterday and when I left, I heard him close the door. They will believe me guilty of the murder!"

"Fear nothing, Sholto," Holmes told him. Take a cab and put the fact in the knowledge of the police, promising to help them in the investigation. We will wait here."

Thaddeus obeyed. and with great leaps, Holmes gained the ladder.

"Now, Watson. let's try to take advantage of the time. In the first place, how did the murderer or murderers get in here, and how did they get out? The door. It hasn't been open since last night; let's look at the window. It is closed on the inside and the hinges are not forced. Let's open. They cannot have dropped down here, there are no gutters, no fireplace chimney and the roof is very high... However, a man has entered through this window: the imprint of his foot is clearly visible on the windowsill... Look at the footprint of a coarse and rude footwear next to the table, and next to it the small, round mark of one wooden leg. The man could not have come up alone, but there was certainly a person in this room who threw down a rope to him, a thick and resistant rope, the one in that corner, after having fastened it to this hook here... Now, how did the accomplice get in? Thanks to him, this matter is out of the ordinary. The door was closed, the window is absolutely inaccessible... Where did he enter? : Look! friend Watson, the hole in the ceiling: we have no other solution to the problem. I'm going to inspect the room above that. As you may recall, this is where the treasure was kept.

Subió al escabel, y...

He climbed onto a footstool, and...

SH-JCS28

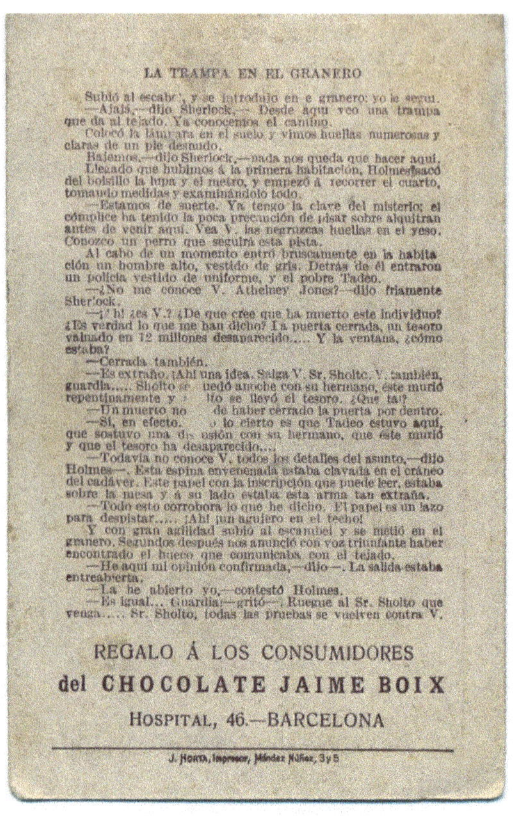

LA TRAMPA EN EL GRANERO

Subió al escabel, y se introdujo en e granero; yo le seguí.
—Ajajá,—dijo Sherlock,—Desde aquí veo una trampa que da al tejado. Ya conocemos el camino.
Colocó la lámpara en el suelo y vimos huellas numerosas y claras de un pie desnudo.
Bajemos,—dijo Sherlock,—nada nos queda que hacer aquí.
Llegado que hubimos á la primera habitación, Holmes sacó del bolsillo la lupa y el metro, y empezó á recorrer el cuarto, tomando medidas y examinándolo todo.
—Estamos de suerte. Ya tengo la clave del misterio: el cómplice ha tenido la poca precaución de usar sobre alquitrán antes de venir aquí. Vea V. las negruzcas huellas en el yeso. Conozco un perro que seguirá esta pista.
Al cabo de un momento entró bruscamente en la habitación un hombre alto, vestido de gris. Detrás de él entraron un policía vestido de uniforme, y el pobre Tadeo.
—¿No me conoce V. Athelney Jones?—dijo friamente Sherlock.
—¡Y tal ¿es V.? ¿De qué cree que ha muerto este individuo? ¿Es verdad lo que me han dicho? La puerta cerrada, un tesoro valuado en 12 millones desaparecido.... Y la ventana, ¿cómo estaba?
—Cerrada también.
—Es extraño. ¡Ah! una idea. Salga V. Sr. Sholto, V. también, guardia.... Sholto se quedó anoche con su hermano, éste murió repentinamente y no se llevó el tesoro. ¿Qué tal?
—Un muerto no puede haber cerrado la puerta por dentro.
—Sí, en efecto. Lo cierto es que Tadeo estuvo aquí, que sostuvo una discusión con su hermano, que éste murió y que el tesoro ha desaparecido....
—Todavía no conoce V. todos los detalles del asunto,—dijo Holmes—. Esta espina envenenada estaba clavada en el cráneo del cadáver. Este papel con la inscripción que puede leer, estaba sobre la mesa y á su lado estaba esta arma tan extraña.
—Todo esto corrobora lo que he dicho. El papel es un lazo para despistar.... ¡Ah! ¡un agujero en el techo!
Y con gran agilidad subió al escabel y se metió en el granero. Segundos después nos anunció con voz triunfante haber encontrado el hueco que comunicaba con el tejado.
—He aquí mi opinión confirmada,—dijo—. La salida estaba entreabierta.
—La he abierto yo,—contestó Holmes.
—Es igual... Guardia,—gritó—. Ruegue al Sr. Sholto que venga.... Sr. Sholto, todas las pruebas se vuelven contra V.

REGALO Á LOS CONSUMIDORES

del **CHOCOLATE JAIME BOIX**

HOSPITAL, 46.—BARCELONA

J. HORTA, Impresor, Méndez Núñez, 3 y 5

He climbed onto the footstool and entered the attic; I followed him.

"Ah ha," said Sherlock. "From here I see a trap that overlooks the roof. We already know the way."

He placed the lamp on the floor, and we saw numerous clear footprints of a bare foot.

"Let's go down," said Sherlock, "We have nothing left to do here."

When we had reached the first room, Holmes took the magnifying glass and the rule out of his pocket and he started to walk the room, taking measurements, and examining everything.

"We are in luck. I already have the key to the mystery; The Accomplice had the little misfortune of stepping into some tar before coming here. See this blackish footprint in the plaster. I know a dog that will follow this track."

After a moment, a tall man, dressed in grey, rushed into the room. Behind him came a policeman dressed in uniform, and poor Thaddeus.

"I think you must recollect me, Mr. Athelney Jones," said Holmes, quietly

'Why, of course I do! What do you think this individual has died from? Is it true what they have told me? He was behind closed doors, a treasure valued at 12 million has disappeared .... And the window, how was it?"

"Closed too."

"It's strange. Ah! an idea. Just step outside sergeant, and you, Mr. Sholto. Sholto left last night with his brother. he died suddenly and Thaddeus took the treasure. How's that?"

"The dead man then got up and locked the door on the inside."

"Yes indeed. the truth is that Thaddeus was here. that he had an argument with his brother, that he died and that the treasure has disappeared ...."

"You still don't know all the details of the matter," said Holmes.

"This poisoned thorn was stuck in the skull of the corpse. This paper with the inscription that can be read was on the table and next to him was this strange weapon."

"All this corroborates what I have said. The paper is hocus-pocus, a blind to mislead... Ah! A hole in the ceiling!"

And with great agility he climbed up the ladder and got into the ceiling. Seconds later he announced in a triumphant voice that he had found the gap that communicated with the roof.

"Here's my confirmed opinion," he said. "The window is partially open."

"I opened it." Holmes answered.

"It's the same ... Guard, " he yelled. Ask Mr. Sholto to step this way .... Mr. Sholto, all the evidence is turned against you."

Series C, Card 29.   THE TRUE TRACK

-   So, he is detained

SH-JCS29

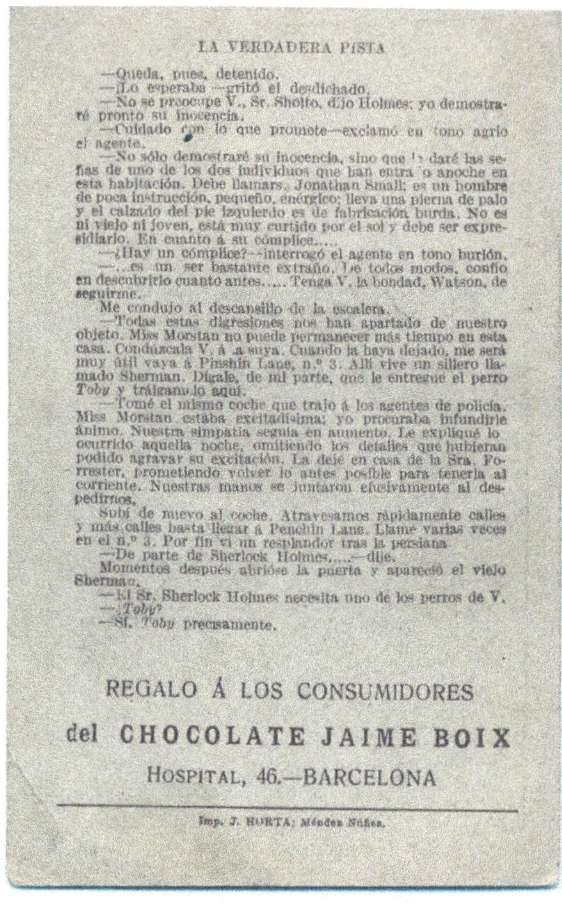

LA VERDADERA PISTA

REGALO Á LOS CONSUMIDORES

del CHOCOLATE JAIME BOIX

HOSPITAL, 46.—BARCELONA

"Remains. Well, stopped."

"I was expecting it!" Cried the unfortunate man.

"Don't worry Mr. Sholto." said Holmes; "I will soon prove your innocence."

"Be careful what you promise," the agent exclaimed sourly.

"I will not only prove his innocence. but I'll give you the name of one of the two individuals Who have entered this room last night. He is called Jonathan small; he is a man of little intelligence. small, energetic: he wears a wooden leg and the footwear on his left foot is of crude manufacture. He is neither old nor young, he is very tanned by the sun and must be an ex-convict. As for his accomplice ...."

"Is there an accomplice?" Asked the agent in a mocking tone.

"He's quite a strange being. I hope before very long to be able to introduce you to the pair of them, Watson follow me."

He led me to the landing of the stairs.

"All these digressions. They have taken us away from our objective. Miss Morstan can no longer stay in this house, take her home, afterwards go to Pinchin lane No. 3. Where their lives a man called Sherman. Tell him. from me, that I need the dog called Toby and bring him here to me.

I took the same car that had brought the police officers. Miss Morstan was extremely excited; I tried to infuse cheer up. Our sympathy continued. on the rise. I explained what had happened that night, omitting the details that would have caused distress. I left her at home of the Mrs. Forrester, promising to return as soon as possible with more news. Our hands clasped effusively as we said goodbye.

I got back in the cab and finally arrived at Pinchin Lane. I knocked multiple times at # 3. At last, I saw a glow behind the blind.

"I was sent by Sherlock Holmes," I said.

Moments later the door opened, and the old man appeared - Sherman.

"Mr. Sherlock Holmes needs one of your dogs."

"Toby?"

"Yes. Toby precisely."

…There were different animals…

SH-JCS30

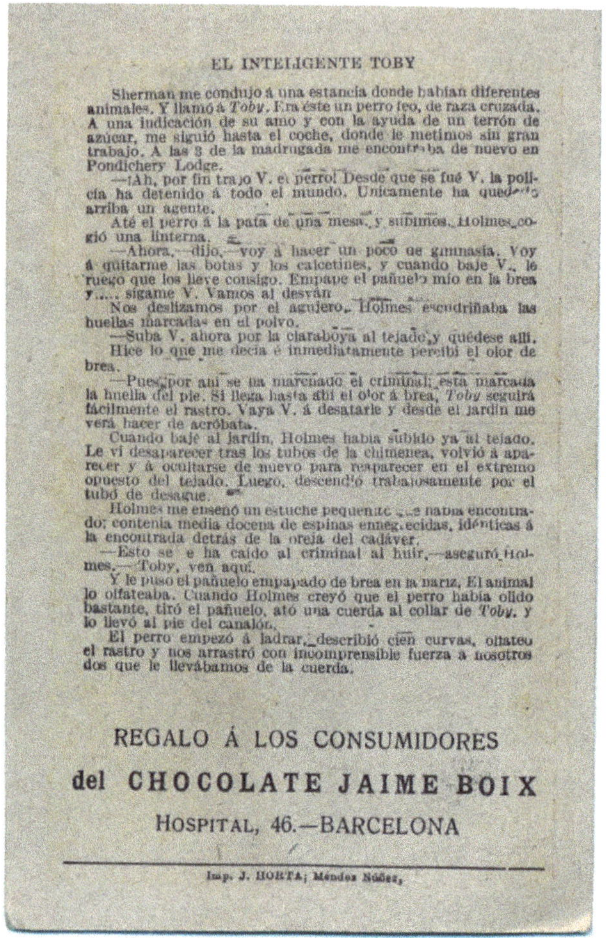

EL INTELIGENTE TOBY

Sherman me condujo á una estancia donde habian diferentes animales. Y llamó á Toby. Era éste un perro feo, de raza cruzada. A una indicación de su amo y con la ayuda de un terrón de azúcar, me siguió hasta el coche, donde le metimos sin gran trabajo. A las 3 de la madrugada me encontraba de nuevo en Pondichery Lodge.

—¡Ah, por fin trajo V. el perro! Desde que se fué V. la policía ha detenido á todo el mundo. Unicamente ha quedado arriba un agente.

Até el perro á la pata de una mesa, y subimos. Holmes cogió una linterna.

—Ahora,—dijo,—voy á hacer un poco de gimnasia. Voy á quitarme las botas y los calcetines, y cuando baje V., le ruego que los lleve consigo. Empape el pañuelo mio en la brea y..... sigame V. Vamos al desván.

Nos deslizamos por el agujero. Holmes escudriñaba las huellas marcadas en el polvo.

—Suba V. ahora por la claraboya al tejado, y quédese allí. Hice lo que me decia é inmediatamente percibí el olor de brea.

—Pues, por ahi se ha marchado el criminal; está marcada la huella del pie. Si llega hasta ahí el olor á brea, Toby seguirá fácilmente el rastro. Vaya V. á desatarle y desde el jardin me verá hacer de acróbata.

Cuando bajé al jardin, Holmes habia subido ya al tejado. Le ví desaparecer tras los tubos de la chimenea, volvió á aparecer y á ocultarse de nuevo para reaparecer en el extremo opuesto del tejado. Luego, descendió trabajosamente por el tubo de desague.

Holmes me enseñó un estuche pequeñito que habia encontrado; contenia media docena de espinas ennegrecidas, idénticas á la encontrada detrás de la oreja del cadáver.

—Esto se le ha caido al criminal al huir,—aseguró Holmes.—Toby, ven aqui.

Y le puso el pañuelo empapado de brea en la nariz. El animal lo olfateaba. Cuando Holmes creyó que el perro habia olido bastante, tiró el pañuelo, ató una cuerda al collar de Toby, y lo llevó al pie del canalón.

El perro empezó á ladrar, describió cien curvas, olfateó el rastro y nos arrastró con incomprensible fuerza á nosotros dos que le llevábamos de la cuerda.

REGALO Á LOS CONSUMIDORES

del **CHOCOLATE JAIME BOIX**

HOSPITAL, 46.—BARCELONA

Imp. J. HORTA; Méndez Núñez,

Sherman led me to a room where there were different animals. And he called Toby. This was an ugly dog. crossbreed. With an indication of his master and with the help of a lump of sugar, he followed me to the cab. where we put him inside without great effort, at 3 in the morning we were back at Pondicherry Lodge.

"Ah, finally, very good, you brought the dog! Since you left, the police have detained everyone. Only one agent has been upstairs."

I tied the dog to the leg of a table, and we went upstairs, Holmes brought a flashlight.

"Now," he said, "I am going to do a little gymnastics. I'm going to take off my boots and socks, and when I come down, I beg you to take them with you. I soaked my handkerchief in the pitch and.... follow me now. Let's go to the attic. We slid into the hole. Holmes scrutinized the footprints marked in the dust.

I'll go up through the skylight to the roof while you stay here."

I did as he told me and immediately smelled pitch,

"Toby will follow easily and follow the trail. Go and untie him And from the Garden you will see some acrobats performed."

I went down to the garden; Holmes had already gone up to the roof. I saw him disappear behind the chimneys, he appeared again and vanished again only to reappear at the opposite end of the roof. Then he trudged down the drainpipe.

Holmes showed me a small box that he had found; it contained half a dozen blackened thorns. identical to the one found behind the corpse's ear.

"This has fallen from the criminal when he fled," said Holmes.

Toby came over and Holmes put the tar-soaked handkerchief on his nose, the animal sniffed it. When Holmes believed that the dog had smelled enough, he threw away the handkerchief, tied a rope to Toby's neck and he took him to the foot of the gutter. The dog began to sniff, and he described six curves, finding the trail he dragged us with incomprehensible force that we were glad he was attached to the rope.

... until you reach the foot of the wall.

SH-JCS31

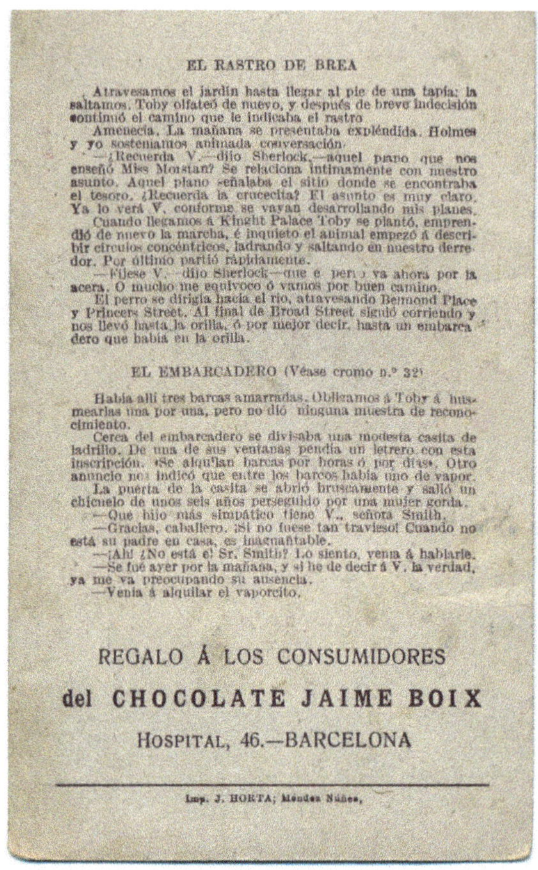

We crossed the garden until we reached the foot of a wall: where we jumped down. Toby sniffed again, and after brief indecision, he continued the path that he indicated the trail
The morning was splendid. Holmes and I had a lively conversation,
"Do you remember," asked Sherlock, "that map Miss Morstan had? It is intimately related to our affair . That map indicated the place where treasure is buried. Do you remember the little cross? The matter is very clear. You will see it as we go: I am developing my plans"
When we arrived at Knight's Place Toby stopped, running back and forth and the restless the animal began to describe concentric circles, barking and jumping around us. Finally, he started again.
"Look at him." said Sherlock "the dog is now going on the pavement. Either I'm wrong or we're on the right track."
The dog was heading towards the river, crossing Belmont Place and Prince's Street.

At the end of Broad Street, he kept running and took us to water's edge. I think it was on the wharf.

THE PIER (See card no.32)

There were three boats moored there. We made Toby sniff them one by one. but he did not show any appreciation. · Near the jetty there was a modest little house of brick. From one of its windows hung a sign with this inscription.
Boats to hire by the hour or day. Another Announcement indicated that there was one steamship among the ships.
The door of the little house was thrown open and a little boy of about six years chased by a fat woman.
"What a nice son you have, Mrs. Smith."
"Thanks. Gentleman. If he weren't so naughty! When his father is not at home, he is unbearable."
"Ah! Isn't Mr. Smith here? Sorry. we came to speak to him."
"He left yesterday morning and if I have to tell you the truth, am really worried about his absence ."
"We came to rent the steamer."

We made Toby sniff them out

SH-JCS32

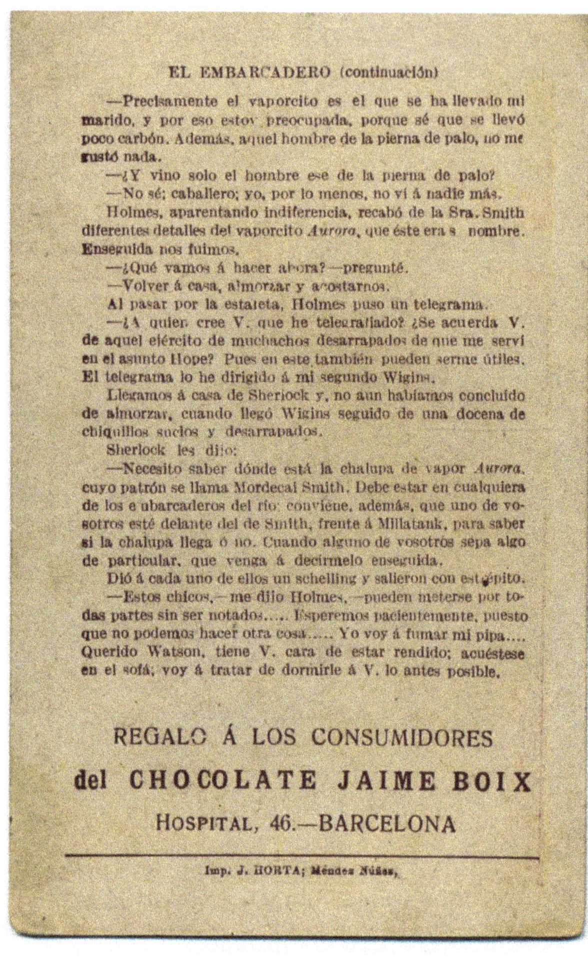

EL EMBARCADERO (continuación)

—Precisamente el vaporcito es el que se ha llevado mi marido, y por eso estoy preocupada, porque sé que se llevó poco carbón. Además, aquel hombre de la pierna de palo, no me gustó nada.

—¿Y vino solo el hombre ese de la pierna de palo?

—No sé; caballero; yo, por lo menos, no ví á nadie más.

Holmes, aparentando indiferencia, recabó de la Sra. Smith diferentes detalles del vaporcito *Aurora*, que éste era s nombre. Enseguida nos fuimos.

—¿Qué vamos á hacer ahora?—pregunté.

—Volver á casa, almorzar y acostarnos.

Al pasar por la estafeta, Holmes puso un telegrama.

—¿A quien cree V. que he telegrafiado? ¿Se acuerda V. de aquel ejército de muchachos desarrapados de que me serví en el asunto Hope? Pues en este también pueden serme útiles. El telegrama lo he dirigido á mi segundo Wigins.

Llegamos á casa de Sherlock y, no aun habíamos concluído de almorzar, cuando llegó Wigins seguido de una docena de chiquillos sucios y desarrapados.

Sherlock les dijo:

—Necesito saber dónde está la chalupa de vapor *Aurora*, cuyo patrón se llama Mordecai Smith. Debe estar en cualquiera de los embarcaderos del río; conviene, además, que uno de vosotros esté delante del de Smith, frente á Millatank, para saber si la chalupa llega ó no. Cuando alguno de vosotros sepa algo de particular, que venga á decírmelo enseguida.

Dió á cada uno de ellos un schelling y salieron con estrépito.

—Estos chicos,—me dijo Holmes,—pueden meterse por todas partes sin ser notados..... Esperemos pacientemente, puesto que no podemos hacer otra cosa..... Yo voy á fumar mi pipa.... Querido Watson, tiene V. cara de estar rendido; acuéstese en el sofá; voy á tratar de dormirle á V. lo antes posible.

REGALO Á LOS CONSUMIDORES

del CHOCOLATE JAIME BOIX

HOSPITAL, 46.—BARCELONA

Imp. J. HORTA; Méndez Núñez,

"Precisely the Steamer that my Husband has taken and I'm worried, because I know he took little coal, also that man with the Wooden leg went with him"

"And only the man with the wooden leg?"

"I don't know; gentleman; I saw nobody else."

Holmes, appearing indifference, sought different details about the little steamer Aurora, which was its name, from Mrs. Smith.

We left immediately.

"What are we going to do now?"

"Go home, have lunch and go to bed."

As we passed the Post Office, Holmes posted a telegram.

"Who you think I have telegraphed? Do you remember that army of ragged boys of which I availed myself in the Hope affair? Well, they can also be useful to me. I have addressed the telegram to my second Wiggins."

We got to Sherlock's house and. we had not yet concluded lunch. when Wiggins arrived followed by a dozen dirty and ragged kids.

Sherlock said to them:

"I need to know where the steamship Aurora is whose Captain is named Mordecai Smith. She must be in at one of the piers. It is also advisable for one of you to be in front of Smith's, in front of Millatank, to know if the boat arrives or not. When some of you know something in particular, let him tell me right away."

He gave each of them a shilling and they ran out with a crash.

"These guys," Holmes told me, "can go all over the place parts unnoticed... Let's wait patiently, we cannot do otherwise… I will. smoke my pipe ... Dear Watson, you have the face of being exhausted; lie down on the couch; I'm going to try to put you to sleep as soon as possible."

… He began to play a sweet sonata…

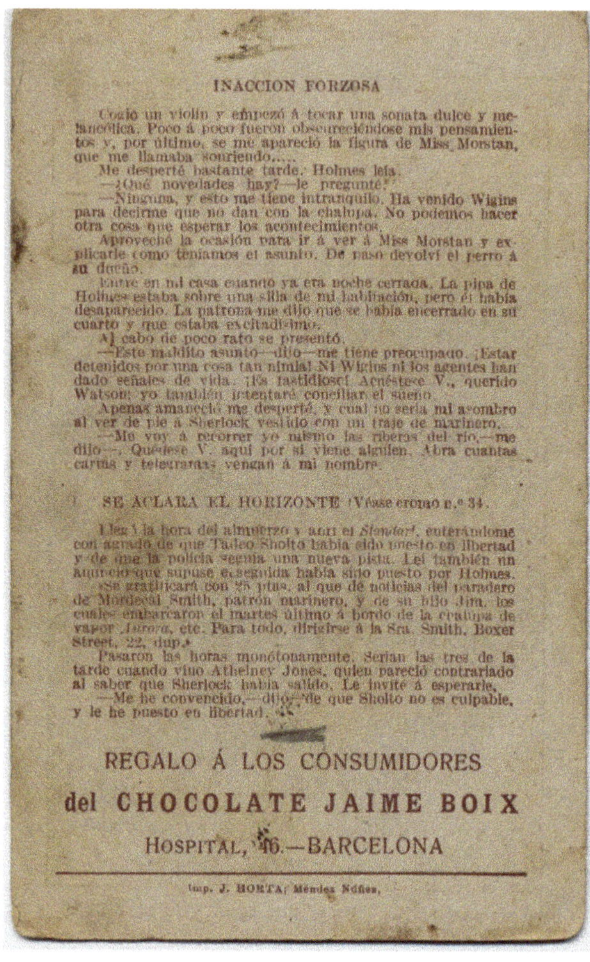

He picked up a violin and began to play a sweet and melancholy sonata. Little by little my thoughts grew darker and, finally, the figure of Miss Morstan appeared to me, who called me smiling...

I woke up quite late. Holmes was reading.

"What's new?" I asked him.

"Nothing and this makes me uneasy, Wiggins has come to tell me they can't find the boat. We can do nothing but wait for events."

I took the opportunity to go see Miss Morstan and explain to her what was happening, in passing I returned the dog to its owner.

I entered our house when it was already dark. Holmes's pipe was on a chair in our room, but he had disappeared. The landlady told me that he had locked himself in his room and that he was very cited. After a little while he introduced herself.

"This damn thing," he said, "has me worried! To be stopped by such a trivial thing! . Neither Wiggins nor my other agents have given me any signs of life.

It's Frustrating! lie down my dear Watson; and try to sleep."

I woke up the next morning and was astonished to see Sherlock standing over me in a Sailor suit.

"I am going to walk the banks of the river myself." he told me- "stay here in case someone comes, open all the letters and telegrams that come in my name."

THE HORIZON IS CLEARED (See Card No.34

Upon opening the Standard, I found with pleasure that Thaddeus Sholto had been released and that the police were following a new lead. I also read an advertisement which I immediately assumed had been placed by Holmes.

Reward of 25 pesetas (£5), to whoever knows the whereabouts of the steam launch Aurora that was last seen last Tuesday. For everything contact Mrs. Smith. Boxer Street, 22, dup.

The hours passed monotonously. it was three in the afternoon, when Athelney Jones came in, who seemed disappointed to learn that Sherlock was out. I invited him to wait for Holmes,

I was happy to be told that Thaddeus Sholto was not guilty and had been given his freedom.

And opened the Standard…

SH-JCS34

Back of Card 34.

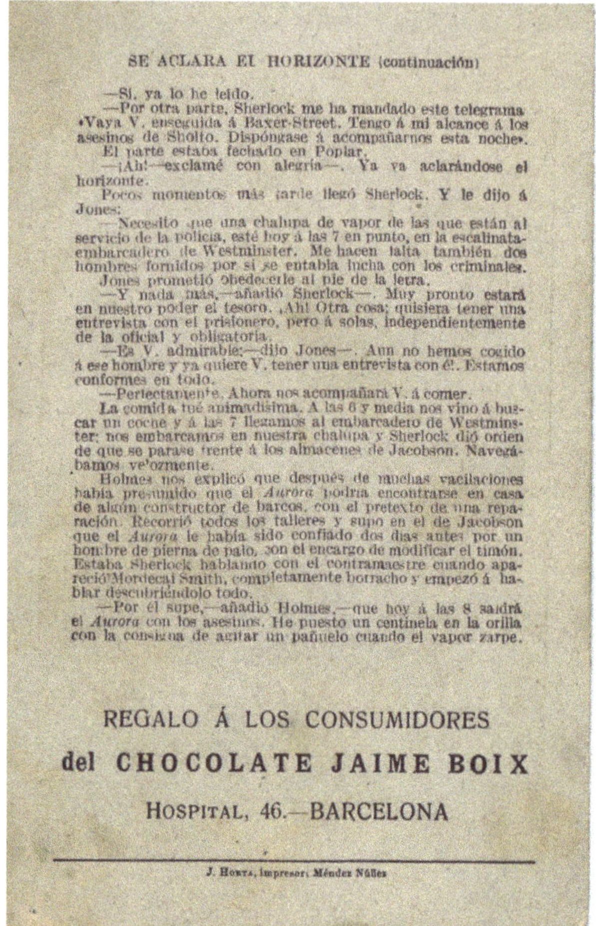

SE ACLARA EL HORIZONTE (continuación)

—Sí, ya lo he leído.

—Por otra parte, Sherlock me ha mandado este telegrama: «Vaya V. enseguida á Baxer-Street. Tengo á mi alcance á los asesinos de Sholto. Dispóngase á acompañarnos esta noche».

El parte estaba fechado en Poplar.

—¡Ah!—exclamé con alegría—. Ya va aclarándose el horizonte.

Pocos momentos más tarde llegó Sherlock. Y le dijo á Jones:

—Necesito que una chalupa de vapor de las que están al servicio de la policía, esté hoy á las 7 en punto, en la escalinata-embarcadero de Westminster. Me hacen falta también dos hombres fornidos por si se entabla lucha con los criminales.

Jones prometió obedecerle al pie de la letra.

—Y nada más,—añadió Sherlock—. Muy pronto estará en nuestro poder el tesoro. ¡Ah! Otra cosa; quisiera tener una entrevista con el prisionero, pero á solas, independientemente de la oficial y obligatoria.

—Es V. admirable:—dijo Jones—. Aun no hemos cogido á ese hombre y ya quiere V. tener una entrevista con él. Estamos conformes en todo.

—Perfectamente. Ahora nos acompañará V. á comer.

La comida fué animadísima. A las 6 y media nos vino á buscar un coche y á las 7 llegamos al embarcadero de Westminster: nos embarcamos en nuestra chalupa y Sherlock dió orden de que se parase frente á los almacenes de Jacobson. Navegábamos velozmente.

Holmes nos explicó que después de muchas vacilaciones había presumido que el *Aurora* podría encontrarse en casa de algún constructor de barcos, con el pretexto de una reparación. Recorrió todos los talleres y supo en el de Jacobson que el *Aurora* le había sido confiado dos días antes por un hombre de pierna de palo, con el encargo de modificar el timón. Estaba Sherlock hablando con el contramaestre cuando apareció Mordecai Smith, completamente borracho y empezó á hablar descubriéndolo todo.

—Por él supe,—añadió Holmes,—que hoy á las 8 saldrá el *Aurora* con los asesinos. He puesto un centinela en la orilla con la consigna de agitar un pañuelo cuando el vapor zarpe.

REGALO Á LOS CONSUMIDORES

del **CHOCOLATE JAIME BOIX**

HOSPITAL, 46.—BARCELONA

J. Horta, impresor; Méndez Núñez

THE HORIZON IS CLEARED
(continued)

"Yes. I've already read it."

"On the other hand, Sherlock has sent me this telegram. Go to Baxer(sic)-Street at once, Sholto's assassins are within my grasp. Prepare to join us tonight."

The telegram was sent from Poplar.

"Ah!" I exclaimed happily. "The horizon is already clearing."

A few moments later Sherlock arrived. And he said to Jones:

- I need a steamboat of the kind that are in the service of the police, to be ready at 7 o'clock today, on the steps-jetty at Westminster. I also need two sturdy men in case there is a fight with criminals."

Jones promised to obey him to the letter.

"And nothing more," Sherlock added, "Very soon the treasure will be. in our possession, Ah! Another thing: I would like to have an interview with the prisoner, but alone. regardless of the official and mandatory."

"You are admirable," said Jones. "We haven't caught that man and yet you already want to have an interview with him! . We are satisfied with everything."

"Perfectly. Now you will accompany us to eat."

The food was very lively. At 6.30 he came to get us a car and at 7 we reached Westminster Pier: we boarded our longboat and Sherlock ordered it to stop in front of Jacobson's warehouses. We were sailing fast.

Holmes explained to us that after much hesitation he had presumed that the Aurora might be in the home of some shipbuilder. under the pretext of. a repair. He toured all the workshops and learned at Jacobson's that the Aurora had been entrusted to him two days earlier by a man with a wooden leg, with a commission to modify the rudder. Sherlock was talking to the boatswain when Mordecai Smith appeared, completely drunk and began to speak, revealing everything.

"Because of him," added Holmes, "that today at 8 o'clock he will return to the Aurora with the assassins. I have posted a sentry on the shore with the. orders to shake a handkerchief when the steam sets sail.

…We arrived at the pier…

SH-JCS35

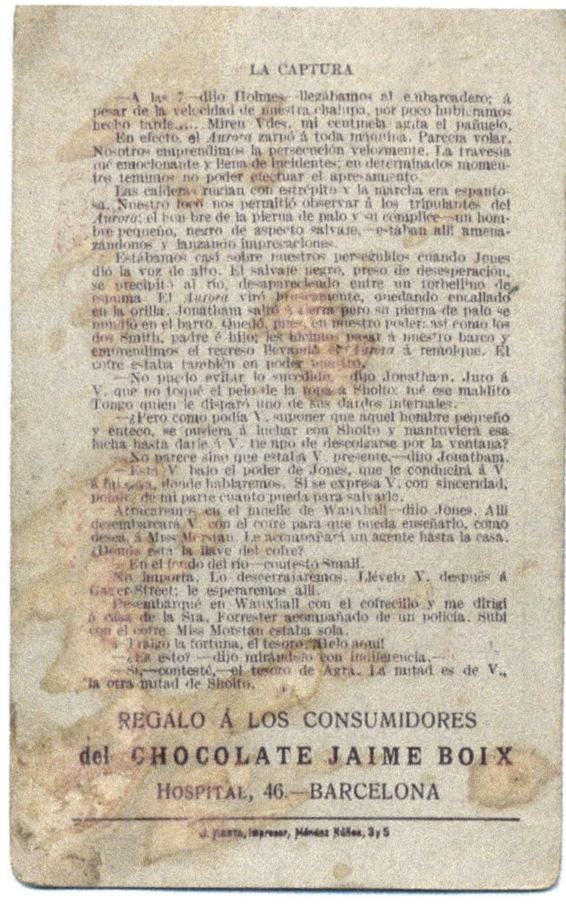

LA CAPTURA

—A las 7 —dijo Holmes— llegábamos al embarcadero; á pesar de la velocidad de nuestra chalupa, por poco hubiéramos hecho tarde... Miren Vdes, mi centinela agita el pañuelo.

En efecto, el *Aurora* zarpó á toda máquina. Parecía volar. Nosotros emprendimos la persecución velozmente. La travesía fué emocionante y llena de incidentes; en determinados momentos temimos no poder efectuar el apresamiento.

Las calderas rugían con estrépito y la marcha era espantosa. Nuestro foco nos permitió observar á los tripulantes del *Aurora*: el hombre de la pierna de palo y su cómplice—un hombre pequeño, negro de aspecto salvaje,—estaban allí amenazándonos y lanzando imprecaciones.

Estábamos casi sobre nuestros perseguidos cuando Jones dió la voz de alto. El salvaje negro, preso de desesperación, se precipitó al río, desapareciendo entre un torbellino de espuma. El *Aurora* viró bruscamente, quedando encallado en la orilla. Jonathan saltó á tierra, pero su pierna de palo se hundió en el barro. Quedó, pues, en nuestro poder; así como los dos Smith, padre é hijo; les hicimos pasar á nuestro barco y emprendimos el regreso llevando el *Aurora* á remolque. El cofre estaba también en poder nuestro.

—No puedo evitar lo sucedido —dijo Jonathan. Juro á V. que no toqué el pelo de la ropa á Sholto: fué ese maldito Tongo quien le disparó uno de sus dardos infernales.

—¿Pero cómo podía V. suponer que aquel hombre pequeño y enteco, se pusiera á luchar con Sholto y mantuviera esa lucha hasta darle á V. tiempo de descolgarse por la ventana?

—No parece sino que estaba V. presente,—dijo Jonathan.

—Está V. bajo el poder de Jones, que le conducirá á V. á su casa, donde hablaremos. Si se expresa V. con sinceridad, pondré de mi parte cuanto pueda para salvarle.

—Atracaremos en el muelle de Wauxhall—dijo Jones. Allí desembarcará V. con el cofre para que pueda enseñarlo, como desea, á Miss Morstan. Le acompañará un agente hasta la casa. ¿Dónde está la llave del cofre?

—En el fondo del río—contestó Small.

No importa. Lo descerrajaremos. Llévelo V. después á Gower Street; le esperaremos allí.

Desembarqué en Wauxhall con el cofrecillo y me dirigí á casa de la Sra. Forrester acompañado de un policía. Subí con el cofre. Miss Morstan estaba sola.

—Traigo la fortuna, el tesoro. Hélo aquí!

—¿Es esto? —dijo mirándolo con indiferencia.—

—Sí,—contesté,—el tesoro de Agra. La mitad es de V., la otra mitad de Sholto.

REGALO Á LOS CONSUMIDORES

del **CHOCOLATE JAIME BOIX**

HOSPITAL, 46.—BARCELONA

J. Pasta, impresor, Méndez Núñez, 3 y 5

"At 7 o'clock," said Holmes, "we arrived at the boathouse; Despite the speed of our boat, we almost would have been late ... Look at that. my sentry waves his handkerchief.

Indeed. the Aurora sailed at full speed. She seemed to fly. We began the chase swiftly. The journey was exciting and full of incidents; at certain times we feared that we would not be able to make the apprehension.

The boilers roared loudly, and the march was dreadful. Our focus allowed us to observe the crew of the Aurora; The man with the stick leg and his accomplice - a small, black man with a wild appearance.-- They were there threatening us and throwing curses.

We were almost on our hunt when Jones called out. The black savage, prisoner of despair. he rushed into the river, disappearing in a whirlwind of foam.

The Aurora turned abruptly, remaining stranded on the shore.

Jonathan jumped to the ground, but his wooden leg fell into the mud and remained in our power: just like the two smiths. father and son; We took them to our boat and started back in tow. The chest was also in our possession.

"I can't help what happened," said Jonathan. "I swear to you, I did not touch a hair of Sholto it was that damn Tongo(sic) who shot one of his infernal darts."

"But how could you suppose that this small and feeble man began to fight with Sholto and continued that fight until he hit him with a dart. I climbed up and in through the window?

"It does not seem that I was present." Jonathan said.

This was under the power of Jones, who will lead you to jail, where you can speak more, if you want.

"Sincerely, I will do everything I can to save you."

"We'll dock at Wauxhall(sic) Pier," Jones said. "With the chest so that you can take it, as you wish, to miss Morstan. an agent will accompany you to the house,"

I disembarked at Wauxhall with the casket and headed to Mrs. Forrester's house accompanied by a policeman. Up the house, Miss Morstan was alone.

"I bring fortune, treasure; hello here"

"It is this?" she said looking at him indifferently.

"Yes, I answered, the treasure of Agra. Half belongs to you. the other half to Sholto."

…If I have this large fortune…

SH-JCS36

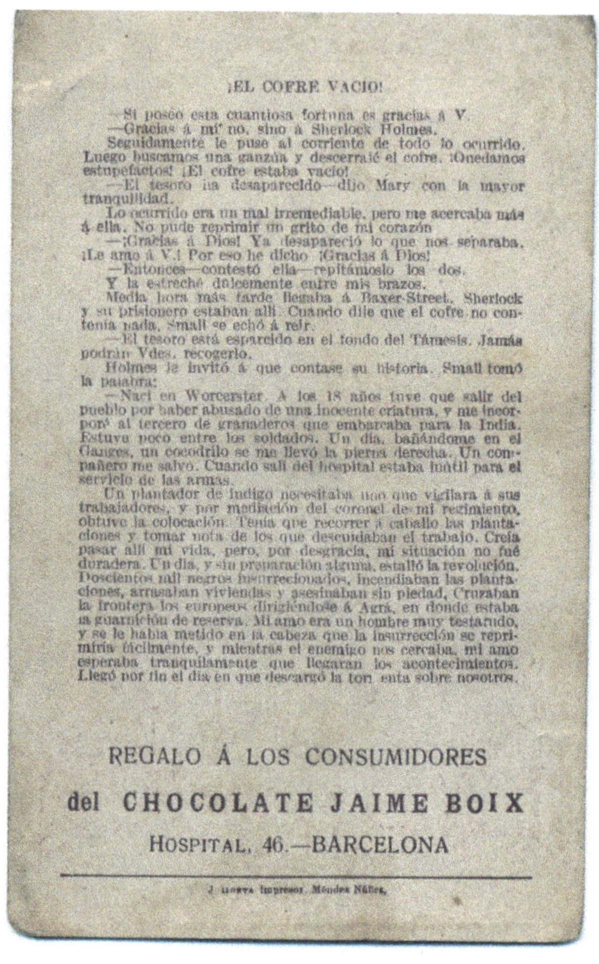

"If I have this large fortune. it's thanks to you."

"Thanks to me no. but to Sherlock Holmes."
Then I brought her up to date on everything that had happened. Then we got a lock pick, and I unlocked the chest. We are stunned! The chest was empty!

"The treasure has disappeared," said Mary with the greatest calm.

What happened was an irremediable evil. but I got closer to her. I couldn't suppress a cry from my heart

"Thanks god! Already. What separated us has disappeared. I love you! That's why I said Thank God!"

"Then," she answered, "let's both repeat it."
And I held her gently in my arms.

Half an hour later she arrived at Baxer(sic) Street. Sherlock and his prisoner were there. When I said that the chest contained nothing, Small laughed.

"The treasure is scattered at the bottom of the Thames. You will never be able to pick it up."
Holmes invited him to tell his story. Small took the floor:

"I was born in Worcerster(sic) At the age of 18, I had to leave town for having abused an innocent creature, and I joined the third grenadier, I embarked for the. India. I was little among the soldiers. One day, bathing in the Ganges, a crocodile took my right leg. A colleague saved me. When I left the hospital, I was useless for the service of arms.

An indigo planter needed someone to watch over his workers and through the colonel of my regiment, I got the placement. I had to ride through the plantations and take note of those who neglected their work. I believed I could spend my life there, but unfortunately my situation did not last. One day, and without any preparation the revolution broke out. Two hundred thousand insurrectionary blacks. plantations were burned. They razed houses and murdered without mercy. The Europeans crossed the border heading for Agra. where there was a reserve garrison. My master was a very stubborn man. and he had gotten it into his head that the insurrection would be easily repressed, and while the enemy surrounded us, my master calmly waited for events to come. The day finally came when he unleashed the storm on us.

In a corner were the corpses…

SH-JCS37

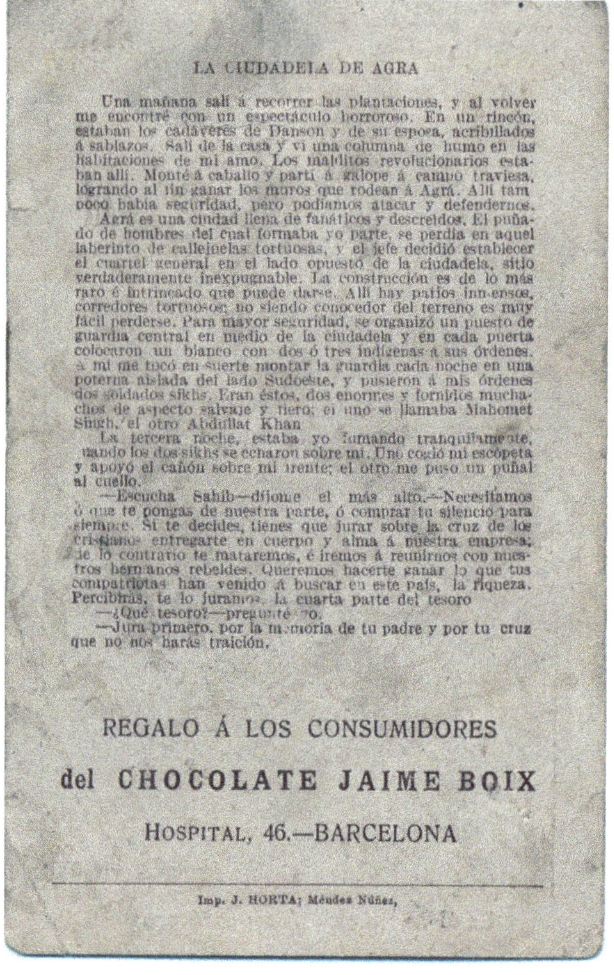

LA CIUDADELA DE AGRA

Una mañana salí á recorrer las plantaciones, y al volver me encontré con un espectáculo horroroso. En un rincón, estaban los cadáveres de Danson y de su esposa, acribillados á sablazos. Salí de la casa y vi una columna de humo en las habitaciones de mi amo. Los malditos revolucionarios estaban allí. Monté á caballo y partí á galope á campo traviesa, logrando al fin ganar los muros que rodean á Agrá. Allí tampoco había seguridad, pero podíamos atacar y defendernos.

Agrá es una ciudad llena de fanáticos y descreídos. El puñado de hombres del cual formaba yo parte, se perdía en aquel laberinto de callejuelas tortuosas, y el jefe decidió establecer el cuartel general en el lado opuesto de la ciudadela, sitio verdaderamente inexpugnable. La construcción es de lo más raro é intrincado que puede darse. Allí hay patios inmensos, corredores tortuosos; no siendo conocedor del terreno es muy fácil perderse. Para mayor seguridad, se organizó un puesto de guardia central en medio de la ciudadela y en cada puerta colocaron un blanco con dos ó tres indígenas á sus órdenes. A mí me tocó en suerte montar la guardia cada noche en una poterna aislada del lado Sudoeste, y pusieron á mis órdenes dos soldados sikhs. Eran éstos, dos enormes y fornidos muchachos de aspecto salvaje y fiero; el uno se llamaba Mahomet Singh, el otro Abdullat Khan.

La tercera noche, estaba yo fumando tranquilamente, cuando los dos sikhs se echaron sobre mí. Uno cogió mi escopeta y apoyó el cañón sobre mi frente; el otro me puso un puñal al cuello.

—Escucha Sahib—díjome el más alto.—Necesitamos ó que te pongas de nuestra parte, ó comprar tu silencio para siempre. Si te decides, tienes que jurar sobre la cruz de los cristianos entregarte en cuerpo y alma á nuestra empresa; de lo contrario te mataremos, é iremos á reunirnos con nuestros hermanos rebeldes. Queremos hacerte ganar lo que tus compatriotas han venido á buscar en este país, la riqueza. Percibirás, te lo juramos, la cuarta parte del tesoro

—¿Qué tesoro?—pregunté yo.

—Jura primero, por la memoria de tu padre y por tu cruz que no nos harás traición.

REGALO Á LOS CONSUMIDORES

del **CHOCOLATE JAIME BOIX**

HOSPITAL, 46.—BARCELONA

Imp. J. HORTA; Méndez Núñez,

One morning I went out to tour the plantations and on returning I found a horrifying sight. In a corner, there were the corpses of Danson and his wife, riddled with sabre blows. I left the house and saw a column of smoke in my master's rooms. The damned revolutionaries they were there. I mounted my horse and set off at a gallop across the country, succeeding in reaching the walls that surround Agra. There was little security there, but we could attack and defend ourselves.

Agra is a city full of fanatics and discreet people. The handful of men of which I was a part, was lost in that labyrinth of winding alleys, and the commander decided to establish the Headquarters on the opposite side of the citadel, a truly impregnable site. The construction is as rare and intricate as can be, there are immense courtyards, tortuous corridors: not being familiar with the terrain, it is very easy to get lost. For greater security, a central guard post was set up in the middle of the citadel, and at each gate they posted a patrol with two or three Indians under a command.

I was lucky to mount the guard. every night in an isolated Gate on the south-west side, and they placed under my command two notorious Sikhs. It was these. two huge, burly boys who looked wild and tender; and one is Ilamba Mahomet Singh, the other Abdullat Khan.

On the third night, I was quietly smoking when the two Sikhs fell on me. One took my shotgun and put the barrel on my forehead: the other put a dagger to my neck.

"Listen Sahib" said the highest, "We need you to take our side, or buy your silence forever. If you decide you have to swear on it. Cross of the Christians, give yourself body and soul to our business; otherwise, we will kill you and we will go to join our rebellious brothers. We want to make you win what your compatriots have come to seek in this country, wealth. you will receive, we swear to you, a quarter of the treasure."

"What treasure?" I asked.

"Swear first for the memory of your father and for your cross that you will not betray us."

-     I swear, I replied.

SH-JCS38

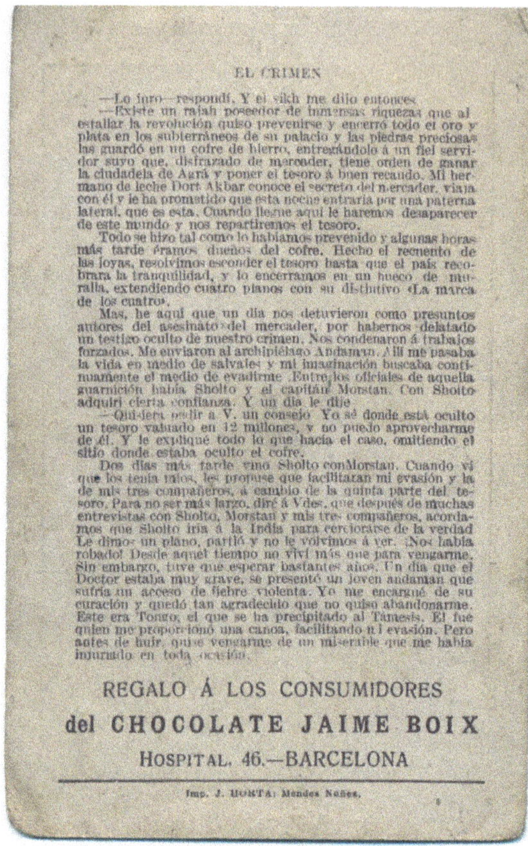

EL CRIMEN

—Lo juro—respondí. Y el sikh me dijo entonces.

—Existe un rajah poseedor de inmensas riquezas que al estallar la revolución quiso prevenirse y encerró todo el oro y plata en los subterráneos de su palacio y las piedras preciosas las guardó en un cofre de hierro, entregándolo á un fiel servidor suyo que, disfrazado de mercader, tiene orden de ganar la ciudadela de Agrá y poner el tesoro á buen recaudo. Mi hermano de leche Dort Akbar conoce el secreto del mercader, viaja con él y le ha prometido que esta noche entraría por una paterna lateral, que es esta. Cuando llegue aquí le haremos desaparecer de este mundo y nos repartiremos el tesoro.

Todo se hizo tal como lo habíamos prevenido y algunas horas más tarde éramos dueños del cofre. Hecho el recuento de las joyas, resolvimos esconder el tesoro hasta que el país recobrara la tranquilidad, y lo encerramos en un hueco de muralla, extendiendo cuatro planos con su distintivo «La marca de los cuatro».

Mas, he aquí que un día nos detuvieron como presuntos autores del asesinato del mercader, por habernos delatado un testigo oculto de nuestro crimen. Nos condenaron á trabajos forzados. Me enviaron al archipiélago Andaman. Allí me pasaba la vida en medio de salvajes y mi imaginación buscaba continuamente el medio de evadirme. Entre los oficiales de aquella guarnición había Sholto y el capitán Morstan. Con Sholto adquirí cierta confianza. Y un día le dije.

—Quisiera pedir á V. un consejo. Yo sé donde está oculto un tesoro valuado en 12 millones, y no puedo aprovecharme de él. Y le expliqué todo lo que hacía el caso, omitiendo el sitio donde estaba oculto el cofre.

Dos días más tarde vino Sholto con Morstan. Cuando vi que los tenía míos, les prometí que facilitaran mi evasión y la de mis tres compañeros, á cambio de la quinta parte del tesoro. Para no ser más largo, diré á Vdes., que después de muchas entrevistas con Sholto, Morstan y mis tres compañeros, acordamos que Sholto iría á la India para cerciorarse de la verdad. Le dimos un plano, partió y no le volvimos á ver. ¡Nos había robado! Desde aquel tiempo no viví más que para vengarme. Sin embargo, tuve que esperar bastantes años. Un día que el Doctor estaba muy grave, se presentó un joven andaman que sufría un acceso de fiebre violenta. Yo me encargué de su curación y quedó tan agradecido que no quiso abandonarme. Este era Tongo, el que se ha precipitado al Támesis. Él fue quien me proporcionó una canoa, facilitando mi evasión. Pero antes de huir, quise vengarme de un miserable que me había injuriado en toda ocasión.

REGALO Á LOS CONSUMIDORES

del CHOCOLATE JAIME BOIX

HOSPITAL. 46.—BARCELONA

Imp. J. HORTA; Mendez Nuñez.

"I swear," I replied. And the Sikh told me then "There is a rajah, possessor of immense wealth who, when the revolution broke out, wanted to save himself and locked up all the gold and silver in the basements of his palace and his precious stones, he kept in an iron chest. Delivering it to a faithful servant of his who disguised himself as a merchant who has orders to reach the citadel of Agra and put the treasure in a safe place. My foster brother Dort Akbar knows the secret of the merchant and travels with him and has promised that tonight he would enter for a paternal lateral(safety) which is this... When he arrives here, we will make him disappear from this world and we will share the treasure."

"Everything was done as we had anticipated and a few hours later we were masters of the chest. Having counted the jewels, we decided to hide the treasure until the country regains tranquillity, and we locked it in a hole in the wall.

We distributed four maps with its distinctive 'Sign of the Four'."

"But behold, one day they arrested us as alleged perpetrators of the merchant's murder, having been betrayed by a hidden witness to our crime. They sentenced us to forced labour. They sent me to the Andaman archipelago, there it happened to me, life in the midst of salvages and my imagination continually sought the means to escape. Among the officers of that Garrison were Sholto and Captain Morstan. Colonel Sholto gained a certain confidence. And one day I told him

I would like to ask you for advice. I know where he is hidden, a treasure valued at 12 million and I cannot take advantage of it, and I explained to him everything that made the case, omitting the site where the chest was hidden.

Two days later Sholto came with Morstan. When I saw that I had them, I suggested that they facilitate my escape and also of my three companions in exchange for a fifth part of the treasure. To not be over long. I will tell you that after many interviews with Sholto, Morstan and my three companions, we agreed that Sholto would go to India to ascertain the truth.

We gave him a map, he left, and we never saw him again. He had robbed us! Since that time, I have lived only to avenge myself. However, I had to wait several years. One day, when the Doctor was very ill, a young Andaman showed up suffering from a violent fever. I took care of his healing, and he was so grateful that he didn't want to leave me. This was Tongo, the one who fell into the Thames. He was true to me; he provided a canoe, facilitating my escape. But before fleeing I wanted to take revenge on a wretch who had insulted me on every occasion."

Series C, Card 39.   WANDERING LIFE

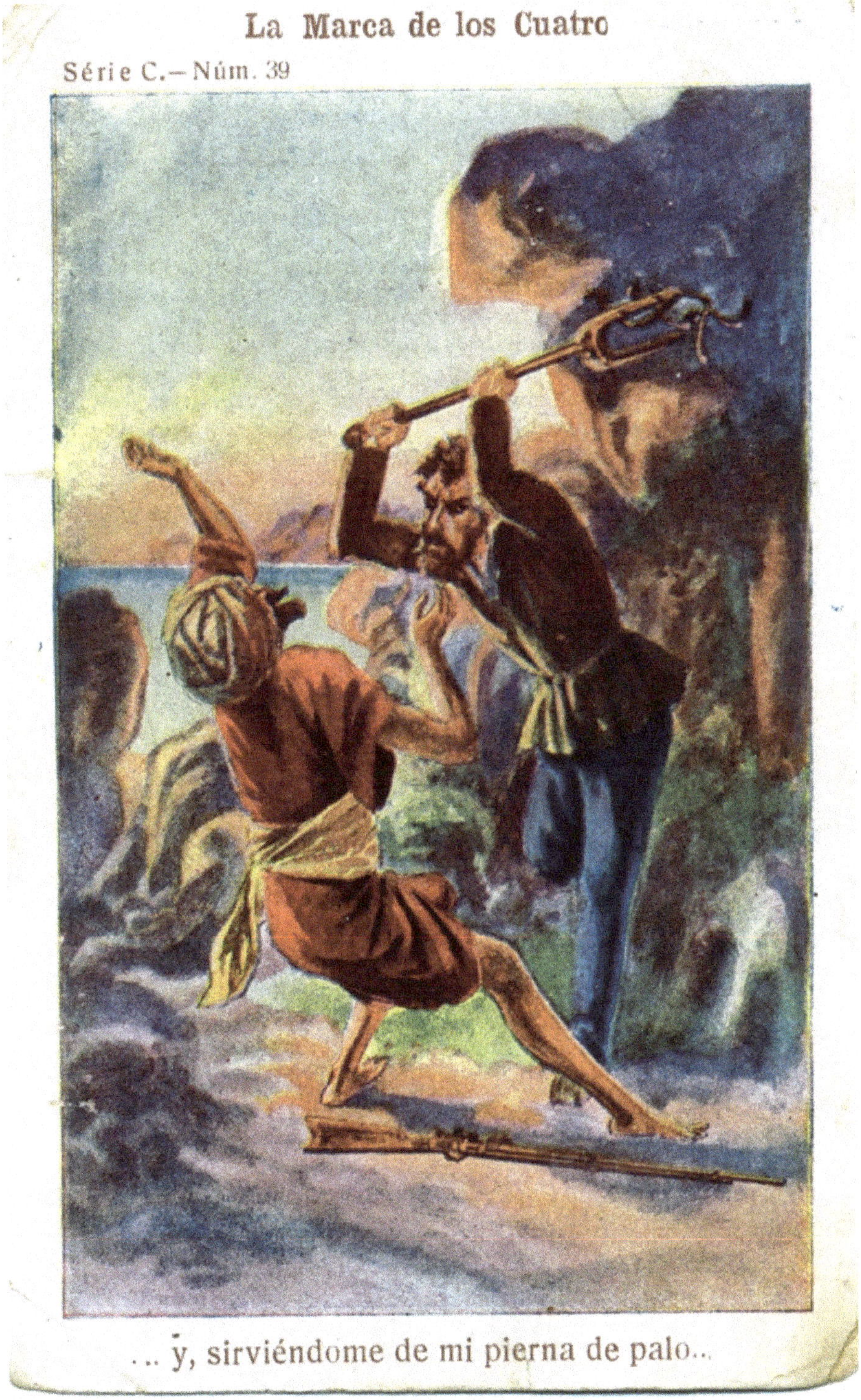

… I swear, I replied.

SH-JCS39

Back of Card 39.

VIDA ERRANTE

Le encontré en el momento de huir y, sirviéndome de mi pierna de palo, le abrí el cráneo.

Durante diez días estuvimos á merced de los vientos, el undécimo fuimos recogidos por un buque que nos condujo á Singapore. No voy á contar las tierras que cecorrimos y las cosas que nos vimos obligados á hacer para volver á Londres; sería cuento de nunca acabar. Al cabo de cuatro años llegábamos á Inglaterra. Ni un solo momento había abandonado la idea de mi venganza. Procuré averiguar el domicilio de Sholto y saber si conservaba el tesoro de Agra. Me asocié á otro que me fué muy útil y no nombro porque no quiero comprometer á nadie. Gracias á mis trabajos adquirí la certeza de que las joyas estabn todavía en sus manos; procuré acercarme á él en varias ocasiones; pero no lo conseguí porque era muy desconfiado y se hacía guardar por dos luchadores de profesión.

Un día me advirtieron que mi perseguido estaba agonizando; corro hacia su casa y me introduzco en el jardín; miro por la ventana y le veo sentado en la cama con sus dos hijos al lado. Iba á precipitarme en el cuarto, dispuesto á luchar, cuando vi desfigurarse su cara y caer inerte. Aquella misma noche me deslicé en su habitación y revolví todos los papeles buscando algún indicio que me pusiera en la pista de encontrar las joyas. No encontré nada. Me marché desesperado, dejando sobre el pecho del cadáver, como símbolo de mi odio, un papel con estas palabras «la marca de los cuatro». Así, por lo menos, se patentizaba claramente la existencia de los que aquel miserable había robado.

REGALO Á LOS CONSUMIDORES

del CHOCOLATE JAIME BOIX

HOSPITAL, 46.— BARCELONA

J. HORTA, Impresor, Méndez Núñez 3.°

"I found him at the moment of fleeing and using my wooden leg. I opened his skull."

"For ten days we were at the mercy of the winds, on the eleventh we were picked up by a ship that took us to Singapore. I am not going to count the lands we crossed and the things we were forced to do in order to return to London; It would be a never-ending story. After four years we arrived in England. Not for a single moment had I abandoned the idea of my revenge. I tried to find out Sholto's address and to find out if he still had the treasure of Agra. I joined someone else who was very useful to me, and I won't name them because I don't want to compromise anyone. Thanks to his help, I acquired the certainty that the jewels were still in his hands; I tried to approach him on several occasions, but I did not succeed because he was very distrustful and had himself guarded by two professional fighters."

"One day they warned me That my persecuted man was dying; I ran to his house and enter the garden: I looked in through the window and saw him sitting on the bed with his two children next to him. I was going to rush into the room, ready to fight. When I saw his face disfigure and fall inert. Later that same night, I slipped into his room and rummaged through all the papers looking for some clue that would put me on the trail of finding the Jewels. I found nothing. I felt desperate, leaving on the chest of the corpse, as a symbol of my hatred. a paper with these words 'The mark of the four'. Thus, to clearly show the existence of those from whom that wretch had stolen."

… Danced Warrior Dancing

SH-JCS40

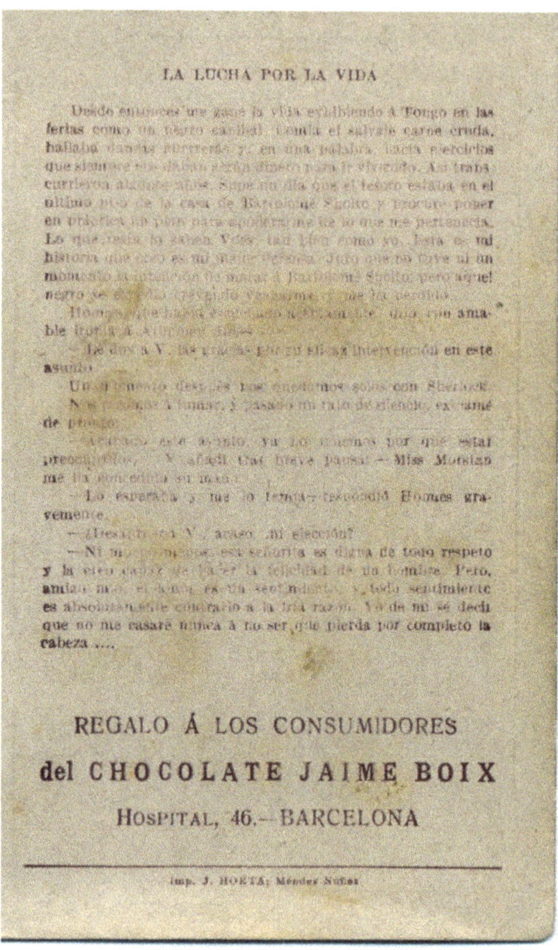

"Since then, I have made a living exhibiting Tongo at fairs like a black cannibal. He ate wild raw meat, danced war dances and, in a word, did exercises that always gave us some money for living. So, some years passed. I found out one day that the treasure was on the top floor of the Bartolomé Sholto's house, and I tried to implement a plan to seize what belonged to me. What remains you know, as well as I do this is my story that I believe is my best defence. I swear I never intended for a moment to kill Bartolomé Sholto. but my negro friend killed him believing I wanted it done."

Holmes, who had carefully scrutinized, said with friendly irony to Atherney Jones. "I thank you for his erudition intervention in this matter."

The others left and I was left alone with Sherlock. We stopped to smoke and after a while of silence, he suddenly exclaimed.

"Finishing this matter, I fear this is the last case we shall work together."

After brief pause, I said "Miss Morstan has given me her hand."

Holmes answered gravely "I feared as much that young lady is worthy of all respect and the only one capable of making a man happy But. My friend, Love is a sentiment, and every feeling is absolutely contrary to the cold reason. I tell myself that I will never get married unless I completely lose my mind..."

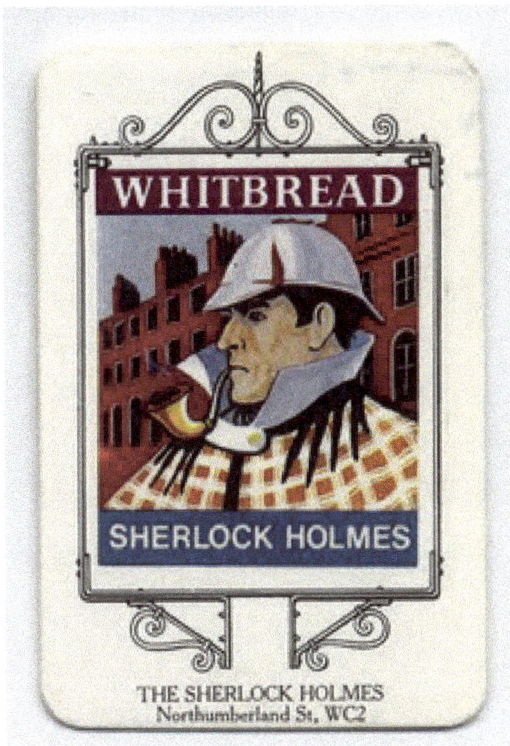

The Sherlock Holmes pub was originally named the Northumberland Hotel back in the 1880s, then its name was changed to the Northumberland Arms and as that was mentioned in the 1892 Sherlock Holmes story "The Adventure of the Noble Bachelor" and could also be the same building named in "The Hound of the Baskervilles". Over the years various Sherlock Holmes memorability has been collected and for Sherlock Holmes fans is a must see in London. This beer mat dates back to the time when Whitbread owned the pub, it is currently owned by the Bury St. Edmunds based brewer Greene King

Player's Cigarettes 1933 Characters from fiction card 25 set– no. 21

Sherlock Holmes

In 1933 john Player & Sons, a branch of the imperial tobacco co of Great Britain and Ireland Ltd produced a 25 cigarette card set from originals by H. M Brock, R.I.
For completeness the set included the following characters

Card No.	Character	Book
1	Adam Bede	Adam Bede
2	Alice	Alice in Wonderland
3	Becky Sharp	Vanity Fair
4	Captain Kettle	Adventures of Captain Kettle
5	Colonel Newcome	The Newcomers
6	D'artagnan	Three Musketeers
7	Don Quixote	Don Quixote
8	Gulliver	Gulliver's Travels
9	John Halifax	John Halifax, Gentleman
10	Long John Silver	Treasure Island
11	Lord Fauntleroy	Little Lord Fauntleroy
12	Lorna Doone	Lorna Doone
13	Midshipman Easy	Mr. Midshipman Easy
14	Mr. Jorrocks	Jorrocks's Jaunts
15	Mr. Pickwick	Pickwick Papers
16	Olivia	Vicar of Wakefield
17	Robinson Crusoe	Robinson Crusoe
18	Rob Roy	Rob Roy
19	Salvation Yeo	Westward Ho!
20	Sam Weller	Pickwick Papers
21	**Sherlock Holmes**	**A Study in Scarlet**
22	Tess	Tess of the d'Urbervilles
23	Tom Brown	Tom Brown's Schooldays
24	Trilby	Trilby
25	Uncle Tom	Uncle Tom's Cabin

But of course, it is only card 21 that we are interested, how many of these characters are known nowaday. Here is Card 21 in all its glory

PLAYER'S CIGARETTES
SHERLOCK HOLMES.
"THE ADVENTURES OF SHERLOCK HOLMES."

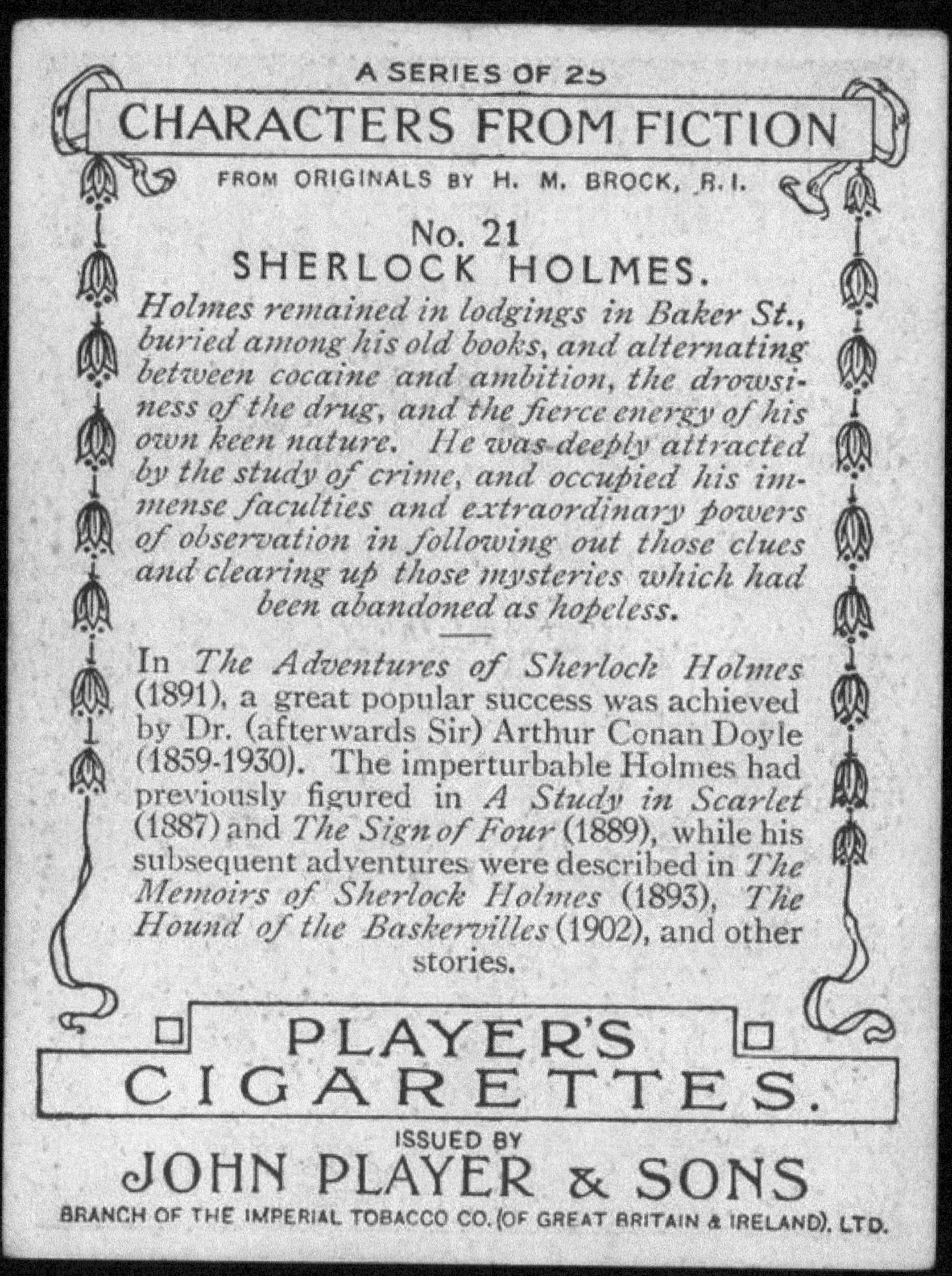

A SERIES OF 25
CHARACTERS FROM FICTION
FROM ORIGINALS BY H. M. BROCK, R.I.
No. 21
SHERLOCK HOLMES.
Holmes remained in lodgings in Baker St., buried among his old books, and alternating between cocaine and ambition, the drowsiness of the drug, and the fierce energy of his own keen nature. He was deeply attracted by the study of crime, and occupied his immense faculties and extraordinary powers of observation in following out those clues and clearing up those mysteries which had been abandoned as hopeless.
In The Adventures of Sherlock Holmes (1891), a great popular success was achieved by Dr. (afterwards Sir) Arthur Conan Doyle (1859-1930). The imperturbable Holmes had previously figured in A Study in Scarlet (1887) and The Sign of Four (1889), while his subsequent adventures were described in The Memoirs of Sherlock Holmes (1893), The Hound of the Baskervilles (1902), and other stories.
PLAYER'S
CIGARETTES.
ISSUED BY
JOHN PLAYER & SONS
BRANCH OF THE IMPERIAL TOBACCO CO. (OF GREAT BRITAIN & IRELAND), LTD.

Wladyslaw Teodor "W.T." Benda

Born 15th January 1873 in Poznań, Poland
Died 30th November 1948 in Newark, New Jersey, USA (Heart Attack)

Graphic Artist famous for illustrating books, short stories, advertising copy, and magazine covers for a number of publications including Collier's, McCall's, Ladies' Home Journal, Good Housekeeping.
He produced 4 illustrations for the Sussex Vampire Short Story that appeared in Hearst's International in January 1924

Images 1/4. Page 30-31. "Fancy anyone having the heart to hurt him" Ferguson muttered as he glanced at the angry red pucker on his bay's throat. All this time Holmes was staring intently at the window across the room.
Ref. SH-WTB1

Images 2/4. Page 33. Holmes, with that quick curiosity which sprang from his eager mind, examined the collection of South American utensils. When he turned away his eyes were full of thoughts.
Ref. SH-WTB2

Images 3/4. Page 34. Mrs. Ferguson kneeling by the cot gave no answer to her husband's reproaches save to gaze at him with a wild despairing look in her eyes.
Ref. SH-WTB3

Images 4/4. Page 35. At the child's cry of pain Ferguson and the nurse rushed to the nursery.
The kneeling figure of his wife by the cot confirmed the horrible accusations of the nurse.
Ref. SH-WTB4

John French Sloan

Born 2nd August 1871 in Lock Haven Pennsylvania.
Died 7th September 1951 in Hanover, New Hampshire.

American Illustrator, Etcher and Painter, best known for this urban genre scenes in the neighbourhoods of New York City.

He did just one Sherlock Holmes Illustration, which appeared in the Philadelphia Press dated 3rd March 1901, with the title 'The Sherlock Holmes Puzzle'

The Puzzle was in the form of a page of script that had to be decoded using a mirror.

John French Sloan Image, taken from 'The Sherlock Holmes Puzzle'
Philadelphia Press 3rd March 1901

(what do you mean, you can't read the letters!)
SH-JFS1

John Sloan Image, taken from 'The Sherlock Holmes Puzzle' Philadelphia Press 3rd March 1901

Message zoomed in and then mirrored.
SH-JFS2 & SH-JF3

You are looking in the wrong book if you want these illustrations.

INDEX

Now this is a handy reference, isn't it?

No.	Code	Name	No.	Code	Name
1	STUD	A Study in Scarlet	31	SOLI	The Solitary Cyclist
2	SIGN	The Sign of (the) Four	32	PRIO	The Priory School
3	SCAN	A Scandal in Bohemia	33	BLAC	Black Peter
4	REDH	The Red-Headed League	34	CHAS	Charles Augustus Milverton
5	IDEN	The Case of Identity	35	SIXN	The Six Napoleons
6	BOSC	The Boscombe Valley Mystery	36	3STU	The Three Students
7	FIVE	The Five Orange Pips	37	GOLD	The Golden Pince-Nez
8	TWIS	The Man with the Twisted Lip	38	MISS	The Missing Three-Quarter
9	BLUE	The Blue Carbuncle	39	ABBE	The Abbey Grange
10	SPEC	The Speckled Band	40	SECO	The Second Stain
11	ENGR	The Engineer's Thumb	41	WIST	Wisteria Lodge
12	NOBL	The Noble Bachelor	42	BRUC	The Bruce-Partington Plans
13	BERY	The Beryl Coronet	43	DEVI	The Devil's Foot
14	COPP	The Copper Beeches	44	REDC	The Red Circle
15	SILV	Silver Blaze	45	LADY	Lady Frances Carfax
16	CARD	The Cardboard Box	46	DYIN	The Dying Detective
17	YELL	The Yellow Face	47	VALL	The Valley of Fear
18	STOC	The Stockbroker's Clerk	48	LAST	His Last Bow
19	GLOR	The Gloria Scott	49	MAZA	The Mazarine Stone
20	MUSG	The Musgrave Ritual	50	THOR	Thor Bridge
21	REIG	The Reigate Squire	51	CREE	The Creeping Man
22	CROO	The Crooked Man	52	SUSS	The Sussex Vampire
23	RESI	The Resident Patient	53	3GAR	The Three Garridebs
24	GREE	The Greek Interpreter	54	ILLU	The Illustrious Client
25	NAVA	The Naval Treaty	55	3GAB	The three Gables
26	FINA	The Final Problem	56	BLAN	The Blanched Soldier
27	HOUN	The Hound of the Baskervilles	57	LION	The Lion's Mane
28	EMPT	The Empty House	58	RETI	The Retired Colourman
29	NORW	The Norwood Builder	59	VEIL	The Veiled Lodger
30	DANC	The Dancing Men	60	SHOS	Shoscombe Old Place

Quick reference to illustrators in these 3 volumes (1,2 & 3)

No	Code	CD	DF	GG	RG	GH	JG	TN	SP	WP	RP	BO	FDS	AT
1	STUD	6	4	3	24		2					21	5	1
2	SIGN			1	24	42		33				24		
3	SCAN			1	5				10					
4	REDH			1	4				10					
5	IDEN				3				7					
6	BOSC				4				10					
7	FIVE				3				6					
8	TWIS				5				10					
9	BLUE				5				8					
10	SPEC				5				9					
11	ENGR				4				8					
12	NOBL				4				8					
13	BERY				4				9					
14	COPP				5				9					
15	SILV				6				9					
16	CARD				4				8					
17	YELL				3				7					
18	STOC				4				7					
19	GLOR				3				7					
20	MUSG				4				6					
21	REIG				5				7					
22	CROO				4				7					
23	RESI				5				7					
24	GREE				3				8					
25	NAVA				9				8+7					
26	FINA				5				9					
27	HOUN				30				60		114		3	
28	EMPT				3				7				8	
29	NORW				3				7				6	
30	DANC				3				7				6	
31	SOLI								7				5	
32	PRIO								9				6	
33	BLAC								7				6	
34	CHAS								6				6	
35	SIXN								7				6	
36	3STU								7				6	
37	GOLD								8				6	
38	MISS								7				5	
39	ABBE								8				6	
40	SECO								8				6	
41	WIST												7	
42	BRUC												5	
43	DEVI													
44	REDC													
45	LADY												5	
46	DYIN									4			4	
47	VALL													
48	LAST												5	
49	MAZA												4	
50	THOR													
51	CREE												8	
52	SUSS												1	
53	3GAR												4	
54	ILLU												6	
55	3GAB												7	
56	BLAN												7	
57	LION												8	
58	RETI												5	
59	VEIL												6	
60	SHOS												8	
Totals		6	4	6	228	42	2	33	356	4	114	45	205	1

Key	Volume	Illustrator
CD	1	Charles Altamont Doyle
DF	1	David Henry Friston
GG	2	Graham Grinham
RG	2	Richard Gutschmidt
GH	2	George Wylie Hutchinson
JG	1	James Greig
TJN	2	Thomas Jeffs Nicholl
SP	1	Sidney Paget
WP	1	Walter Paget
RP	2	Raymond Pallier
FS	3	Frederic Dorr Steele
TO	1	The Boston Observer
AT	2	Arthur Twidle